MAD, BAD AND BLONDE

MAD, BAD AND BLONDE

CATHIE LINZ

THORNDIKE
CHIVERS

This Large Print edition is published by Thorndike Press, Waterville, Maine, USA and by BBC Audiobooks Ltd, Bath, England.

Thorndike Press, a part of Gale, Cengage Learning.

Copyright © 2010 by Cathie L. Baumgardner.

The moral right of the author has been asserted.

The text of this Large Print edition is unabridged.

Other aspects of the book may vary from the original edition.

Set in 16 pt. Plantin.

LIBRARY OF CONGRESS CATALOGING-IN-PUBLICATION DATA

Linz, Cathie.
    Mad, bad and blonde / by Cathie Linz.
      p. cm. — (Thorndike Press large print romance)
    ISBN-13: 978-1-4104-2939-1 (hardcover)
    ISBN-10: 1-4104-2939-3 (hardcover)
    1. Large type books. I. Title.
PS3562.I558M33 2010
813'.54—dc22   2010016595

BRITISH LIBRARY CATALOGUING-IN-PUBLICATION DATA AVAILABLE

Published in 2010 in the U.S. by arrangement with The Berkley Publishing Group, a member of Penguin Group (USA) Inc.

Published in 2010 in the U.K. by arrangement with the author.

U.K. Hardcover: 978 1 408 49215 4 (Chivers Large Print)
U.K. Softcover: 978 1 408 49216 1 (Camden Large Print)

Printed in the United States of America
1 2 3 4 5 6 7 14 13 12 11 10

DEDICATION

This book is dedicated to the many incredible librarians in my life starting with Joyce Saricks, who became my mentor and good friend. To John Charles, who rates a 21 out of 10; Shelley Mosley, who always makes me smile; Kristin Ramsdell, who is priceless; and Mary K. Chelton, who is so smart and has attitude. I could say so much more but won't, because I know you're all blushing.

There are many other librarians who have been so supportive — from all over the country as well as close to home. I wish I could thank you all personally. But please know you all rock! And you have my sincere gratitude. If I could send you all chocolate, I would. Please come visit me on Facebook.

Special thanks to children's librarian Stacey Freedman for her help, to Susan Frank for the Marine Corps input and to "Linzie" Andrea Markell for the baseball info. Any mistakes aren't theirs . . . or mine, because this is fiction <grin>. More gratitude goes to Techno-buddy Liz Verrill and BlackBerry Goddess Lynne Yulish for their support and the push to get me on Facebook. Thanks to Chilibabes Susan Elizabeth Phillips, Lindsay Longford, Suzette Vann and Margaret Watson for their brilliant brainstorming. And hugs to Jayne Ann Krentz for the years of friendship.

This book is also dedicated to the many Marines who are serving our country and to their families who give up so much. Semper fi!

CHAPTER ONE

It was the perfect day for a wedding. Too bad the groom didn't show up.

Faith West shivered in the beam of May sunlight streaming through a small window in the bridal anteroom of the historical Chicago Gold Coast church. Fingering the rich white satin skirt of her wedding dress, she sat very still, unable to believe this was really happening to her. Alan Anderson, the man she'd agreed to marry, was late for his own wedding.

There had to be a reasonable explanation for Alan's absence: car trouble, a dead cell phone, maybe even an accident, heaven forbid.

Faith caught sight of herself in the large mirror on the opposite wall. A few wisps of her brown hair had escaped the confines of her upswept hairstyle, and her blue eyes appeared haunted despite her perfect makeup. Did she look like the kind of woman a man would leave at the altar? Possibly. She was certainly no raving beauty. She was just a librarian. A librarian with a rich private investigator father.

Faith's family flitted around her like a skittish school of fish, coming and going — offering help, offering suggestions, offering vodka. She remained calm in the center of all the chaos, strangely distant from her surroundings. The reality was she was probably going into shock and should accept the offer of alcohol purely for medicinal purposes.

The question was: What would Jane Austen do in this situation? Whenever Faith was in trouble, she looked to her favorite author for the solution. And Faith was armpit deep in trouble at the moment.

"I bet you scared the poor man away," Faith's pain-in-the-butt Aunt Lorraine interrupted Faith's racing thoughts to declare. "A children's librarian whose father taught her how to shoot a gun. A big mistake."

Aunt Lorraine, also known as the Duchess of Grimness, was the bane of the West family's existence. With her demonlike black hair and Hellboy eyes, she was scarier than anything written by Stephen King. Not exactly the model wedding guest, but Faith's mom had insisted on inviting her.

For a wild second Faith wondered if Alan had stayed away because he was afraid of Aunt Lorraine, having met her for the first time at the rehearsal dinner the night before. Maybe she was the reason he hadn't shown up. Could Faith really blame him for wanting to avoid Aunt Lorraine's stinging barbs?

Hell yes, she could blame him! How could Alan leave her sitting here wondering what had happened to him? How could he be so cruel? How could anyone, aside from Aunt Lorraine, be that cruel?

Alan wasn't just anyone. He was her fiancé, a reliable and respectable investment banker she'd known for two years. They'd been engaged for the past eleven months. They were perfectly suited for each other, sharing the same interests, values and aspirations. Neither one of them was blinded by passion or prone to wild behavior.

That's not to say that the sex between them hadn't been good; it had been. Not great but good. She loved him. He loved her. Or so he'd said last night before kissing her.

Faith looked around. Someone had led Aunt Lorraine away. She was replaced by Alan's shamefaced best man. "Alan just sent you a text message."

"Where is he? Is he okay?"

Instead of answering her anxious questions, the best man hightailed it out of the room, heading for the nearest exit and no doubt the nearest bar.

"Where's my BlackBerry?" Faith asked her maid of honor, her cousin Megan, who was like a sister to her. Faith and Megan were born two days apart, grew up within a few blocks of each other, and had been known to complete each other's sentences. Their dads were brothers. Faith had only had one bridal attendant, and of course that was Megan.

"I'm sure Alan has a good reason for being late." Megan had always been the optimist in the family. "Maybe he was in an accident. Your dad is still checking the area emergency rooms."

Faith's uber-workaholic father owned the most successful investigative firm in Chicago. If Alan wasn't in an emergency room, then her father would be tempted to put him in one.

"Where's my BlackBerry?" Faith heard the edge of hysteria in her voice but couldn't do anything to stop it.

"Here. It's right next to you." Megan handed it to her. Sure enough, there was a text message from Alan that had been sent two minutes ago.

"thought i wanted marriage. i don't. i need to find who i really am. I want adventure and excitement. Don't want u. Sorry."

Alan hadn't left her because she could shoot a gun. He'd left because he didn't think she was exciting enough. She'd scared him away by *boring* him to death.

"What did he say?" Megan demanded.

Her cousin was her best friend, but even so, Faith was too humiliated to show her what Alan had written. Instead she turned the BlackBerry off with trembling fingers. "I've been dumped in a text message," she said unsteadily. "And not just dumped, but left at the altar."

"We never actually walked down the aisle."

"Close enough." Faith angrily wiped away the tears that were starting to stream down her face. "There are people waiting out there. Lots of them. And they're all expecting a wedding."

"They'll all be on your side."

That was cold comfort at this point. Faith welcomed the anger starting to surge through her. It kept the pain and humiliation at bay.

So much for her happy ending. Faith had continued to believe in her fairy-tale wedding even when Alan hadn't shown up for the preceremony photographs, even when his best man had refused to look her in the eye, even when the minister had approached her privately to ask if she wanted to delay the proceedings.

"He'll show up," Faith kept saying. "You'll see. He'll show up. And he'll have the lamest excuse for being late."

Her belief in Alan and her faith in a positive outcome had lasted longer than it should have and was now as tattered as the lace handkerchief she'd nervously shredded with her beautifully manicured fingers.

Last night he'd claimed he loved her, yet today he didn't want her. How did that work? Did Alan love her like he loved fine wine and the Cubs instead of the way you loved the person you were supposed to marry? Weren't Cubs fans supposed to be the most loyal guys on the planet?

Faith was having a hard time thinking coherently, and she felt cold enough to get frostbite. The man she loved didn't want her. She couldn't think about that, or she'd dissolve into a sobbing mess. But she could think of nothing else.

Her parents burst into the anteroom. "I finally tracked him down," Jeff West said. His usually smooth brown hair was messed from his running impatient fingers through it. "The bastard took a flight to Bali an hour ago. One-way."

Alan has gone to Bali searching for adventure and excitement, because he couldn't find any with me. So much for love and commitment. I guess those things don't matter to him. I don't matter to him.

What had she done to make him change his mind about marrying her? He couldn't have thought she was boring when he'd proposed. So what had changed?

Would Alan have stayed if he'd known she was a crack shot with a gun? Her dad had taken her to the firing range and taught her himself when she was ten. Faith had never told Alan about her weapons training because she didn't like to brag about the marksmanship awards she'd won. Maybe she should have. Maybe then he'd have thought twice about dumping her. Maybe then he'd have thought she was more exciting. A children's librarian who had a gun and knew how to use it. Yeah, that ranked right up there on the excitement scale with . . . what?

What *was* Alan's definition of exciting? Interest rates and the stock market? Sex in the middle of Wrigley Field? A blow job in Bali?

"You poor baby." Faith's mother, Sara, sat beside her and hugged her. "He seemed like such a nice investment banker."

"There was nothing in his background to indicate he'd bolt like this," her dad said. "I had him thoroughly checked out. Other than being a Cubs fan instead of a Sox fan, there didn't seem to be anything wrong with him. He wasn't seeing another woman — or another man — wasn't defrauding the bank or his clients."

"Maybe he just got a case of cold feet," Megan said. "He could still come back."

"And when he does, I'll beat the crap out of him," Jeff growled.

Faith would have thought that her fiancé would be smart enough to figure out that dumping her at this late date meant there was no place he could hide. Not even Bali. Her father would track him down and make him pay . . . big time.

Only one person was more imposing than Jeff West, and that was Aunt Lorraine, who was now trying to push her way back into the room.

"Get rid of her," Faith begged her parents.

"Gladly," her dad said. "Do you think I haven't wanted to make her disappear for years now? But your mother would never let me."

"She's my much older sister," Sara said apologetically. "She practically raised me."

"And she scares you shitless," Jeff said. "Believe me, I get it."

"She implied it was my fault Alan left," Faith said. It turned out the Duchess of Grimness was right. According to Alan's brief text message, it was obvious that he blamed Faith for being too dull for him.

"Your fault? That does it." Sara glared at Lorraine, who was still trying to get in the room but was prevented by Megan. "She's gone too far this time." A curtain of fierce determination fell over Sara's face. "Don't worry, I'll handle her." She marched over and moved Lorraine out of the room.

Watching her mother's totally uncharacteristic behavior, Faith realized anything was possible. Anything but her wedding. There was no saving that now.

"What are we going to do?" Faith asked her dad. "All those people are out there waiting. We've got the wedding reception at the Ritz-Carlton. You paid so much for everything." Tears welled again, but she dashed them away. Alan had said there were only a handful of people he wanted to invite. His parents were dead, and he had no other close family. Since almost all of the guests were from her side of the family,

Alan had been perfectly happy to have Jeff foot the bill, and her dad had done so with boatloads of paternal pride.

Again, what would Jane Austen do? She would take control.

"Tell the people in the church that due to circumstances beyond our control, the ceremony has been canceled," Faith said. "Tell them the reception is still on. Don't cancel it. You might as well enjoy it."

"That's my girl," her dad said. "We'll get our money's worth as a celebration of friends and family. And it makes good business sense, since a lot of West Investigations' top clients are also in the audience and will be at the reception."

"Are you nuts?" her mom said, having rejoined them in time to hear Faith's request.

"Probably," Faith muttered.

"I was talking to your father." She turned to face him. "Your daughter is suffering, and all you can do is talk about business and money?"

"I could put out a hit on Alan," Jeff growled, "but I'm restraining myself."

"I know people who could do the job," Faith's paternal grandmother spoke up for the first time. Her blue eyes and high cheekbones proclaimed her Scandinavian heritage, while her gelled spiky haircut revealed her rebel nature. "They're in the Swedish mob."

Jeff frowned. "I never heard of the Swedish mob."

"Of course not. They're very discreet. Not like the Finnish mob."

"I appreciate the offer, Gram, but it's not necessary," Faith said.

"Well, if you change your mind, the offer stands," Gram assured her.

"I'll keep that in mind."

"You do that." She patted Faith's hand. "I'm sorry things didn't work out."

"Thanks." She took a deep breath but felt the walls closing in on her. "Listen, you guys don't have to stay with me. Go on to the reception, and please give everyone my regrets, but I just can't . . ." She shook her head, unable to go on.

"You have nothing to be regretful about," her mom said.

"Except regret at ever hooking up with Alan the Asshole to begin with," her dad said.

"Are you sure you want us to go?" Her mom looked uncertain.

"Yes, I'm sure. Megan will stay with me, right?"

"Of course I will."

"See, I'll be fine."

"Of course you will . . . in time." Gram patted her hand again. "A year or two should do it."

When they finally left, Megan looked at her with concern. "Are you okay?"

"Not yet. But after a few mojitos I will be. Now please help me get me out of this damn dress!"

Faith woke with a hammering headache and the sound of intense roaring in her ears. Her eyelids didn't seem to want to open, but she was able to sneak a peek through a narrow slit. The limited view was not enough to tell her where she was.

"This is your captain speaking. We'll be landing in Naples in about an hour."

Her eyes flew open.

"The flight attendants will be going through the cabin . . ."

Faith didn't pay attention to the rest of the announcement as the events of the day and night before came rushing back. Left at the altar. Humiliated, brokenhearted, angry. She and Megan downing several mojitos at a neighborhood bar before heading to Faith's Streeterville condo only to trip over Faith's suitcases just inside the door. A matched set of luggage packed with carefully chosen outfits for her dream honeymoon to the Amalfi Coast in Italy.

Alan wanted to spend their honeymoon elephant riding in India because his boss at the bank had done that and raved about it. Personally, Faith was not that fond of pachyderms. Had he left her because of that? Because she didn't want to boogie with the elephants?

It wasn't like her choice was dull or boring. Who didn't like sunny Italy? Faith had longed to go to the Amalfi Coast ever since she'd seen the movie *Under the Tuscan Sun* and watched Diane Lane get swept off her feet in the beautiful town of Positano.

She distinctly remembered shouting at her living room wall last night, "Alan ruined my wedding, but he's not going to ruin this too! I refuse to allow him to mess up any more of my life! I'll show you exciting and adventurous! I'm going to Italy! *Solo! Solo mio!*"

Faith spent the last two years trying to please Alan. This trip was one of the few times she'd stood her ground and refused to back down. Once he didn't get his way, Alan had completely lost interest and told her to handle all the arrangements. Gladly, she had — which was why she had possession of the nonrefundable tickets and the rest of the travel reservations.

Megan had been supportive as always. "Go for it! I'd come with you, but I can't get away from work right now."

Sitting on the plane, Faith felt as if she'd just woken up from a long, drugged sleep. Unlike Sleeping Beauty, she hadn't been brought back to life by a kiss from a handsome prince. Instead, she'd been brought back to reality by the handsome prince screwing her over.

The ironic thing was that Faith was usually a worst-case scenario specialist, always prepared in case things went wrong. One of her dad's favorite mottos was, "Expect the worst, and if it doesn't happen, you'll be pleasantly surprised." Her relationship with Alan was the one time she'd allowed herself to believe . . . and look what happened.

She ended up on a flight to Italy. Alone. Her first solo trip ever. But it was better than moping in her condo, crying her eyes out. She'd taken action. She'd left the mayhem behind in Chicago, calling her dad and telling him she was fleeing the country.

There was no time to reflect further on her actions as the flight attendants prepared for their landing. Her arrival in Naples went smoothly as she cleared customs with no problem. Two aspirins and a bottle of Pellegrino water took care of the headache. Her rental car was ready . . . and so was she.

She *was* ready, right? She wasn't going to let fear hold her back, right?

She could do this. She *would* do this.

Faith put her iPod into the sound system and moments later Gnarls Barkley's song "Crazy" blared out of the sporty little red Italian convertible's speakers. She'd had to put her smaller suitcase in the passenger seat next to her, since it didn't fit anywhere else.

The instant she hit the road, all the other drivers seemed determined to hit *her.* She refused to let them. She'd handled rush-hour traffic in Vegas not to mention on the Kennedy Expressway in Chicago during construction season. The crazy Italian drivers didn't scare her. Being alone on her honeymoon scared her if she thought about it. So she refused to think about it and instead stepped on the gas, cranked up the sound system and sang along with her favorite Bon Jovi CD, *Lost Highway.*

Caine Hunter had his instructions. Keep an eye on Faith West, keep track of her actions and report them back to Chicago. He knew a lot about her already: children's librarian, jilted bride, handy with a gun. Her team from the library in Las Vegas where she'd

21

worked two years ago had come in second place in the city's Corporate Challenge, an event where organizations compete in various sporting events. She'd aced the shooting event.

Caine was only mildly impressed. She still seemed like a spoiled little rich girl to him, with her fancy wedding in one of the most prestigious churches in Chicago, a fancy banker fiancé and a condo in Chicago's trendiest Streeterville neighborhood. Not that the wedding or the fiancé had panned out for her in the end. Too bad, so sad.

No one had ever accused him of being the sentimental type.

He'd say this for Faith West: she didn't drive like a librarian . . . more like race car driver Danica Patrick. Driving in Italy, especially around Milan, was not for wimps.

Yet here she was, weaving in and out of traffic, music blaring. Was she really that reckless or just plain stupid? Hard to tell at this point, but Caine aimed on finding that out . . . among other things.

Faith's knuckles were permanently white by the time she reached the small town of Positano. The infamous road of a thousand curves on which she'd been traveling clung precariously to the steep cliffs and was narrower than her parents' driveway at home. That didn't stop huge tour buses from barreling around blind curves, hogging the entire road and making her fear for her life and her sanity.

But she'd done it. She'd made it here. Alive. In one piece. Jane Austen would be so proud.

"Welcome to the Majestic Hotel, Mrs. Anderson." Huge terra-cotta urns filled with flowers bracketed the reception desk adorned with colorful majolica tiles. The lobby, with its antiques and artwork, was a study of understated elegance. "We have the honeymoon suite all ready for you and your husband."

Her stomach clenched. This was no honeymoon, and she had no husband. But she did have sunshine, breathtaking views and the scent of citrus blossoms in the air. "It's Ms. West. Faith West. Not Mrs. Anything. I called ahead to explain the change . . ."

"Oh yes, I see the note here. I'm sorry for the confusion, Ms. West. If you could show me your passport, please." He raised his hand, and a uniformed bellman immediately appeared with her luggage. "Paco will take you to your room."

She'd spent hours over the past winter,

poring over guidebooks and surfing websites trying to decide where to stay — the Grand Hotel in Sorrento or the Capri Palace Hotel on the island of Capri? But Positano had held her under its spell and, while she planned on visiting both Sorrento and Capri during her stay, this was her ultimate destination. The room didn't disappoint with its private terrace displaying a colorful bougainvillea-framed view of the pastel, sunlit town hugging the rugged cliffs that plunged down to the blue waves of the Mediterranean.

John Steinbeck was right. This place was a dream.

The dream was interrupted by the sound of her stomach growling. She needed to eat something and fast. The hotel dining room was serving for another hour, Paco the bellman informed her in a sexy Italian accent, his liquid brown eyes gazing at her with Latin approval.

Faith was starving. But not for male attention. She handed Paco his tip and showed him the door.

She barely had time for a fast bathroom stop where she looked at the thick towels and large tub longingly before hurrying down to eat. Knowing that nearby Naples was the birthplace of pizza, she quickly ordered a pizza Margherite.

And waited. And waited. Other diners were seated on the sunny terrace dining area. Two guys in particular made a point of staring at her sitting all alone. She wasn't pleased to see their food arrive before hers. They hadn't even ordered Italian but steak and fries. The skinnier of the two men gave her a leering look. He poured ketchup onto his plate and then dipped a fry into it, holding it up and taunting her with it before chomping into it with gusto.

Normally Faith would have looked away and ignored him, but she wasn't feeling very generous toward the opposite sex at the moment.

Faith gave the man her best withering librarian look.

He responded by smacking his lips at her.

She made an *Eww-yuck* face.

He dipped another fry in the ketchup and waved it at her before sucking it into his mouth in one go. An instant later the man grabbed his throat and started turning red then blue.

Before she could react, a man smoothly moved past her and gave the choking man the Heimlich.

Faith sank into her chair. She felt guilty that while trying to impress her, the idiot had ended up choking and nearly killing himself. Was there some kind of Italian curse that was reserved for brides who came to the Amalfi Coast without their grooms?

Then all thought went out of her head as she got her first good look at the rescuer. Dark hair, dark eyes, stubble-darkened cheeks and chin. A dark knight. A man meant to get a woman's juices flowing.

He stopped at her table and stared down at her before saying with amusement, "I'll say this: you sure know how to make an impression on a guy."

CHAPTER TWO

"Thank you, uh . . ." Faith paused, waiting for him to provide his name, which he finally did.

"Caine," he said. "Caine Hunter."

The name suited him. He looked like a hunter, someone who went after what they wanted. "Well, thank you, Caine Hunter."

"Are you thanking me for saying you know how to make an impression on a guy?"

"No, I was thanking you because you saved that man's life. I wasn't trying to make him choke."

"Good to know."

A waiter hovered nearby. "I'm so sorry, signore. All the tables are taken. You will have to wait," he said apologetically.

"Would you like to join me?" Faith heard herself ask.

A second later the waiter scooted forward to hold a chair out for Caine invitingly.

Caine didn't bother looking at the menu

before ordering in fluent Italian. She'd meant to learn more of the language, but there had never been enough time, what with all the planning for the wedding. The wedding that never happened.

She glanced down at her hands, glad to see they weren't shaking. Her left hand looked so bare without her engagement ring. She'd yanked it off at her condo and stuffed it in a bottom drawer.

"Is this your first trip to Europe?" Caine asked.

She looked up. "No. My first trip was with my grandparents when I was thirteen. We didn't come here to the Amalfi Coast, though. We visited the capital cities and some of the battlefields where my grandfather fought in World War II. After V-E Day he was called back to the States to do top secret work — intelligence gathering, code breaking, that sort of thing. After the war he started his own investigation business in Chicago. He passed away two years ago." She took a deep breath. She still missed her grandfather and couldn't believe she'd just babbled all about her background the way she had. She was normally a pretty private person. "Anyway enough about me and my family. What about you? Is this your first trip to Europe?"

"No." He didn't elaborate the way she had. In fact, he didn't elaborate at all.

A man of few words. That suited her just fine. Unless it meant that she was the one who had to do all the talking to fill in the awkward silence. She was rapidly running out of energy here, and if she didn't get some food in her soon, she'd pass out at the table, and Caine would have to do a second rescue.

"Here." He shoved some fresh bread still warm from the oven at her. "Eat some of this."

She did so gladly. Where had the plate of sliced crusty bread come from? She'd been sitting here for twenty minutes and gotten nothing. He'd only been there three minutes.

"I'm still jet-lagged," she explained in between big bites. "I flew in this morning and then drove straight here from Milan."

"That must have been exciting for you."

She shrugged. "I handled it."

"You seem like the kind of woman who could handle just about anything."

His comment surprised her. "What makes you say that?"

"The Italian roads aren't for wimps."

"That's true. There were a few moments there when I feared for my life."

"Only a few?"

She laughed and reached for more bread. "Okay, quite a few times. Was it just me, or were the other drivers actually trying to drive me off the road? I was already going much faster than the speed limit."

"Italian drivers consider that more a suggestion than an actual speed limit. They pretty much go as fast as they want to or are able to. You've got to keep up or get out of their way."

"There are some drivers in Las Vegas who feel the same way."

"I thought you were from Chicago?"

She frowned, trying to remember if she'd told him that.

"You said your grandfather started his business there, so I assumed . . ."

Faith nodded. "Right. I did grow up there and I do live there now, but I took a break for a few years after I got my degree and went to work in Las Vegas."

"Doing what? Dealing blackjack?"

"No. I'm a librarian."

"What were you doing in Las Vegas?"

"Working at the library there. Oh good!" She almost grabbed the plate out of the waiter's hands. "Food."

His pasta arrived a moment later along with a bottle of white wine and two glasses.

She savored the subtle taste of tomato, cheese and basil in her pizza even as she appreciated the look of his lean fingers cradling the glass of wine he was handing her. "Want a taste?"

She did. She wanted more than a taste. She wanted to gobble him up. What was wrong with her? She hadn't even had any alcohol yet, and she was already dazed. Just because a man was looking at her. Not just any man. Paco and French Fry Boy hadn't had this effect on her. Only Dark Knight Caine seemed to have the ability to get to her.

She must be jet-lagged. That had to be it. She took the glass he offered, startled that the slight brush of his fingertips against hers created a mega-reaction with plenty of inner zing and heat. She gulped at her wine like a novice.

"Do you approve?" he asked.

Of her reaction to him? No, not really. She didn't approve at all. She hadn't come to Italy to have a fling with a rebound man. Had she? No, of course not. How shallow would that make her? Not as shallow as her runaway groom.

"The wine is lovely. It has a nice fruity bouquet with an underlying hint of nuttiness." She was certainly nuts to be thinking

31

seductive thoughts, but at least she sounded coherent and together. Again, Jane Austen should be proud. "So, are you here on vacation?" She took the nonchalant movement of his head as a nod. "You're traveling alone?" Another nod. "Me too." Oops. Her dad would have a stroke. Rule number one in travel security: Never admit you're alone. "But people know where I am, of course."

Caine watched her nervously press her napkin to her lips. She had a sexy mouth, even if she was telling him more than he thought she would. You'd think her father would have trained her better.

Even though he knew her work history, he'd had to play it dumb about her time in Las Vegas. He noticed she didn't mention that she'd occasionally worked part-time for West Investigations. As the daughter of the owner, it wasn't like she had to fill out time sheets or punch a time clock. She could work when and where she wanted.

He wasn't sure why she'd been so talkative about her background. Was that her normal behavior, or was exhaustion playing a part? She'd been talking a mile a minute before he gave her wine, so he couldn't blame the alcohol.

Not that he was complaining. Having her freely offer information was much better than his having to pry it out of her.

All in all, this job was turning out to be easier than he'd expected. She hadn't eyed him at all suspiciously, and that idiot choking had provided him with an unexpected yet perfect entrée. He couldn't have set it up any better if he'd tried.

Now he just had to convince her that sticking close to him was a really good idea. He'd seen her blue eyes widen when their fingers had touched a moment ago. He'd felt the jolt of electricity too. Sexual chemistry. That might prove useful later. For now, he didn't want to push her too hard.

So he sat back in his chair and watched her as she nervously chatted on about some movie and how she'd always wanted to visit Positano. She spoke as if coming here was her mission in life.

Caine knew all about missions. As a former Force Recon Marine, he was part of a brotherhood that valued honor, courage and commitment. He'd learned a lot in the Special Forces. Secrecy, subterfuge and surveillance were a way of life to him. He knew two dozen ways to kill with his bare hands. He'd seen things and done things that still gave him nightmares. He was battle-hardened — some might even say battle-scarred. But he'd survived. Plenty hadn't. Too many had died.

Caine reminded himself he'd survived for a reason. He had a mission of his own: a personal mission that went far beyond this professional assignment to keep tabs on Faith. There was no going back now.

Faith didn't sleep well. Given how exhausted she was, she should have had no problem. But unpacking her honeymoon trousseau had turned out to be more stressful than she'd anticipated.

She was confused, depressed and maybe even a little bit . . . relieved? Had she been more in love with the *idea* of love and marriage than the reality? Was Alan *really* the only man for her, her complete soul mate? Maybe not, she admitted to herself. That didn't mean that his defection and desertion didn't hurt.

The tears had started again, leaving her eyes puffy and red. She'd jammed the sexy lingerie and nightgowns into a bottom drawer before stubbing her bare toe in her hurry to get away from the antique, hand-painted cabinet in her hotel room.

She'd dreamed about Alan heading off into the sunset on the back of Dumbo the elephant while Caine the Dark Knight swooped down to rescue her . . . or kill her.

She couldn't be sure. Which was why she woke up shaking.

Sleep had been impossible after that. Dawn was lighting the sky as she got up and had a nice long soak in the old-fashioned tub. The hotel had provided a selection of lemon-scented oils and lotions to which she could easily become addicted. Lemon-adorned ceramic tiles marched across the bathroom walls in a beautiful display. Maybe she'd buy some tiles while she was here and have them put in her bathroom at home. Dressing in a colorful chiffon halter top and white Capri pants made her feel a little more cheerful.

The lobby was deserted as she headed out to take a walk through the lush gardens. Her delight at arriving at her dream location yesterday was diminished today as the reality of her situation hit her. She was alone. There was no one at her side to rave about the view or to smell the flowers. No one to hold her hand when she stumbled, no one to catch her if she fell. By the time she reached the outdoor terrace, she was blinking back the tears as she bumped into someone.

"Are you okay?"

She nodded furiously. It was Caine. He looked as good as he did last night, maybe even better. He had his hands braced on her arms to steady her. The sizzle of attraction was so powerful it was scary.

"You probably just have something in your eye, right?"

She nodded again and hurried off. She felt like an idiot. She didn't want to make a fool of herself in front of him or anyone else.

By the time she returned to the safety of her own room, she had her emotions more under control. She was pleasantly surprised to find a breakfast tray waiting for her, filled with warm flaky croissants and rolls as well as creamy butter and a selection of jams. The delicious food helped fight off her depression. So did a quick call from Megan.

"Are you okay? How's the view?" her cousin asked. "Is it as good as you hoped?"

Faith looked out the window and nodded. Sunshine poured down on the pastel-colored houses clinging to the rocky cliffs. Here and there splashes of bougainvillea added more color. "It's even better than I expected."

"And how about you? How are you doing? No regrets about going?"

"I can't believe I'm really here. And I don't regret coming, no. It's as spectacular as I always dreamed it would be. Even the bathroom is awesome. I'd tell you more, but I signed up for a tour to Pompeii, and I just realized it leaves in a few minutes. Tell my parents I'm fine. I'm just not up to talking to them myself. I came here to forget, not to rehash the past. I've got to go. I'll call you later."

Her tour of the eerie ruins of Pompeii left her feeling depressed at the disaster that had struck out of the blue. Sure, being left at the altar wasn't as bad as a having an erupting volcano like Mt. Vesuvius spewing hot lava all over you, but both events had come without any warning and caught the victims completely unprepared.

Faith left the area with a cloud of melancholy hanging over her. She could see the sadness on her face as she entered the lobby and caught her reflection in a gilded mirror: the dark circles under her eyes, her blah brown hair. That moment reminded her too vividly of sitting in the church anteroom waiting for Alan.

She'd never had a panic attack, but she felt one coming on. Her chest hurt, and she couldn't breathe.

"Did you want an appointment, signorina?" someone asked her. "We have an opening now."

"What?" Faith looked away from the mirror and realized she was standing near a hair salon tucked into a corner of the lobby next to the hotel's spa. She stared at the photo in the window of a blonde model with a trendy haircut that reminded her of Ellen Barkin's in *Ocean's Thirteen*. "Yes, I want an appointment." She pointed to the photo. "Make me look like her."

Caine watched Faith enter the ritzy salon. No surprise there. A rich princess like her would be looking to have her nails done and all that other pampering stuff.

He'd discreetly trailed her at Pompeii, noting her body language. With her bent head and arms wrapped around her middle, you'd think she was genuinely upset at the mass tragedy that had occurred there nearly two thousand years ago . . . if he remembered the date correctly. And he always remembered correctly. That was part of his job: to notice and remember the details. For a Marine, details could mean the difference between life and death. The mission had to be completed, no matter the cost. Failure was not an option.

He sat in the lobby and made himself comfortable. He almost didn't recognize Faith when she finally stepped out of the salon. Her hair was cut shorter and glimmered with sunlight. Amazing what hair coloring and highlights could do. Had he been a poetic kind of guy, he might have come up with some line about her being a Greek goddess or something. But no one had ever accused him of being poetic and lived to tell the tale.

Instead, he gave her a nod of approval and said, "You look good." Meanwhile, his body was saying, *Take her to bed.* He wanted her. Badly. Suddenly. Because she was a blonde now? Because she smelled like lemons? How demented was that?

Her smile lit up her entire face and made her blue eyes gleam. "Thanks." She moved her head back and forth, making her hair fall across her cheek. "I'm still getting used to the new me."

He reached out to remove a strand of hair that clung to the corner of her mouth. More sizzle. His body hardened. "Would the new you like to join me for dinner on the terrace tonight?"

"That sounds nice."

"Good." He planned on the evening being more than merely nice.

Caine wasn't disappointed. Faith looked great in a black jersey dress that clung in all the right places. The librarian had awesome breasts. Why hadn't he noticed that before? That wasn't usually the kind of thing that got past him. This job just kept getting better and better.

Faith noticed the way Caine was looking at her . . . and she liked it. He was dressed all in black, and he had that sexy stubble thing going on again. This was clearly a man who had to shave twice a day. No metrosexual here. Caine was totally, ruggedly masculine.

The *risotto agli scampi e punte d'asparago* she ordered was culinary perfection — the prawns and asparagus tender and fresh. She didn't think dessert could be any better, but it was. She and Caine shared bites of the *ravioli al limone.* The ravioli filled with a lemon-flavored ricotta cheese was a Positano specialty.

The divine dish wasn't the only thing making her mouth water. Caine kept eyeing her as if he wanted to taste her instead of the food. The heat was tangible, and it wasn't coming from the candlelight on the table.

The minute their meal was over, Caine took her by the hand and led her to the hotel's private garden. This morning she'd been achingly alone, and now she ached for something else.

Caine stopped at the first shadowy corner they reached. Cupping her face in his hands, he lowered his mouth to hers. The kiss was magical. He tasted of lemon and forbidden sex, of dark temptation and wine.

Her knees trembled as she held on to his shoulders. She parted her lips and moaned with pleasure as he expertly seduced her with his tongue. A French kiss in an Italian garden. Heaven.

She was no longer boring or blah. She was a new woman, a powerful blonde woman desired by this man with a raw hunger that was exhilarating and irresistible. Their kiss rapidly intensified, their embrace becoming increasingly intimate.

Caine cupped her breasts in the palm of his hand, and his touch burned through the jersey of her dress and her bra. She shivered with delight when he brushed his thumb across her hardened nipple. She wanted him to take her right there and then.

This wasn't like her at all. She wasn't the type to jump into a man's bed at the drop of a hat. She'd never been so wild with passion that one kiss made her long to have a man make love to her.

But this was more than just a mere kiss. This was an erotic revelation.

Unfortunately, it was interrupted by the arrival of a group of people strolling along the garden walkway. Still dazed and distracted, Faith nodded her agreement after Caine said, "Come with me, because it's hard to find unless you have someone who knows the way."

His dark eyes gleamed with a sensual promise. This was definitely a man who knew his way.

Wait, what had she just agreed to? "What's hard?" She almost swallowed her tongue. "Wait, that came out wrong. What's hard to find?"

"The walk along the Via Positanesi d'America." The Italian words fell from his lips with sexy skill. He had the kind of voice that made reading a shopping list sound wicked. "The views from there are great. I can take you tomorrow . . . if you'd like."

She'd definitely like. She wanted him to take her. Was that wise? Did she care? This moment was the beginning of the rest of her life. "I'd like," she said.

They spent the rest of the week together — exploring the narrow pedestrian pathways along the edge of the cliffs, sharing a pistachio gelato on the Marina Grande, jumping aboard the shuttle boats to take them island hopping.

Faith fulfilled her dream of seeing Capri and visiting the Blue Grotto. Caine fulfilled her desire to forget her humiliating past in

Chicago and live in the moment with a man who evoked a fiery passion within her — the kind of passion that she never even knew existed.

His long, leisurely kisses and heated caresses left her breathless and aching for more. Even though Faith talked to Megan every day and heard all about her father's dissatisfaction with her not calling him, Faith didn't mention Caine to her cousin. She wanted to keep Caine to herself. She didn't want to talk about him, to be logical about being on the rebound. She didn't want her father telling her to be sensible, reminding her of her responsibilities back home.

She just wanted to forget . . . and Caine made her do that. Made her forget everything but her need for him. Neither one of them talked about their past, although he did tell her he was a lawyer from Philadelphia. Instead, they focused on living in the moment. Sunshine and seduction. Laughter and desire.

And so it was only right, only natural that on Faith's next to last night in Positano she found herself in Caine's bed, peeling his shirt off as he stripped her naked. He worked faster than she did, but she did her best to catch up. Hard to do when he kept distracting her by lowering his open mouth to her bare breast and lapping at her nipple with his velvety rough tongue. She arched her back as sharp delight speared through her.

The view from his room might not be as stunning as hers, but the sight of him standing nude beside the bed a moment later was beyond words. He was built like an Italian statue sculpted by Michelangelo. Grabbing his lean hand, she tugged him down to her.

Neither of them spoke, using kisses instead to convey their thoughts and needs. He shoved the tangled sheet out of his way and slowly made his way to the place where she ached the most.

Faith closed her eyes and surrendered to the moment as he treated her to the most wickedly intimate of touches, first with his devilishly talented fingers and then his illegally hot tongue. Her pleasure skyrocketed until she was consumed by a climax that held her so tightly in its grip that she wasn't sure it would ever end.

She was still gasping for breath when he fumbled for a condom from his wallet on the bedside table and quickly rolled it on, surging into her before her last wave of pleasure diminished. The powerful friction Caine created, moving in and nearly out, was almost more bliss than she could bear. She was catapulted into a new level of ecstasy, raw and magical.

Her orgasm hit her with the force of a velvet fist clenching the walls of her vagina, the tip of her clitoris, and the other million G-spots she hadn't even known existed until that instant.

No wonder people became addicted to sex. She got it now. She never had before. But now . . . she knew.

Would Jane Austen think it prudent to have incredible sex with a man like Caine? Probably not, which was poor Jane's loss . . . and Faith's utterly satisfying gain.

Caine woke at dawn the next morning to find Faith still sound asleep, curled up in his arms with a smile on her face.

He carefully slid his arms from around her and headed for a cold shower. He needed to figure out what the hell he was supposed to do now, aside from having sex with her again. How many times had they done it last night? He'd lost count. This wasn't part of his plan. *She* wasn't part of his plan.

Ice-cold needles of water hit his body as he stepped into the shower. For the first time since taking this assignment, he felt a wave of guilt. What kind of man had he become?

The kind to get the job done.

His personal mission remained clear and unchanged. His goal was etched into his very soul with the acid of a bone-deep need for revenge. He scrubbed soap over his body, trying to decide if having sex with Faith was a plus or minus regarding his ultimate mission. As far as pleasure went, there was no contest. She was not only hot, but she also got to him. And that could be a problem.

Caine heard a muffled thud over the roar of the shower. "Faith? Are you okay?" he called out. No answer. Maybe she hadn't heard him. Wait, was that the outer door slamming shut?

He jumped out of the shower, grabbing a towel on his way. Sure enough, Faith was gone.

Shit. He'd left his wallet on the nightstand. What a rookie mistake. She'd removed his Illinois driver's and private investigator's licenses and tossed them onto the middle of the rumpled bed. His wallet had been thrown against the far wall, explaining the thump he'd heard.

He garnered all that intel in a second while racing toward the door she'd just

46

slammed on her way out. He yanked it open and stepped into the hallway. The door slammed behind him, leaving him stranded wearing nothing but shower water and a towel.

Caine used every one of the creative curses he'd learned from his years in the Marine Corps. He was so screwed.

Faith called her father the instant she got to her room. "How could you! Megan told me you were upset with me not talking to you on the phone. So instead of trusting me, you sent one of your minions to spy on me!" During their week together, Caine had told her he was a lawyer from Philadelphia, but his driver's license listed a Chicago address. Ditto for his private investigator's license. Obviously the man lied. "His name is Caine Hunter. Ring any bells?"

"Oh my God!" her father bellowed. "He doesn't work for me. He works for that low-down thieving bastard Vince King from King Investigations!"

Great. Faith's heart sank. She'd just slept with and had mind-blowing sex with the enemy.

CHAPTER THREE

"Are you still there? Did you hear what I said?" Faith's father demanded, his voice so loud she had to hold her cell phone away from her ear. "Caine Hunter works for that bastard Vince King!"

"Yes, I heard you."

"You said this guy has been spying on you? Have you had direct contact with him?"

"Yes." You couldn't get any more direct than she'd gotten with Caine last night. The heated memories filled her mind and weakened her knees. She sank onto the bed. Her contact with Caine had been intimately direct and extraordinarily sensual, not that she was about to tell her father that.

"Did he threaten you? Intimidate you in any way?"

"No, nothing like that." Although Caine's ability to give Faith pleasure had been so intense that it had threatened her self-control and left her flying to orgasmic planes she'd never visited before.

Sensing she wasn't telling him everything, he demanded, "Do I need to come over there and get you?"

"Of course not."

"You're obviously not in a clear state of mind."

Hey, you wouldn't be clear if you'd gone through what I have in the past week, she wanted to tell her father but didn't. She'd already left her family with the mess caused by her ruined wedding. Instead of facing the music and handling things herself, she'd hopped on a plane and left town.

Not the action of a responsible adult, perhaps, and she felt guilty about that . . . along with the fact that she'd just slept with her father's enemy. Or to be more precise — she'd slept with an employee of his enemy.

"You haven't forgotten why that bastard King is our enemy, have you?"

"No, Dad, I haven't forgotten." How could she? Their rivalry was legendary.

"He worked for me. He was my best friend, and he betrayed me."

Yeah, Faith sure knew how betrayal felt. She'd had more than her fair share lately.

"After swearing he'd never start his own

49

agency, he did just that. He's been out to get me ever since — stealing clients, sabotaging cases, messing with our investigators. When Alan the Asshole went missing, my first thought was that King had gotten to him. I don't think that's what happened in that instance, but I will certainly check it out again. This case with Caine Hunter showing up in Italy is another matter. Hunter isn't just any employee. He's got a sick grudge against us. He blames me for his father's death."

"What? Why would he do that?"

"His father was involved in a major case of ours, one involving corporate theft in the millions of dollars. We were about to turn our information over to the authorities when the guy committed suicide."

"How can Caine blame his father's suicide on us?"

"Because he doesn't think his father was guilty, which is ridiculous. Listen, Faith, this Hunter guy is not to be messed with. He's a former Marine with revenge on his mind. That's a dangerous combination."

And here she'd been thinking Caine's dark eyes and broad shoulders were a dangerous combination. Silly her.

"You need to get away from that bastard immediately," her father said.

"I fly home tomorrow."

"Don't wait until then," he ordered before hanging up.

Faith's first inclination was that she wasn't about to let Caine force her out of her dream trip — even if it was now threatening to turn into a nightmare. Here was yet another man who'd messed things up for her. Yet another betrayal.

Maybe she *should* just leave. Was it really worth hanging around for another day?

Before she could make that decision, the door to her room opened. Because the door had a habit of not latching all the way, she usually made sure it was shut after she entered her room, but today she'd been too upset.

Caine stood there, wearing a towel and a scowl.

"Get out of my room!" She still held her cell phone in her hand, and while a part of her wanted to throw her BlackBerry at him, she needed it to get help. Wait; dialing 911 wouldn't do a thing for her in Italy.

"I can explain —" he began.

She cut him off. "I'm sure you can come up with some additional lies to add to the pile you've already told me. Don't bother. My father already told me all about you."

Caine's face darkened. "Your father

wouldn't know the truth if it bit him in the ass."

"That sounds like a more accurate description of you. I know that you work for Vince King. You're not going to try to deny that, are you?" Was some small part of her hoping he'd say there had been some terrible mix-up? Yeah right. That was like hoping that Alan would show up at the church last week.

"No. I don't deny that," Caine said. "Vince had me follow you because he was suspicious of you going to Italy on your own. Come on, you have to admit it doesn't fit your pattern of behavior. You've never traveled on your own in your entire life."

"And because I haven't taken a solo trip before, your boss sends you all the way to Italy to spy on me? Talk about paranoid. That's sick."

"I was already here in Italy. On personal business."

Faith wasn't buying one word Caine said. That brief flicker of hope had died, stomped out completely. "Why don't you admit what your real job was?"

"I already told you —"

"Lies. You've already told me a bucketful of lies. The truth is that Vince sent you here to seduce me in order to get even with my father. Because Vince hates my father. He and my father have been bitter rivals for years, just like the Montagues and Capulets." And with the same tragic outcome. At least she hadn't guzzled a load of poison. No, she was sooo over having her heart broken by a man.

"Having sex with you was not part of the plan," Caine angrily denied. "I'm not some gigolo for hire."

"A gigolo would have done a better job," she retorted.

"I didn't hear any complaints last night."

"Well, you're hearing them now."

"I didn't come here for a postcoital postmortem."

"Why *did* you come here? Did you really think that I'd buy your lame excuses and fall into bed with you?"

"Why not?" he drawled. "It worked before."

She slapped him. Hard. Her palm stung and turned red. Had Jane Austen ever slapped anyone? Damn, it hurt. She wiggled her hand to shake the pain off.

Caine apparently thought she was going to hit him again, because he grabbed her wrist to prevent her from repeating her attack.

"Get your hands off me!" she yelled.

"Gladly. Once you calm down."

"People need to stop telling me to calm down," she growled.

She was considering kicking his shins when he tugged her against his body, which was now naked, the towel having fallen to the floor.

She froze. How dare he be aroused at a time like this? Did the man have no shame? Clearly not, or he wouldn't have barged into her room practically nude.

Well, she wasn't going to respond. She refused to be impressed or aroused or anything but furious — coldly, logically furious.

"Listen to me, because I'm only going to tell you this once." His voice was as hard as the rest of his body. "No one told me to have sex with you. That wasn't planned. It was a mistake. There's no way I'm telling Vince or anyone else about what happened last night. No one has to know. Unless you blabbed to your father?"

She refused to acknowledge Caine or the question he'd asked. Instead, she was reciting the titles of Jane Austen's books in her head, in chronological order.

Sense and Sensibility — *1811.*
Pride and Prejudice — *1813.*

Mansfield Park — *1814*.
Emma — *1816*.
Northanger Abbey — *1817 posthumous*.
Persuasion — *1817 posthumous*.

Clearly frustrated by her silence, Caine tightened his hold on her. "Did you tell your father?"

"That you're a bastard? No, I didn't have to tell him that. He already knew."

"You've got a lot of attitude for a librarian."

"So I've been told." She hadn't, but that was about to change. "So be afraid. Be very afraid."

"Oh yeah. I'm just trembling in my boots here. Can't you tell?"

Betrayed by two different men in ten days, Faith had had it. No more Ms. Nice Girl. "Unless you want me to hurt you, you'll release me immediately."

"Hurt me? Yeah right. Ouch! Shit!" He released her to rub his nipples that she'd just pinched and nearly ripped off his chest.

"I did warn you." She picked up the towel and threw it in his face. "Now get out." She yanked the door to her room open. "And don't come back. I already know everything I need to know about you and the grudge you have against my family."

"Did your rich daddy tell you he's the reason my father died?"

"He said you mistakenly blame him for your father's suicide."

Caine's face darkened, and a muscle jumped in his clenched jaw. "The only mistake is the one Jeff West made in accusing my dad. That's a mistake he's going to pay for big time."

"And you made me pay big time too by seducing me when you knew I was vulnerable. Yeah, that's the sign of an honorable man, all right," she mocked him bitterly. "Honor, courage, commitment — aren't those the requirements of a Marine? You're sadly lacking in all three of those traits."

"You don't know what the hell you're talking about, lady." His words hit her like bullets. "I've got more honor in my little finger than your entire family has ever had. And my commitment is to my dad, who was falsely accused."

"So you say."

"So I plan on proving."

"That will never happen."

"Watch me." He marched out of her room.

She slammed the door after him, only to have it bounce open again and for her to find Paco the bellman standing there. "Do you need help, signorina?"

"Yes, I need to be moved to another room, one with a door that closes properly." And keeps dangerously seductive men out.

Faith didn't start crying until fifteen minutes later in her new room when she called Megan. "I'm sorry to wake you up," she sobbed. "I know it's after midnight there. But I had to talk to you." She bit her lip and attempted to scrub the tears from her cheeks.

"Are you okay?"

"No." She gulped, trying to regain her control. "Not really."

"Faith, you're scaring me. Did you have an accident? Are you in the hospital? Hurt? What happened?"

"First you have to swear not to tell anyone. Pinkie swear."

"Pinkie swear. What happened?"

"I had sex with the enemy."

"What? Were you raped?"

"No. I had rebound sex with a guy, and I just found out he works for King Investigations."

"Uh-oh."

"Yeah, that's putting it mildly. You know this isn't like me at all. I don't jump into bed at the drop of a hat."

"I know you don't. So who is this guy?"

"His name is Caine Hunter."

"When did you meet him?"

"The first day I arrived."

"Why didn't you mention him before now?"

"Because I was stupid. I wanted to forget the mess my life was in. And he made me feel sexy and attractive. I fell for the act. He totally played me."

"I don't understand."

"He was specifically sent here to have sex with me."

"What? But why? Who would do that?"

"Vince King."

"Why go after you?"

"For revenge. You know how King hates Dad. And this guy, Caine, hates Dad too. Blames him for his father's suicide. It's ridiculous, of course. As if Dad would ever falsely accuse someone of a crime. You know how good my father is at what he does."

"I think I remember this case," Megan said slowly. "It was right before you came back from Las Vegas. I don't know the details, but it was a very tragic situation. As I recall, the guy's son was serving in Iraq in the Marine Corps at the time of his father's death."

"Was there any question about it being a suicide?"

"I don't think so, but I'm not sure. Let's get back to you and this guy."

"He got to me in a vulnerable moment. Normally I'd never have sex with a guy I'd only known for a week. Never in a million years. But after the way Alan dumped me, I was just feeling so terrible. Caine knew that and took advantage."

"The bastard."

"The rat bastard." Faith wiped away the remaining dampness on her face and lifted her chin with newfound resolve. "The total rat bastard."

"So what are you going to do now?" Megan asked.

"I don't know. I'm trying to decide if I should leave today and come home a day early. But then I let him win. What do you think?"

"I wish I was there to help you."

"Yeah, me too."

"I should have taken a leave from work and gone with you to Italy. If I'd been there, that scumbag wouldn't have gotten to you. I'd have had your back."

"I know you would."

"I feel so guilty —"

Faith interrupted her. "No, it's not your fault. Not at all. You have nothing to feel guilty about. I, on the other hand, have quite a bit to feel guilty about. Number one: that I didn't tell you about Caine before now. Number two: that I was so stupid to fall for this guy's act. Number three: that I didn't just stay in Chicago and face the music. Number four: that I left you all to deal with it for me."

"Don't worry about us. Everything here is fine. You know how organized your mom is. She's handled everything just fine."

"Is she mad that I haven't called her?"

"No, she understands."

"Well, she wouldn't understand this new mess I'm in, so don't tell her about it."

"Don't worry. I already pinkie swore, remember?"

"Thanks, Megan, for being there for me when I need you."

"I just wish I really was there and not here."

"You better get some sleep. You've got to work in the morning."

Megan groaned. "Don't remind me."

"Love you, Cuz."

"Love you too."

Faith ended the call and stepped to the window, where she had a new view of Positano, similar to the one in her previous room but now one floor lower. She remembered her arrival here in Positano when she'd first seen the picture-perfect display of bright white buildings and pastel houses perched against the cliffs. So much had changed since then. If only she hadn't met Caine, hadn't fallen for his fake charm, hadn't ended up in his bed. That had changed everything.

One thing was still the same, though. Her stomach was growling.

Paco, bless his heart, had made sure that a delicious breakfast was brought to her new room along with her packed bags. Faith wasn't really hungry, despite her noisy tummy, but she needed to keep her strength up, so she nibbled on a flaky croissant smothered with lemon marmalade.

She wasn't about to waste her final morning moping around her room.

When the going gets tough, the tough go shopping. Not that Faith had ever really gone for that saying before, but she was a new woman now.

No more frumpy librarian clothes for her.

Okay, so she'd never worn frumpy clothes, but she'd never gone for edgy look-at-me outfits before. That was all about to change. Positano had plenty of specialty boutiques, and she was going to hit all of them her last day here.

■ ■ ■ ■

"I'm telling you, Vince, she's no threat," Caine told his boss over the phone. "Hell, she's spent most of her time here sightseeing."

Well, there had been some incredible sex last night, but he wasn't sharing that intel with his boss. That was strictly on a need-to-know basis, and Vince didn't need to know that Caine had compromised his impartiality by letting his dick think for him.

Not that having sex with Faith had diminished Caine's determination to clear his father's name. In fact, her overconfident claim that she knew her father was right about everything had only served to reinforce Caine's drive to prove her wrong. His mission remained the same: clear his dad's name.

"You're sure she hasn't contacted Stalotti in Naples? He hasn't signed on the dotted line yet for us to do the work for his new Chicago office."

"I checked her cell phone yesterday. The only calls have been to her cousin in Chicago."

"What about her father? Hasn't she called him?"

"No. Not before today."

"That seems strange," Vince, ever the paranoid, said. "Why wouldn't she call her father more frequently than that?"

"Do you have any proof that West even knows about Stalotti?"

"I don't need proof. I trust my gut on these things. Stalotti's headquarters are in Naples. He has a summer house in Positano. What's the West daughter doing now?"

"Shopping." Caine had followed her from the hotel to the heart of Positano, where he'd watched her buy a watercolor painting of the harbor area from one of the many artists displaying their work along the bougainvillea-covered lane there.

"So you're willing to bet your job that she's no threat?"

"Affirmative. She's a children's librarian."

"A great cover. Who's going to suspect the librarian? No one except me."

"You suspect everyone," Caine said.

"That's what's made me the man I am today: Chicago's leading investigator. The story was in the *Chicago Tribune* today, page two. West's days as top dog in this business are numbered."

"Hmmm." Caine wasn't really paying attention. Faith had wandered into a shop that sold clothes, and she hadn't come out yet. But a woman with a big hat and giant sunglasses was strolling out. She wasn't wearing any of the clothes Faith had worn earlier, but something about the way she walked, the sway of her hips . . .

His gaze went down her tanned legs to her shoes. She was wearing the same sandals Faith had worn this morning. She'd had them handmade three days ago by a wizened guy in a skinny storefront barely wide enough to stand in. She'd picked the blue fake gems that dotted the tops because they were the color of the water here.

"Gotta go," Caine told Vince before following the woman as she made her way up the street.

"Nice try," he muttered under his breath.

He saw her go into another tiny boutique. "Two can play that game, sunshine." He tugged a baseball cap out of his back pocket and bought a sleeveless T-shirt from a vendor's outdoor stand next door, all the while keeping an eagle eye on the boutique. By the time Faith came out ten minutes later, wearing the same bogus huge hat, sunglasses and telltale sandals, he had changed his appearance and his posture.

He saw her nervously glance over her shoulder and look right past him. Damn, he was good. The surveillance techniques he'd learned in the Marine Corps served him well in his current position.

She ducked into another store. This time she came out with a backpack and two bags filled with her purchases.

Another store, another bag and an escort. An elderly couple, the man on the left, the woman on the right, bracketed her like bookends. As the street narrowed and the crowd grew, they stood behind Faith to let her go ahead.

Caine kept track of her hat, which he could see above the crowd. Thank God Faith was tall. She wove in and out of the throng of tourists filling the area, turning it into a pedestrian traffic jam.

Shit, he'd lost her.

No wait, there she was. On the move again. Fine by him. He wasn't about to let her go.

Jeff West stared at the phone in his home office. It wasn't quite eight in the morning here in Chicago, but he couldn't wait any longer. Faith had called at midnight last night and told him about Caine.

Vince had gone too far this time. Jeff had to do something about that. He couldn't let that bastard get away with it.

Jeff had already put one of his best agents

to work overnight digging up information on Vince. And he'd set his best computer geek to hacking into Vince's e-mail files. Illegal, certainly, but necessary. It's not as if Vince hadn't done the same to Jeff, which is why he was constantly updating his firewalls and security systems.

Jeff picked up the phone and dialed. Vince answered as Jeff had known he would.

"I know why you're calling," Vince preempted him by saying. "You saw the article in the *Trib* describing me as Chicago's leading investigator."

"You're Chicago's leading bastard! How dare you send one of your thugs to trail my daughter on her vacation to Italy."

"What's wrong, West? Afraid of what I'll find?"

"Going after me is one thing, but going after my family . . . That's low, even for you."

"You taught me everything I know," Vince said.

"You know nothing."

"I know more than you think."

"If I find out you had a hand in my daughter being left at the altar —"

"Save your empty threats. I didn't have anything to do with that mess. You and your daughter created that debacle all by yourselves."

"Why go after Faith in Italy? Might it have something to do with a potential new Italian client of yours?"

"I have no idea what you're talking about."

"Yes, you do. The ironic thing is that I had no idea about Stalotti and wouldn't have, if you hadn't tipped your hand by spying on Faith. My daughter is innocent. But your operative isn't. Caine Hunter has a grudge against me."

"So do plenty of other people."

"Well, my daughter was smart enough to know that Caine wasn't some regular tourist."

"Really? She sure spent enough time with him. He swept her off her feet. Just like I told him to."

Jeff saw red. He swore vehemently. "If you thought we had a rivalry before, that was child's play compared to what you're in for now. This is war."

"Oh yeah?" Vince said. "Go ahead. Bring it on."

"I thought you said West's daughter was no threat to me," Vince bellowed over the phone to Caine. "I should fire your sorry ass right now! She made you, didn't she? Don't bother denying it. Why didn't you tell me? Then I would have been better prepared for Jeff West's call. He knows about Stalotti. He claims he didn't know until he tried to figure out why I was having Faith watched, but I don't believe him. Do not let that woman out of your sight. She's due back here in Chicago tomorrow, or I'd send someone else. How did she find out who you are?"

"Does it matter?"

"If you weren't so damn good, and if having you on my payroll didn't drive West nuts . . ."

Caine ignored the unspoken threat. Working for King Investigations gave him access to information about Jeff West that would be harder to get otherwise. Harder but not impossible. As a former Marine, Caine knew how to filter out distractions in order to focus on succeeding in the mission. "I made a mistake. It won't happen again."

"It better not. Hell, it wasn't that difficult an assignment, Caine. Especially for a man with your credentials. Don't screw up again."

"I won't."

Faith was so proud of herself. She'd outsmarted Caine. The adrenaline high brought with it a sense of accomplishment that she hadn't felt for a long time. "You rock!" she told herself.

Her cell phone rang. "Vince King just admitted that he sent Caine there to sweep you off your feet, was the way he put it." Her father's voice vibrated with lingering anger.

Even though she'd suspected as much, hearing it confirmed still hit her hard. Talk about a buzz kill. "You talked to Vince?"

"Damn right I did. No one messes with my family. I'm taking that bastard down. What about you? Will you be okay?"

"Don't worry about me," Faith said. "I've got everything under control." In one week, Faith had gone through two rotten, life-changing experiences that had turned her into a different person — a stronger, tougher person on a new life path.

She stared down at her brand-new Italian leather spectator pumps. She'd just beaten Caine at his own game. He was still trailing the woman wearing her sandals and clothes, including the big sun hat. The salesclerk had been glad to help out by pretending to be her. Faith had also enlisted the help of an elderly couple to throw Caine off. She'd paid them all well.

Meanwhile, Faith was currently in the backseat of a sleek black Mercedes sedan whisking her back to Naples, where she planned on getting a flight home this afternoon. Sure, she'd had to pay more to leave her rental car in Positano, but it was worth it.

It felt so good to beat Caine at his own game. Better than good. It felt damn *great*. Utilizing the tricks of dumping a tail reminded Faith of her PI training. The thrill of successfully evading him brought with it a surprisingly strong feeling of satisfaction along with a newfound sense of confidence.

All of which left Faith knowing what she had to do next.

CHAPTER FOUR

"I quit," Faith told her boss, Maria Sanchez.

Maria wasn't someone easily startled. As the branch manager of the River North branch of the Chicago Public Library, she couldn't afford to get rattled. When the library's women's bathroom toilet backed up last month, Maria was Ms. Calm. When eighty-nine-year-old geezer Oscar O'Hara flashed Maria in the nonfiction section of the library, she merely said, "Put that away."

And so Maria was currently bestowing the same look of tranquillity upon Faith. You'd think that having five kids would make Maria a little more stressed-out, but no . . . quite the opposite. Nothing surprised her. "I realize you've been through a rough patch," Maria said in that soothing voice of hers. "This is no time to be making major life changes."

"It's the perfect time to make major life changes."

Maria frowned. She wasn't accustomed to being contradicted. Her composed exterior showed the first tiny signs of cracking as a flush rose beneath her flawless olive skin and the feathery lines around her eyes deepened. "But you're so good at your job. You're a great children's librarian."

"No, I'm not. I don't even like *Charlotte's Web.*"

Now Maria did look surprised. "You don't?"

Faith shook her head. "I've always hated it. I'm not a fan of spiders."

"Even so, that's no reason to quit. Give yourself some time to think things over. Don't make the decision now. You're still jet-lagged."

"No, I need to move on. I'm sorry it's such short notice, but I can't stay. It's a new day, and I need to make a new start."

"If this is about your salary —"

"It's not. Trust me, it's not."

"Then I don't understand."

Now Faith was the calm one. "I don't expect you to."

"I thought you enjoyed working here."

"I did. But it's time for me to move on. Today. Right now. I'm sorry." She placed her official letter of resignation on Maria's desk before turning and heading down the hallway for her own cubicle. She grabbed an empty cardboard box along the way and started quickly packing up her things — her Jane Austen action figure and her What Would Jane Do? coffee mug. Her Fancy Nancy tiara and glitter sunglasses. Her personal collection of favorite children's books including *Scaredy Squirrel* and the classic *Harold and the Purple Crayon*. Her poster of the cover of *Little Polar Bear* by Hans de Beer. The READ poster of Jeffrey Dean Morgan she bought at the ALA store. Her props for story time. So much jumbled together. She was thinking in fragmented sentences, but her decision remained firm. She had to leave.

Faith walked out of the library without looking back, clutching the box to her chest while two tote bags filled with the rest of her stuff hung from her arms. This condition made flagging a cab more of a challenge than usual during lunch rush, but she managed.

During the ride from the library to her Streeterville condo, she turned to her iPod and played Madonna's "Jump" repeatedly. Faith was ready to jump — to jump from the life she'd known before to a new one. She was ready, willing and able.

Able . . . which got her thinking of Cain

and Abel. Caine . . .

No, that thought pattern had to stop immediately. To help herself along with that goal, Faith touched the screen of her iPod, skipping ahead to "I Hate Everything About You" by Three Days Grace, her most recent musical download.

She didn't realize she was mouthing the lyrics "I hate, you hate" until she caught the nervous look the cabbie gave her in the rearview mirror.

She felt the need to apologize. "Sorry. I was just singing along with a song . . . never mind." Removing the buds from her ears, she safely stowed her iPod away. If only she could stow away her thoughts of Caine as efficiently.

"I quit my job at the library today," Faith told her father as she sat in his corner office with a great view of the Picasso statue in Daley Plaza. "I'm taking you up on your standing offer to come work here." She was pleased with how confident and forceful that came out.

Her father jumped up and came around his desk to hug her. "Hey, that's great! You know I've always wanted you to join the family business." He beamed at her. "You're the best researcher we've ever had. No one does background checks as thoroughly and efficiently as you." He headed back to the Aeron ergonomically designed chair behind his desk, the one she'd picked out for him his last birthday, and turned his attention to a file on his desk. "Go see my assistant, Gloria, and she'll set you up."

"Thanks, but I don't want to just sit in front of a computer all day. I want to work real cases. In the field."

"Sure. Eventually you can work up to that." He transferred his attention from the file to her. "Hey, have you done something to your hair?"

"Yes." Her boring hair of the past was a distant memory now. She still loved the new look, the way her hair moved when she did, swinging against her neck. The multilayered, sophisticated style continued to be a huge confidence boost. "I used to be a mousy brunette, and now I'm a tough blonde. But don't change the subject. Are we agreed?"

"On what? That you're a tough blonde?"

"No, that I get assigned to a real case by the end of next week." She made a note of the date on her BlackBerry. "I've got my PI license, and it's still valid."

"I know."

It was just now occurring to Faith that the last time her BlackBerry and her father were in the same room together had been on her wedding day.

"Have you heard from Alan?"

She blinked. "No. Why? What have you heard?"

"About Alan, nothing. But I've heard plenty about Caine. What happened over there in Italy? You still haven't told me."

"Caine tried to tail me, but I successfully evaded him. Why does he think that his father is innocent? Does he have any grounds for such an assumption?"

"Of course not."

"That's what I told him."

"You talked to him about the case?"

"Only briefly. He was making accusations, and I was defending you."

"That's my girl." He flashed her a smile.

"He seems very determined about clearing his dad's name."

"He doesn't have a leg to stand on."

"Did you review the case?"

"I didn't have to."

Her father sounded a bit defensive, which was unusual for him. The confidence was still there, as it always was. But there was a new underlying tension she hadn't picked up on before.

"Don't bother your pretty head about this," he continued. "You stay focused on

76

your new job here in the family business."

"This is what the library was paying me." She wrote an amount on a piece of paper. "I'd need to make at least that much here."

Her father just smiled. "Honey, you'd make nearly twice that much here."

"Really?" she squeaked.

"Really."

She eyed him suspiciously. "Because I'm your daughter?"

"Because that's what we pay our top talented investigators. I told you that you should have left that job a long time ago."

The door opened, and her uncle Dave entered the office. He was taller than her father by two inches and younger by two years. He was in charge of the accounting side of the business, a role that suited his mathematician self-proclaimed nerdy side. A fan of Thurber's short stories, he readily admitted that he was often in his own world. His love for mathematics explained his quirky tie filled with rows of gold and silver pi symbols on a red background. He had another tie with the same design on a blue background. They were the only two ties he owned.

"Oh, sorry to interrupt," he said.

Faith jumped up and gave her uncle a hug. She hadn't seen him at the wedding, although she knew he'd been there. She also knew he liked to keep a low profile and avoided drama whenever possible.

"Faith is joining the company," Jeff said proudly. "She finally saw the light and dumped that go-nowhere librarian job of hers."

Her father never had been thrilled with her chosen profession.

"Now you just need to get Megan to do the same thing," Jeff told his brother.

"Megan loves her job." He looked at Faith. "I thought you loved your job too."

"I needed a change," Faith said.

"I can see that." Dave frowned. "You've changed."

Faith touched her hair. "Yes, I'm blonde now. Hair color and highlights can do amazing things."

Dave slowly shook his head. "That's not all."

"You're right. The stylist cut my hair as well."

"No, that's not what I meant. It's not just your change in appearance. It's your change in attitude. The way you're sitting in that chair with confidence."

Instead of sitting in the anteroom of the Gold Coast church shredding her lace handkerchief. Not that her uncle had seen her in that sorry state.

"It's a change for the better," she said.

"Absolutely," her father agreed.

Her uncle didn't look as sure.

"Is there a reason Faith West took an earlier flight than you did?" Vince demanded when Caine showed up in his office straight from the airport.

"She was trying to aggravate me."

"From the look on your face, it seems she succeeded. You want to know how she spent her day today?"

"Not really."

"The mild-mannered children's librarian just quit her day job and has gone to work for our mutual enemy, her father. I told you not to underestimate her."

Caine couldn't get over how much she'd messed up his mind. And in such a short time. Here he'd been feeling guilty for having slept with Faith in Italy when she was still vulnerable after being jilted by her ass of a fiancé. Caine hadn't intended to take advantage of her. His attraction to her had taken him by surprise and continued to do so.

And there Faith was, sneaking out on him in Positano, evading his surveillance, making him feel and look like a total idiot.

Caine was not a man accustomed to making mistakes. Hell, he even owned the T-shirt — To Err Is Human. To Forgive Is Divine. Neither Is Marine Corps Policy.

Had Faith been leading him on the entire time? Did she have some kind of hidden agenda of her own?

It had been a long time since he'd been played the fool. She'd totally taken him in.

"Now you look aggravated and surprised," Vince noted.

Caine immediately schooled his expression, putting his war face on.

"Better," Vince said approvingly.

Caine had never been one to wear his emotions on his sleeve, and the fact that he'd shown them made him doubly angry. But he had his feelings under control now. And he'd keep them that way. Because he wasn't about to be distracted by a sexy blonde with deception up her sleeve. She might have won their previous skirmish, but the war wasn't over by any means. He was just getting started.

Faith kept walking along Michigan Avenue as she checked her incoming call. It was her mother.

"Hi, Mom."

"Your father just told me you quit your

job at the library!"

"That's right."

"Why didn't you speak to me before doing something so drastic?"

"Because I knew you'd try to talk me out of it."

"Of course I'd talk you out of it. Why would you do a dumb thing like that?"

"Gee, Mom, tell me what you *really* think."

"I'm sorry. It's just that you loved your job."

"I loved Alan too, and that didn't work out so well either."

"Did something happen at work? Did you have a disagreement with a coworker?"

"No."

"With your boss?"

"No."

"Jane Austen would never quit her job at the library."

Faith had forgotten that her What would Jane Austen do? philosophy had originally come from her mom. "Probably not. But I did."

"I don't understand why."

"It was time." Faith entered the Crate and Barrel store.

"Time for what?"

"Time for a change. You know . . ." Faith

looked around. "The beds look different in person."

"Where are you?"

"Crate and Barrel. I'm buying a new bed."

"What's wrong with the old one?"

"Alan slept in it."

"Oh."

"Is that your daughter on the phone?" Aunt Lorraine bellowed in the background. "You tell her how selfish it was to leave you to handle the mess after her wedding. And then she didn't even call you from Italy."

"I'm sorry," Faith's mom murmured.

"Tell Aunt Lorraine she's right," Faith said. "It was selfish of me to dump everything in your lap that way."

"I didn't mind."

"And I should have called you from Italy."

"Megan explained about that. And you did e-mail me. But, honey, I'm worried about you."

"Don't be."

"This leaving your job thing. It's not like you."

"Yeah, I'm different." Faith held the phone away from her face and took a photo before e-mailing it to her mom. "What do you think?"

"Who's the photo of?"

"Me, Mom."

"The light must be funny in that store." Her mother sounded confused. "You look blonde in this picture."

"I am blonde now."

"Why are there beds behind her?" Aunt Lorraine shouted in the background. "I told you I wondered what kind of work she was really doing in Las Vegas. Prostitution is legal there. Tell her it's not legal here in Chicago. Make sure she knows that."

"Assure Aunt Lorraine that I do know that. Why is she there?"

"Her condo is being painted, and she had to come stay with us for a few days."

"Thanks for warning me. I won't be stopping by. How are you holding up?"

"I'm managing." Her mother's voice sounded strained, but then Aunt Lorraine did that to a person.

"Come visit me and see my new bed." Faith indicated which one she wanted to the salesclerk with her free hand. "They should deliver it tomorrow." She'd already checked that out online ahead of time.

"Won't you be working tomorrow?"

"Right. That's not a problem for the delivery. The doorman is great."

"Yes, he was most helpful when we were there."

"Again, I'm really sorry I dumped everything on you that way. I'll make it up to you."

"I may hold you to that."

"I'm not going back to my library job," Faith said.

"We'll see," her mother said.

Faith had her condo door open as Megan stepped off the elevator with a Giordano's pizza with extra mushrooms in her hands. "I met the delivery guy in the lobby."

Faith hugged her before grabbing the cardboard box from her. "I know Italy is the birthplace of pizza, but there's nothing like a Chicago-style deep dish."

"My dad told me you quit your job. Is that true?"

"Yes." Faith opened the box and grabbed an extralong knife from the kitchen's dark brown granite countertop. A regular pizza cutter couldn't handle the job of this big-boy pizza. She also grabbed a pair of wineglasses from her cherry wood kitchen cabinet.

"Why?" Megan asked. "Why would you quit?"

"Because I wanted to."

"Is this because of Caine? Or because of Alan?"

"It's because of me. I'm tired of getting

kicked in the teeth. I'm fighting back. Turning over a new leaf. Out with the old blah and boring me, in with the new mad, bad and blonde me."

"You were never blah and boring," Megan hotly defended her.

"Alan sure thought so. That's why he left."

"He left because he's a bastard!"

"Why didn't I see that something was wrong?"

"Love is blind. But don't let Alan's actions make you quit your job."

"That's not why I left the library. I need a new start." After opening the bottle of 3 Blind Moose Merlot she'd chosen, Faith filled Megan in about how Caine had tailed her that last morning in Positano and how she'd evaded him. "It felt good flexing my investigative skills again. Vince actually told my father that he'd sent Caine there to 'sweep me off my feet' were his exact words."

Megan's eyes widened. "Vince and your dad spoke? I thought they hadn't talked to each other in over a decade."

"My father initiated the call and warned Vince that he'd crossed the line."

"Does your dad know that you went to bed with Caine?"

"No."

"Does Vince know?"

"Caine claimed he wouldn't tell him."

"Do you believe him?"

"I don't know. I do know that Caine was my first and last dumb blonde moment."

"I meant to tell you it looks good on you."

"What does? Being a dumb blonde? Gee, thanks."

"You know what I mean. The new hair color. It looks really good."

"Thanks." Faith ran her hand through her shorter do. "I'm still not totally used to it, but I do love it."

"What's this?" Megan asked, pointing to a beautifully wrapped small jeweler's box on the table.

"I brought you something back from Italy. Open it."

Megan looked down at the delicately carved cameo pendant. "I love it! Help me put it on."

Faith did and received a hug before she and Megan once again focused on their meals.

Once most of the pizza and bottle of Merlot were gone, the talk became more emotional.

"What kind of cheap slut am I to be in love with Alan and about to marry him one week and then have sex with Caine the next? What does that say about me?"

"That you were badly hurt by Alan and were taken advantage of by Caine."

"But if I really truly loved Alan, then Caine shouldn't have been able to tempt me, no matter what."

"Are you saying you weren't in love with Alan?"

"I don't know. I couldn't face sleeping in the same bed I shared with Alan, so I donated it to charity and bought a new one. That's how I spent my afternoon. They deliver it tomorrow, so I'm sleeping on the couch tonight." Faith paused for a moment. "Hey, get up and help me move the dining room table."

"What?"

"You heard me."

"What about the plates?"

She whisked them off the table as well as their glasses and the wine bottle. "There. Now, take hold of the other end, and we'll rotate it so that it's going the other way."

"Why?"

"To get a new perspective."

"We have to move the chairs out of the way first."

"Right." Faith released her hold on the edge of the table and headed for the nearest dining room chair, setting it aside. "Okay, that's done. Now, let's move the table."

Megan said, "Watch the —"

Faith swore as she hit her head.

"— hanging lamp."

Faith set down the table and rubbed the back of her head. "Maybe we should leave it like this."

"At an angle?"

"The decorating magazines all say not to keep things all straight and commonplace." She returned her plate and their glasses to the table before tugging a chair closer and sitting down.

"Is the view different enough?"

"It was *perspective* not *view*." She automatically looked out the immense floor-to-ceiling window, where she could see Lake Michigan and the Ferris wheel at Navy Pier. Several sailboats dotted the blue water, while the greenery of a nearby park's trees provided a welcome splash of color. "I love the view here. I don't want to change that."

"I should hope not. That view is worth a mint."

Talking about views reminded her of the view from her hotel room in Positano and Caine. She blocked him from her mind and returned her attention to her final slice of pizza. It was bad enough that her ex-fiancé was haunting her, now she had a mad

88

Marine doing the same thing.

"We packed up all Alan's stuff and sent it to his address as you requested when I talked to you in Italy," Megan said. "His condo is still on the market."

"He was going to move in here with me because I have more room."

"And because your condo is a lot better than his. Better view, better neighborhood, better everything."

"Yet he dumped me. The former me. He wouldn't have a chance with the new me."

"Good to hear. After hurting you so badly, Alan doesn't deserve another chance."

"Neither does Caine. I feel like such an idiot. A week ago I was eating pizza with Caine in Italy." Faith left her last half-eaten pizza slice on her plate. She'd suddenly lost her appetite. She should have lost it sooner, but she was too damn tempted by the deep-dish specialty. Giving in to temptation was turning out to be a big problem with her lately. And not just with food but with men too. One man in particular.

"Did you fall in love with Caine at first sight?" Megan asked. "I mean, it's just . . . well, you don't usually give your body without giving your heart."

"I know. What's wrong with me?" Faith sniffed back the sudden threat of tears.

"How could I have messed up this badly?"

"It wasn't easy. You must have really been working hard to mess up this much."

Astonished by her cousin's reply, Faith blinked before cracking up.

"I mean it's bad enough being a jilted bride," Megan continued. "But how many women can claim to be a jilted bride and then have a fling go bad in Italy? Not many."

"I know."

"And it's Italy. I mean come on. The home of David. Well, the statue of David. The birthplace of hunks like . . . help me out here."

"Uh. . . . Michelangelo?"

"Come on. Hardly a hunk. Think of someone else."

"I can't."

"You're a librarian. If you don't know the answers, you know where to find them. Where's your BlackBerry?"

"Why?"

"Because we're gonna Google hunky Italian men."

"No, we are not. You do that, and I'll be getting e-mails for penis enlargements by the thousands."

"Really? How do you figure that? Have you done this before?"

"No. That's one mistake I'm not going to

make." Faith had already made enough mistakes to last her a lifetime.

The next morning, Faith woke up and rolled off the living room couch, only to clutch her head and wonder why her dining room table was at a weird angle that way. *Too much wine. Headache. Elbow ache.* She'd hit it on the hardwood floor when she'd fallen, and now her funny bone was making her entire arm tingle.

Faith felt better after she'd taken a shower and drank her first cup of coffee. She wore one of her new Italian outfits for her first day of work. Most of the boutiques in Positano specialized in summer resort and swimwear, but she'd managed to find a few things she liked. The bold red wraparound jacket and black embroidered skirt weren't so avant-garde that they would make her look like a runway model. Okay, so it would take more than an outfit to make her look like a runway model. It would also take more than a change in hair color and style. But she didn't want to look like a runway model so that was fine. She wanted to look more like Jennifer Garner in *Alias* and less like Jane Austen.

Faith practiced the stiletto catwalk she'd seen a woman demonstrate on the *Today*

Show once. Her four-inch heels were not at all practical for walking the distance to West Investigations' office. But damn, they made her feel powerful.

She packed them in her bag and reluctantly put on more comfortable shoes. Her black Keds weren't librarian shoes. They were comfortable and sensible.

She went back and forth, switching between her Keds and her stilettos until she caught sight of the clock and realized she was in danger of being late her first day on the new job. She hurried out, still wearing the stilettos. They went better with her outfit.

Oh yeah, she felt like one confident woman. Until she stepped outside her building and saw Caine waiting for her.

He eyed her approvingly, his head-to-toe look up and down her body incredibly intimate. "Nice move, sunshine," he drawled.

CHAPTER FIVE

Faith gave Caine a dismissive look before taking out her iPod, inserting the white earbuds and playing Carbon Leaf's "A Life Less Ordinary."

"You can ignore me, but I'm not going away," Caine said.

"You are going away if I sic Yuri on you."

"Who's that? Your bodyguard?"

"Close enough. Yuri is my doorman." She looked over her shoulder to wave him toward her only to find that Yuri wasn't at his post at the moment.

"I heard you've gone to work for your father," Caine said.

She paused her music. "Why do you care?"

"I don't."

"Then why are you here bothering me?"

Instead of answering, Caine said, "Was that your plan all along? Was your sob story as a jilted bride just a cover for your real reason for visiting Italy? To steal one of King Investigations' clients?"

She stared at him in amazement. And not the complimentary kind of amazement. "You are as delusional as your boss."

"Did you tell your father about us?"

"There is no *us*."

"There was. In Positano that night."

"Why are you so nervous about my father finding out? Are you afraid he'll beat you up?"

"Your father is the one who should be afraid."

"How dare you threaten him!"

"How dare your father mess up the investigation so badly that he killed my father."

"My father assures me that the investigation was very thorough and no mistakes were made."

"Did he offer to show you the case file? No? I didn't think so."

"He would if I asked him to."

"Dream on."

"You're just trying to make trouble. Stop following me around."

"I'm not following you."

"So you just happened to be standing here outside my condo building?"

"No, I wanted to find out why you lied in Italy."

"Me? *You're* the one who lied."

"You said you were a children's librarian."

"I was. I'm not anymore."

"Why?"

She almost blurted out a litany of reasons. Because she wanted to teach Caine a lesson. Because she wanted to prove that her father had done nothing wrong. Because she wanted to be tougher and meaner so that no other man would ever take advantage of her again.

There were tons of reasons.

"Why?" he repeated.

That, sir, is no business of yours. That's what Jane Austen would say. But Faith wasn't Jane Austen, and she needed a tougher author mentor now. Unfortunately, she couldn't think of one right at the moment, but she would soon. Her ability to channel Jennifer Garner from *Alias* seemed to have disappeared.

Since Faith couldn't think of something stinging and brilliant to say, she turned her back on Caine and looked for Yuri again.

Removing her earbuds, she called out, "Yuri, I need you."

The doorman quickly appeared at her side. He was a stocky man built like a wrestler. "Is there a problem?" he asked.

Faith nodded. "This man is giving me a

hard time."

"Yo, Bentley, is that you?" Caine said.

Yuri glared at Caine before blinking. "Hunter? Caine Hunter? What the hell are you doing here?"

"Me? What about you?" Caine slapped him on the back. "What's with the uniform? What happened to your dress blues, Gunny?"

"That was a long time ago."

"You two know each other?" Faith had to ask, even though the answer seemed obvious.

Caine nodded. "Bentley here was a Marine. Semper fi."

She turned to look at her doorman. "You were a Marine?"

Yuri shrugged. "Like I said, that was a long time ago. Nearly ten years."

Faith eyed both men suspiciously. "Did you pay Yuri off to say he knew you?"

Her question was directed to Caine, but both men gave her an offended look.

"What?" she said.

"You don't pay someone off to say they were a Marine," Caine stated.

"Why not? Yuri does a lot of community theater work. He's a good actor."

"I'm just starting out," Yuri said modestly.

"He was an extra on an episode of *ER* last

year," she said.

Caine frowned. "Gunny, you're an actor?"

Yuri nodded sheepishly.

"Why are you calling him Gunny?" she asked.

"He was a gunnery sergeant in the Marines."

"What about you?" Yuri asked Caine. "I thought you'd be a lifer."

"It was time. I had important business here at home that I had to take care of."

"It must be something *really* important to make you leave the Corps."

"Affirmative. My mission here doesn't get any more urgent or more personal." Caine's look made it clear to Faith that no one and nothing would get in his way.

Yuri said as much. "You always excelled at getting the mission accomplished."

"His mission is deeply flawed," Faith said.

Yuri looked at her in surprise. "You know the nature of his mission?"

She nodded.

"How did you obtain that piece of intel?" Yuri asked.

"Caine told me himself," she said.

"Is that right?" Yuri asked Caine.

Caine nodded.

Yuri shifted uncomfortably. "Uh . . . this seems personal between the two of you."

"You could say that." Caine's voice was curt. "Her father is responsible for my father's death."

"That's not true," she vehemently denied.

"It *is* true," Caine said. "And I aim on proving it."

"And I aim on proving you wrong," Faith said.

"You're welcome to try, sunshine, but you're bound to be disappointed."

"Yuri, do not let this man into my building."

"So you own the entire building now, do you?" Caine said.

"This is private property, and you have no business trespassing on it," Faith said.

"I'm standing on a public sidewalk," Caine pointed out.

"I've got to go or I'll be late," she muttered.

"Late for your new job working for your daddy? Why don't you just admit it? You were working for him all along."

"I'm not admitting anything to you. You're the one who lied to me continually." Her eyes widened as a new possibility occurred to her. "Wait a second. What about that guy who was choking at the hotel that first day? Was he your plant? Did you pay him to pretend to choke so you could save the day and get my attention?"

"No, but that would have been a good idea."

You, sir, are a blackheart and a cad. Okay, she had to stop channeling Jane Austen here. The problem was that Faith had never been good at insults. She'd never really had the need before.

It's not as if she hadn't heard plenty of salty language in Las Vegas. But she'd never bothered to pay attention to it. The words had gone in one ear and out the other.

She wished the same could be said about the things that Caine said. But no, those phrases stuck like Super Glue. What had he called her? Sunshine? It hadn't sounded like a compliment. It had sounded both condescending and demeaning.

Faith stepped off the curb only to be yanked back by his hand on her arm.

"Careful, sunshine. You don't want to throw yourself under a car on my account."

"I'd rather throw *you* under a car," she muttered.

"I'm sure you would."

"I mean if I were a violent person, which I'm not."

"You're just a crack shot."

"I don't go around shooting people."

"Not yet anyway."

"What's that supposed to mean?"

"Children's librarian by day, tough PI by night. Not your usual combination of professions."

"You already know that I'm no longer a librarian."

"Once a Marine, always a Marine. Once a librarian, always a librarian."

"How would you know?"

"I'm good at reading people."

"Right. Is that why you trailed the wrong person that last day in Positano? Because you're so great at reading people?"

"I said I was *good,* not great. But hey, if you want to say I'm great, that's okay with me."

"You're neither good nor great at anything."

"You know, a more sensitive guy might be hurt by those words. Good thing I'm not sensitive."

"I can't imagine a less sensitive human being on the entire planet."

"That's a little extreme, isn't it?"

"Go away." She put her earbuds back in.

He gently removed one of them to tell her, "That's a good way to get your wallet stolen, holding your purse like that." He waved her wallet at her.

She grabbed it back from him. "Are they

teaching pickpocketing techniques in the Marine Corps now?"

"Any rookie knows that you always secure your valuables." He lifted the strap over her head and shifted the bag so it was across her body instead of hanging from one shoulder.

When his hand brushed over her breast, he looked as stunned as she felt. Her body was still humming disloyally from the mere touch of his hand on her arm earlier. Now her hormones were on full alert and sizzling.

What was wrong with her? Did all jilted brides feel like this? Somehow she doubted that. Or if they did, it was because of their fiancé's touch. Not a stranger's.

But Caine didn't feel like a stranger. Had Megan been right when she'd wondered if Faith had fallen in love with Caine at first sight? If that were true, then Faith had better get over it pronto.

You'd think that finding out that Caine had been sent to Italy to seduce her would be enough to make her immune to his sex appeal. But noooo, her rebellious hormones continued to rock 'n' roll. Jane Austen would be so ashamed. So would Jennifer Garner.

"Leave me alone." She marched off.

He ambled right along behind her.

She turned and confronted him. "Stop following me."

"I'm not."

"You already know I'm headed for work."

"So am I. We can walk together."

"No, we can't. You are not going to harass anyone at West Investigations, including me."

"I'm just heading for work." He held out one arm in a sweeping gesture meant to invite her to go ahead of him. "You go ahead."

"I will."

She walked two blocks with him behind her. She could feel him eyeing her derriere, which made her self-conscious. As if that wasn't bad enough, she was also quickly getting a blister from the stilettos. She should have worn the Keds.

He followed her all the way to the building housing West Investigations.

She turned, ready to berate him for his idiotic behavior, when he smiled at her and said, "You do remember that King Investigations is located across the street from West Investigations, right?"

Damn, Faith had forgotten that for the moment. She said nothing but did bestow a look intended to reduce him to meaningless status. Caine's confident grin told her that he wasn't impressed.

The man had fooled her once. He wouldn't get a second chance.

"I can't believe you quit your job at the library," Gloria Gibbs said.

Faith eyed her father's long-time administrative assistant cautiously. "You're not going to lecture me, are you?"

"*Moi?* Never."

Faith had to bite her lip to prevent herself from laughing out loud. Gloria looked like Oprah during her heavier phases and, like Oprah, she enjoyed administering what Gloria called "suggested paths to a better life."

"I see you're wearing red today." Gloria nodded approvingly. "A good power look. And my signature color." She patted the lapel of her vibrant chili pepper red pantsuit jacket. "But those shoes." Gloria shook her head. "What were you thinking?"

"These are my kick-ass stilettos."

"You kick anyone's ass in those, and they'll have to go to the hospital for stab wounds. Are you wearing them because of Alan?"

"Why does everyone think that my every move or decision is caused by some man?"

"Did I hit a tender spot?"

Faith nodded.

"Does it have anything to do with the fact that your father told me to call security should a certain Caine Hunter show up on the premises?"

"What?"

"Your tender spot and killer shoes —"

"Have nothing to do with Caine or Alan. I am capable of making my own decisions, you know."

"Right."

"Okay, I do admit that some of the —"

"— crap," Gloria inserted.

"Some of the crap I've been through in the past week or so has been life changing."

"I approve of you taking that trip to Italy on your own, by the way," Gloria said.

"It was cowardly of me to take off like that."

"No way. It was brave of you. You wanted to go to Italy, so you did. Nothing cowardly about that. Getting back to the subject of work, I really don't know why your dad wants me to show you around, you already know where everything is. Here's your new office."

"Office? I thought I'd have a cubicle or something."

"A cubicle? For the owner's daughter? Surely not."

"Whose office was it?"

"Why do you want to know?"

"Because I don't want to move someone else out. Just give me an empty cubicle someplace."

"But your father . . ."

"I'll deal with my father. Is he in?"

Gloria shook her head. "He has back-to-back off-site meetings all morning."

"Good." She saw an empty cubicle near the windows. "Is that one open?"

Gloria nodded.

"Great." Faith made her way over.

"Do you believe the boss's daughter booting Lawler out of her office?" The young woman speaking had her back to Faith. "I guess those are the perks you get when your daddy owns the company."

"Actually, he and my uncle have joint ownership," Faith said. "And I'm not booting anyone out of their office."

"She wants to be your cubicle buddy instead," Gloria took obvious pleasure in saying. "Faith West meet Abs Boyce."

"Abs?" Faith said.

"Short for Abigail," Gloria said. "Isn't that right, Abs?"

"That's right." Abs looked as tough as she'd sounded. No girly ruffles for her. Her dark hair was cut short and her side part accentuated her narrow face. Her expression was defiant, reminding Faith a bit of a four-year-old who refused to participate during story time at the library.

Faith wanted to reassure Abs that she wasn't here to make trouble for anyone. But she had the feeling Abs wouldn't believe her. She seemed the type who preferred proof to promises. That was a goal that Faith hoped to achieve. Maybe Abs could teach her a thing or two.

"I'm here to learn," Faith said.

"I'm here to work," Abs said.

"Right. Me too," Faith said.

"Really? What are you working on?"

Okay, Abs had her there. "What are you working on?"

"Too many cases."

"I can help."

"You think so? Fine. Here." Abs handed her a pile of files. "Log in and get started." She pointed to the computer. "You do know how to log in, right?"

Faith not only knew how to log in, she finished working on the pile of files within an hour. "What's next?" she asked Abs.

"You're done with all those cases?"

Faith nodded. "I guess you didn't hear that in addition to my father being one of the owners of this business, I'm also one of the best researchers in background checks."

"And Faith's entry was also one of the finalists in the Pimp My Bookcart contest," Gloria said proudly as she passed by with a fresh cup of coffee from the staff room nearby. "What?" This as Faith gave her a look. "I'm just saying —"

"That was in my past life," Faith said.

"What is a Pimp My Bookcart contest?" Abs appeared intrigued then suspicious. "Did you make that up?"

"It's a contest where book carts are decorated, sort of the way people decorate parade floats. Check it out for yourself," Faith said. "Go ahead. Google it."

"I will." Abs quickly typed on her keyboard. "Wow. I'm impressed." She seemed to be telling the truth.

"Yes, well I was just part of a team that created that. Just like I want to be part of the team here. I could clearly learn a lot from you if you'd be willing to teach me."

"Show me how to pimp up a cart for the staff break room and you've got a deal."

Faith returned home to find her new bed and mattress set up just as she'd requested. She loved it when things went according to plan. Heading straight for her linen closet, she dug out the floral sheet set that Alan had said was "too girly" and refused to let her use.

Dancing across the bare cherry-stained hardwood floor, she put her sheets on her bed. Hers. All hers. Only hers.

When she shifted the nightstand a bit, something fell onto the floor. She glared at Alan's compact discs before scooping them up and taking them into the kitchen where she dumped them into a Restoration Hardware shopping bag. Then she spent the next hour scouring the condo looking for other hard-to-find things he might have left behind — like the beer making kit she found in the back of her kitchen cabinet or the mustache trimming kit hiding in the bottom of the linen closet. Not that Alan actually ever had a mustache, but he wanted it in case he decided to grow one.

She gathered it all up and was tempted to just dump it in the garbage. Kick it to the curb. Instead, she took what she considered to be the more responsible adult choice and carried the bag down to Yuri's station in the lobby. Then she took out her BlackBerry and texted Alan for the first time since the botched wedding.

"Have left final bag of your stuff with my doorman. Have someone pick up in 24 hours or it all goes."

She was responsible but not a saint. She wasn't going any further out of her way than this. The ball was in Alan's court now. She was done.

"If someone doesn't come in twenty-four hours to pick this bag up, just get rid of it." She handed the shopping bag to Yuri and felt ten tons lighter.

"Okay."

"So you and Caine really do know each other?" Faith said.

Yuri nodded.

"I can still count on you keeping him out of this building, right?"

Yuri appeared insulted by her question. "Of course."

"I'm sorry, but I had to ask. I mean, you two go way back, apparently. And you probably have some secret handshake Marine thing going on."

"Yeah, we share Secret Decoder Rings," Yuri said dryly.

"I'm sorry. I sounded condescending, and I didn't mean to."

"That's okay."

Faith casually inquired, "So, was Caine always as impossible as he is now?"

"I don't know what he's like now, but he was a rock when I knew him."

"Unemotional, you mean."

"The words *Marines* and *emotions* aren't usually used in the same sentence."

"Right."

"By rock I meant you could count on him, put your life in his hands, and he'd have your back."

Caine had had more than her back; he'd had her entire body. And she couldn't seem to forget what that felt like.

She looked down at her BlackBerry and was startled to find a text message from Alan. "Give me more time."

She instantly texted back, "NO."

To which he instantly texted "Be reasonable."

Reasonable? She stared at the screen. How could she have thought this was the man she wanted to marry? What did that say about her judgment? That she was an idiot.

"24 hours," she texted back. "Or your Wagner operas CD collection is smoke."

Then she programmed her BlackBerry to ignore any more messages from Alan.

"Bad news?" Yuri asked.

"If someone doesn't pick up that bag in twenty-four hours, can you see that it's donated to Goodwill? Or thrown away. Whatever."

"Sure. No problem."

Faith sighed. "Could you tell Alan was an ass?"

"Let's just say he wasn't at the top of my Facebook friends list."

She blinked. "Yuri, you're on Facebook?"

"Sure. Isn't everyone these days? Great networking for my acting friends and me."

"I'm impressed."

"But you're not impressed with Caine?" Yuri asked.

"Absolutely not. That's why I'm asking you to keep him out of the building. Remember, if someone doesn't pick up the bag, do whatever you want with it. I never want to see it again."

She never wanted to see Alan or Caine again either. Since Alan was still in Bali, that was a done deal. Getting rid of Caine was proving to be more difficult.

CHAPTER SIX

Faith began her second day at her new job by returning to her old job. Just temporarily. To pick up something important that she'd left behind — the pair of wings her favorite story time group had made for her out of cardboard, tissue paper, lots of pink paint and silver glitter with a bunch of feathers stuck on. The wings didn't really fit and were totally lopsided, but they had great sentimental value for Faith. She asked the cabbie to wait and was in and out of the library in record time. Ten minutes, tops.

Unfortunately, the cabbie and his vehicle were nowhere to be seen.

Instead, Caine stood there looking entirely too sexy in well-worn jeans and a plain black T-shirt. "So you decided to turn in your stilettos for a pair of fancy wings, huh?"

"No. I turned in my wings for a pair of stilettos."

"Yet here you are in sandals and wings."

"It's only temporary. I'm merely transporting them home."

"Right. Because who doesn't need a pair of wings at home? You probably have several pairs of wings. One pair for work, another pair for play. One set more casual, another more formal. Is that a smile? Yes, it is. No, it's too late to try to hide it now. I saw your lips go up."

"You're imagining things."

He sure was. Imagining her wearing those wings and little else. Maybe the wings, a thong and those stilettos she'd worn yesterday. Oh yeah, she'd give some of those Victoria's Secret models a run for their money. Not that the wings were actually that sexy, now that he got a closer look. But Faith sure was hot.

Caine was extremely frustrated that he couldn't get over Faith. He was frustrated period.

Faith's smile turned into a frown as she very belatedly asked him, "What are you doing here? Are you following me again? You can't use the excuse that you're heading for work."

"It wasn't an excuse. I work across the street from your office."

"I don't have an office."

"A penthouse suite?"

"I have a cubicle just like any other employee."

"Right."

"It's the truth. And you don't work across the street from the library. So I'll ask you again. What are you doing here?"

"Helping you."

"I don't need your help."

"How do you plan on getting those wings of yours home? Are you gonna fly?"

"I'm going to hail a cab."

"Right. Good luck with that. It's still morning rush. My car is right here." He pointed to a black Mustang.

"You're illegally parked."

"I'd be happy to give you a lift."

"No way am I getting into a car with you."

"Afraid?"

"Damn right."

"There's no need to be."

"Yeah right. You seduced me in Italy because you think my father had something to do with your father's suicide."

"Is there a problem?" Maria Sanchez asked as she joined them on the sidewalk.

Great. Now Faith's former boss saw her standing there making a fool of herself. She should have just abandoned the wings and left them at the library.

No, that's what the old Faith would have

114

done to avoid a confrontation. The new Faith could handle anything.

"No problem," she assured Maria even as the wings started shedding some of their excess glitter. "I've got everything under control here."

"I'm giving her a lift," Caine said.

"If that's your black Mustang, you're parked illegally," Maria told him.

"We're leaving right now," Faith said.

"Right. Here, let me take those for you." He reached for the wings.

She stepped back. "Don't touch my wings."

"Has she always been this touchy about her wings?" Caine asked Maria, shooting her a killer smile that clearly left the otherwise unflappable librarian a bit dazed.

Faith couldn't believe it. Maria actually blushed. And was that a giggle? Surely not.

Caine held his car door open for Faith. "The faster you and your wings get in, the faster we can get going."

Faith got in. She was determined to prove to him that he didn't intimidate her.

She was equally determined not to let him bend her fairy wings out of whack . . . or any further out of whack.

Caine hopped in and smiled at her. "Where to, sunshine?"

"My condo."

"Not taking your wings to your new job?"

"They aren't necessary there."

"Only one day on the job, and you already know that?"

"Yes."

"I don't know. Props can come in handy in investigative work. Like that sun hat in Italy. Smart move on your part."

She glanced over at him, checking his profile for any sign of mockery.

"What?" he said. "You can't accept a compliment?"

"From you? I find it a little hard to believe. As in nearly impossible."

"A flaw you'll have to work on."

"It's not a flaw. It's based on past experience. You just missed our turn."

"I know a shortcut."

"I'll bet you do."

"What's that supposed to mean?"

"That I was an idiot to ever get in this car with you. Stop right now."

"Why? We're only two blocks from your condo."

"I'll walk."

"With those?"

"If I have to."

"You don't have to. Just stay calm. Don't panic."

"I don't panic."

"Right. See, here we are. At your front door."

Yuri stepped up and opened the car door. "Good morning, Ms. West." If he was surprised at finding her with Caine, he hid it well. Having a pair of glitter-encrusted wings thrust at him didn't faze him either. "Having a good day?"

"Just peachy." She stepped out of the Mustang.

"I'm glad to hear that." Yuri's face was blank, but there was a hint of laughter in his voice.

By the time she regained possession of her wings from Yuri and turned to grudgingly thank Caine for the lift, he'd already driven away without saying a word.

"Your friend Caine isn't big on formalities." And he never had told her why he was standing outside the library just when she needed a ride. The man had an uncanny knack of turning up when she needed him.

Wrong. She didn't need him. And it wasn't a knack. He was stalking her because he thought she was a link to getting revenge against her father.

Yet Caine had shown flashes of kindness and humor, not to mention that damn sexiness.

Caine was still stuck in her mind when Faith got to work. Seeing him made her want to know more about his father's case. So as soon as she got to her cubicle, she started searching through the system.

It took some digging, but she found it. On the surface it looked like an open-and-shut case. Dr. Karl Hunter was a chemist working for the American Research Corporation on a project to develop an affordable biofuel. He was in charge of the project. There were only three other people directly involved in it. Details were sold to a rival company. A large amount of money showed up in an offshore account in Karl Hunter's name.

But something niggled at her. She couldn't put a finger on what it was exactly. So she copied the file onto a small thumb drive she kept in her purse — a break in company policy and protocol. She discreetly slid the drive into her pocket.

"Looking at old cases?" Abs said, leaning over Faith's shoulder to view the computer screen.

"I thought I could learn something from studying some previously solved cases."

"I remember that one. It was a big deal. I didn't work on it personally, but I heard the buzz about it. I mean, the guy ended up offing himself. Committed suicide."

"Yes, I know."

"Kinda sad, I guess."

"Yes."

"Faith, your father would like to speak to you," Gloria joined them to say.

Faith cleared the computer screen and headed for her dad's office. "You wanted to see me?"

"Why didn't you move into the office I provided for you?"

"I didn't think it was fair to move someone else out just so the boss's daughter could move in."

"Hmmm. Well, I've got a new assignment for you today. You said you wanted to do more than just sit in front of the computer screen, right?"

"Absolutely."

"Good. Then I want you to head over to Thompson and Associates for a sales pitch. They are an up-and-coming law firm, and they need to hire a top-notch investigation company. I want you to convince them that they need to sign on the dotted line with us. Think you can handle that?"

"Of course."

"I e-mailed you a list of talking points about why West Investigations is their best choice. The appointment is for eleven thirty, so you'd better get a move on. I'm counting on you to get this deal done."

Thompson and Associates was located in the Dirksen Federal Building, a short walk away. Once inside, she went through the security checkpoint with its metal detectors before heading for the bank of elevators. A slight jostling at her side had her looking in that direction. "You don't take direction well, do you," Caine said. It was a statement, not a question, as he pointed to her purse and waved her wallet at her.

She grabbed it back for the second time in as many days. She belatedly noticed that Caine had changed clothes since she'd last seen him a few hours ago. Gone were the jeans and T-shirt, replaced with a dark suit, white shirt and black tie.

She hadn't seen him in business attire. He cleaned up nice. Real nice. Hot, hot nice. He still had that Dark Knight thing going on.

"I see you left the wings at home," he said. "And before you ask, no, I'm not following you. I'm here for a business meeting."

"Me too."

She stepped into the elevator and punched the button for the eleventh floor. "What floor do you want?"

"Eleven."

"Where's your business meeting?"

"Sorry, I can't tell you that. Confidential information."

He held out his hand for her to precede him out of the elevator. Instead, she reciprocated the gesture right back at him. "No, you go first. Please."

This gave her the chance to admire him as he walked in front of her. He had the upright military posture of a Marine. And he walked right into the offices of Thompson and Associates.

"I have an appointment with Mr. Kneeson," Caine said.

"So do I," Faith said, hurrying to stand beside him at the elegant reception desk. "At eleven thirty."

"I'll let his assistant know you're here," the receptionist said.

Faith stepped away from the desk to study the ACHIEVE poster elegantly framed on the wall.

"Small world, huh," Caine said.

"I can't believe they send you out as a sales rep."

"They don't usually, but the regular guy got sick."

"Sure he did." She shook her head. "This is just another chance for you to hassle me."

"I'm sorry for this mix-up," the administrative assistant, a woman in her late fifties with a choppy haircut, said. "Usually we don't book these kinds of appointments so close together. And usually Mr. Kneeson doesn't get a flat tire on the Edens Expressway. It's just been one of those crazy days. He should be in shortly. Again, I'm sorry for the confusion."

"No problem." Caine smiled at her and held out his hand. "I'm Caine Hunter with King Investigations, and I know all about crazy days."

The assistant, who was old enough to know better, melted. "I appreciate you being so understanding, Mr. Hunter."

"Call me Caine."

"Can I get you a refreshment while you wait, Caine? Some coffee or tea?"

"I was here first." Faith said, sounding like one of the kids in her story time group. "Hi. I'm Faith West with West Investigations. I have an eleven thirty appointment with Mr. Kneeson."

"As I just stated, he's not here yet. He had a flat tire. Would you like to reschedule your appointment?"

"No, I'll wait."

"Caine, would you like some coffee or tea while you wait?"

"Why didn't you ask him if he wanted to

reschedule?" Faith said.

"Because she's smart enough to know the answer would be no," Caine replied on the assistant's behalf. "And some black coffee would be great, thanks."

"Do you have any chai tea?" Faith said even though the assistant, whose name Faith had yet to discover, hadn't asked her if *she* wanted anything. "And I'm sorry, but I didn't catch your name."

"Linda Dennis. And no, I don't believe we have any chai tea."

"That's okay," Faith said. "I'm fine."

The look Linda gave Faith indicated that the assistant doubted that. "I'll get your coffee, Caine. I won't be long."

Caine sat in one of the elegantly upholstered chairs and made himself right at home. Faith sat next to him, to once again prove that she wasn't intimidated or turned on by him.

"Flat tire. Bad timing," Caine said.

"Bad luck," Faith said.

"You'd know all about luck," he said.

"I certainly know about bad luck. I've had a run of that lately."

"Bad luck or bad judgment?"

"You're right for once. My bad luck was caused by my bad judgment. But I'm fixing that. I definitely learn by my mistakes, and

I do not repeat them."

"Good to know."

Could he tell that she was saying that going to bed with him was a mistake? Did he even care?

"Here's your coffee, Caine. And I just spoke to Mr. Kneeson. He should be here in a few minutes."

"Thanks," Caine said.

"Yes, thank you, Linda." Faith smiled at her. Linda didn't smile back.

Caine calmly sipped his coffee while Faith kept checking her BlackBerry, reviewing the talking points while making sure Caine couldn't see the screen.

With every minute she became more and more tense while Caine seemed to become calmer and calmer.

"Hi, I'm Chuck Kneeson. I'm so sorry for this mix-up and delay." He gave both Caine and Faith a strong handshake. "Let me take you out to lunch to make it up to you. Both of you."

"No, that's not necessary," Faith said.

"Sounds like a great plan to me," Caine said.

Great. She couldn't very well leave him alone to have lunch with the client. Now she was stuck with him. Caine, not the client.

"I understand if it's too much for you, Faith," Caine said as if she couldn't cope with him or the client, she wasn't exactly sure.

"Lunch sounds good," Faith said.

"And King Investigations will pay," Caine said.

"No, West Investigations will pay," Faith insisted.

"How does the Palmer House sound to you? I've got a seminar to give there at the hotel later this afternoon."

"Sounds great," Faith said. *Just peachy.*

They walked the several blocks to one of Chicago's iconic locations. Once inside the impressive Beaux Arts–style hotel lobby, Faith blushed when Caine caught her gawking like a tourist at the painted ceiling murals depicting Greek mythology.

"I haven't been here since the big renovation," she explained. "Did you know the Palmer House is the oldest continuously operated hotel in the country? And legend has it that the brownie was invented by the chef here when Bertha Palmer, the wife of the original owner, wanted a dessert for ladies to easily eat at Chicago's 1893 Columbian Exposition. Bertha was a very smart woman. She traveled to Europe and came back with the newest paintings by those rowdy Impressionists. She bought over two dozen Monet paintings and nearly a dozen by Renoir. After her death, her art collection was donated to the Chicago Art Insitute, and the paintings became the basis for their Impressionist collection, which is now one of the best in the world. Oh yeah, Bertha was really something. Her husband built this hotel for her as a wedding present, but it burned down almost two weeks later in the Chicago Fire in 1871. So he built it again. And then the hotel was enlarged in the twenties. So this place has a lot of history."

Damn. Her inner librarian was showing — the one who beat the rest of the staff at Trivial Pursuit and had a thing for local history.

"I read someplace that knowing trivia like that is a good trait for an investigator to have," Mr. Kneeson said. "*Tangential knowledge*, I believe it was called."

Faith proudly threw her shoulders back and stood a little straighter. "It is a good trait to have, because you never know when you'll need to call on a bit of information to start a conversation."

"Or a con," Caine said.

"You'd know more about cons than I would," she said.

"Right. I do have more experience as an investigator than you do," Caine said.

Damn. Score one for him.

"Caine doesn't usually do the sales pitches for his employer," she said.

"Neither does Faith."

Mr. Kneeson's gaze volleyed back and forth between Faith and Caine. "I gather you two know each other pretty well?"

"You could say that," Caine said while Faith was saying, "Not really."

Mr. Kneeson just laughed. "Okay then. Let's get lunch, shall we?"

They were quickly seated at the restaurant on the lobby level. Faith ordered the Amish Chicken Club Waldorf sandwich, while Caine and Mr. Kneeson both ordered the Diablo Burger.

Whenever she attempted to bring up the reasons why West Investigations was the best choice for Thompson and Associates, Caine was right there to distract Mr. Kneeson. The food, especially the truffled potato chips, was delicious, but the company was turning out to be extremely frustrating.

"Excuse me a minute," Mr. Kneeson said, glancing down at his BlackBerry. "I've got to take this call." He stood and moved to a quieter corner to speak.

Faith glared at Caine. "Stop trying to

sabotage my business lunch."

"It's not *your* lunch."

"You're monopolizing the conversation."

"You're just angry because you're losing."

"I am not losing. Losing patience maybe, but not losing my cool or losing this client."

"He isn't your client yet."

"He will be."

"You sound pretty confident about that."

"I am confident."

"Then you shouldn't be afraid that I'll get Mr. Kneeson to go with King and not West."

She eyed him suspiciously. "Did you somehow arrange this? For him to get a flat tire?"

"You've really got a vivid imagination. Is that because you're a librarian?"

"A *former* librarian."

"Right."

"You won't win."

He just smiled. "We'll see."

She smiled back, even as she gritted her teeth. "Yes, we will."

"Sorry about that," Mr. Kneeson said as he returned. "Where were we?"

"I was about to tell you why someone smart enough to be a White Sox fan like yourself would want to choose West Investigations for your firm."

"How did you know I'm a White Sox fan?"

She pointed to his BlackBerry screen with the Sox logo. Then pointed to her own screen with a matching logo.

"Do you have some of the ball players as clients?"

Faith smiled discreetly. "You know I can't answer that question. He's a Cubs fan." She nodded toward Caine. "You know what that means."

Mr. Kneeson nodded. "That his team is going to lose again."

She nodded too. "The sports franchise that's gone the longest without a championship. And that's not just in baseball, that's all the sports combined. When did the Cubs last win the World Series? Was it 1904?"

Now Caine was the one gritting his teeth. "No, it was 1908."

She and Mr. Kneeson exchanged a knowing look.

Talk about a momentum shift. Things were totally going Faith's way now as she and Mr. Kneeson talked baseball — recent games and the bullpen, pitching stats and RBIs.

Caine called the server over. "I'll take the check now."

"It's already been taken care of by the young lady," the server said.

Faith just smiled. She'd cornered the

server earlier and made the payment arrangements with the corporate credit card.

"I hate to eat and run," Mr. Kneeson said, "but I've got to get to that workshop I told you about. Caine, it was great meeting you. Faith, get the paperwork to my assistant Linda, and we'll get things wrapped up."

Faith waited until Mr. Kneeson was out of sight before punching a fist into the air. "Yes!" She'd done pretty damn well for only her second day on the job.

"That was dirty, bringing in the Cubs that way. Is nothing sacred?"

"Hey, there's no crying in baseball," she countered, quoting the movie *A League of Their Own.*

"No crying in the Marine Corps either," he said.

"Yeah, I figured."

"So how did you know I was a Cubs fan?"

"I went through your wallet, remember."

"Right. In Italy. You saw my season ticket stubs, right?"

She nodded and shifted uneasily. Why did she have to go and bring up Italy? The moment of strained silence seemed to last forever. "Well, I uh . . . I have to get back to the office."

"You know, sunshine, we could have been

130

a great team, had circumstances been different."

But circumstances weren't different, and she'd be wise not to forget that. More stood between Caine and her than merely rooting for rival baseball teams. Some things couldn't be forgotten . . . or forgiven.

CHAPTER SEVEN

"Your dad is over the moon about you joining the firm," Faith's mom, Sara, said as
she joined Faith in her condo on Saturday.
They sat together on Faith's couch, sipping
herbal tea. "He's probably given you a
prime corner office with a view."

"Actually, I insisted on having a regular
cubicle. Didn't Dad tell you?"

"No. He just keeps gloating about you
working with him. Your father was never
happy with you working as a librarian," Sara
said.

"I know. He wanted me working with him.
But I didn't quit because of him. He never
asked me to leave the library."

"Of course not. He would never do that.
You know I was a librarian when I married
your father."

"Right. And you left your job when you
had me."

"I planned on going back to work when

you started kindergarten," she said wistfully.

"Really? You never said that before. What stopped you?"

"Your father needed my help and support because West Investigations was just starting to take off then. Your grandfather had run a small-scale operation, but it doubled in size during that time. Anyway, enough about all that."

"Dad didn't manipulate me into quitting," Faith assured her mom. "The only men who have manipulated me are Alan and Caine."

"Who's Caine?"

"Didn't Dad tell you?"

"No. Who is Caine?"

Faith jumped to her feet. "Your tea is cold. Let me make a fresh pot. Would you like a chocolate-and-Brie panini with that panini maker you got me? Is it okay that I kept it, even though I didn't get married? Was that rude? I know it was rude to have you do all the work of returning the wedding gifts."

"The gifts were still in their boxes, so it wasn't all that difficult. And Megan was a big help."

"I owe both of you big time. Here." Faith handed her mom a delicately wrapped jeweler's box. "I got this for you in Italy."

In addition to the two cameos she'd bought for her mom and Megan, Faith had also chosen one for herself. Instead of the traditional profile, Faith's cameo depicted the Bay of Naples. She had yet to wear it. The cameo for her mom was the most intricately done of them all.

Her mother held up her large cameo pin. "It's lovely. Thank you so much, honey."

They shared a heartfelt hug. "You're welcome."

Her mom pinned the cameo on her sunshine yellow cotton sweater and then said, "But let's get back to Caine. You still haven't told me who he is."

Faith shrugged. "He's a guy I met in Italy."

"He's an Italian?"

"No. American."

"You said he manipulated you. How?"

"By lying to me. He told me he was a lawyer from Philadelphia, but he was really a private investigator from Chicago."

"Did your father send him? If he did, I'll —"

"No need for threats. Dad didn't send him. Vince King did."

"Vince?" Sara blinked, clearly startled by this news. "But why?"

"To spy on me. You know how paranoid that guy is. He thought I was trying to steal some new Italian client of his. Which is ridiculous."

"So this Caine lives here in Chicago?"

"Yes."

"Is he the reason you joined the firm and left the library?"

"Why do people keep asking me that?"

"What people?"

"Megan. You. Caine."

"This Caine seems to know you pretty well, even if he hasn't known you very long. What about Alan?"

"Huh?" The abrupt change in subject threw her.

"Alan. The man you were going to marry. The man who broke your heart. Unless Caine did that too? Did he break your heart?"

"I only knew him for a week."

"You haven't seen him since you've returned to Chicago?"

The look on Faith's face gave her away.

"I thought so," her mother murmured.

"What do you mean?" Faith knew she was saying that a lot, but she couldn't help herself. She was having a hard time keeping up.

"Just that you seem . . . different."

"It's the hair."

"Don't give me that. It's not the hair," her mother said. "You seem . . . I don't know . . . angry."

"You'd be angry too if you'd been dumped on your wedding day."

"I don't know," Sara said. "Sometimes when your dad is being a bear, I do wonder . . ."

Faith blinked. "What? What do you wonder?"

"Nothing. I was just kidding," Sara said, standing to join Faith. She put her arm around her daughter. "How about that panini you talked about? I could use some chocolate about now."

Faith spent the rest of her weekend studying, catching up on her investigative skills. Her first week on the job had gone very well, all things considered. She'd gotten Thompson and Associates to sign on the dotted line as West Investigations' newest client. Her dad had been proud.

She set aside the files she'd been studying and reflected on what her mother had said yesterday. Did her mom really wonder what her life would have been like if she hadn't married Faith's dad? And if she did, was it a sign that her parents were having marital trouble? They'd argued in the past but never for long and never in a way to make Faith question their love for one another.

Maybe her mom was just in a funk. After

all, Aunt Lorraine was staying with her all week, and that was enough to drive the most cheerful person into the depths of depression. Not that Faith's mom had seemed depressed. Faith was probably blowing everything out of proportion.

Her thoughts were interrupted by the sound of her cell phone's ringtone of the opening of the World Series White Sox theme song, "Don't Stop Believin" by Journey. Checking the screen, she saw that it was her grandmother calling.

"Hey, Gram. How are you doing?"

"I was going to ask you that," Gram said. "How are you doing? Do you need me to put a hit on Alan with the Swedish mob?"

"No."

"The Swedish mob is better than the Finnish mob."

"So you've said."

"You don't believe me?"

"I believe you. Gram, how did you know that grandfather was the one for you?"

"I've told you the story before."

"Tell me again."

"We met in London toward the end of the war. I was fifteen. He was a lot older than I was. Twenty years older. My parents worked at the Swedish Embassy in London. They'd sent me out to the countryside when the bombing was so bad, but by this time late in the war, London was no longer being bombed. Your grandfather was so charming. We danced together. One dance. He said he'd come back for me when I was older and that I should wait for him."

"You knew when you were fifteen?"

"He was my first love."

Faith thought back to her first love — Danny Montgomery in kindergarten. He said he didn't like girls, so Faith had gone home and gotten a pair of scissors to chop her long hair off so she'd look more like a boy. Her crush on Danny was gone by the time she entered first grade.

"How did you know it would last?" Faith asked.

"I didn't. But I was young and an optimist. I knew your grandfather was special."

"How? How did you know? Was it something in his personality? What traits did he have that made you so sure?"

"He had kind eyes and the ability to be a leader, to make people believe. He was pragmatic. Even-tempered."

"Alan was even-tempered," she pointed out. "He was pragmatic."

"He didn't have kind eyes. And he always talked about himself all the time."

"Yeah, I guess he did."

138

"Don't pine for him. He's not worth it. You need to go out and find yourself some sexy young man to distract you. I could set you up with someone. My bridge partner has a nice grandson who's single."

"No thanks, Gram. I'm not ready to start dating."

"You haven't told me about your trip to Italy yet. Was it everything you hoped?"

"Dad didn't say anything to you about it, did he?"

"No. Why should he? Did something happen over there I should know about?"

"No. I just wondered. Uh, the Amalfi Coast was beautiful. Even better than the pictures I'd seen."

"So you had a good time?"

"Positano was amazing. The place makes you want to sit down at a local café and just let the beauty and magic envelop you."

"And you had a good time?"

Faith continued to avoid directly answering her grandmother's question. "Great food. The food is to die for."

"I have to confess I was nervous when I heard you took off like that out of the blue. I mean that's not like you. But it sounds like you made the right choice going there."

Faith wondered what her life would be like right now if she hadn't gone to Italy. What if she'd stayed in her condo and cried about her ruined wedding, surrounded by unreturned wedding gifts? Would she have left her job at the library? Or would she have sunk into one giant pity party and not climbed out?

Had Caine actually been good for her? Wow, that was a weird concept, one she couldn't quite wrap her mind around at the moment.

"Faith, are you still there?" Gram asked.

"Yes, sorry. I was just thinking."

"About your new job? You dad is so happy."

"Yeah, I know."

"And when he's happy, I'm happy. That's what moms do. They are happy when their child is happy. Their grandchild too. I want you to be happy."

"Thanks, Gram." After disconnecting the call, Faith was left wondering what it would take to make her happy.

She knew in investigative work, sometimes you never found the answer or the information you needed, no matter how hard you tried. Too often, life was like that too.

"We're in a rut. We need to mix things up more," Faith said as she joined Megan in the elegant foyer of Faith's condo building a few days later. They were meeting for their customary dinner nearby.

"I don't want to mix things up. I want sushi," Megan said. "It's the second Tuesday of the month, which means it's Sushi Tuesday."

"But we're in a rut."

"We are *not* in a rut. Stop saying that."

"We're creatures of habit."

"Oh puh-lease. You changed your hair, your job, your man, your bed. That's enough. It's Sushi Tuesday, and we are having sushi, got it?"

"Got it." Faith held open the door for Megan and motioned her to go ahead of her. "Jeez, you can be stubborn."

"Me? You're the one with the stubborn streak. I'm the optimist in the family."

"Sure, it's easy to be an optimist when Aunt Lorraine isn't your mother's sister."

"True." They started walking toward the Sushi Place a few blocks away. The early evening weather was perfect — sunny and in the mid-seventies without the humidity that could turn the coolest woman into a sweating blob . . . even a mad, bad blonde with the best haircut in the world. Shaking her head, Faith enjoyed the silky swing of her hair against the back of her neck. She still sometimes caught a glimpse of herself

141

in a mirror and would do a double take for an instant. Changing her look was one of the smartest things she'd ever done.

"I need another author mentor," Faith said.

"Does it have to be a dead author? A dead *female* author? I've got it." Megan snapped her fingers. "How about Beatrix Potter?"

"Right. Like she's a kick-ass role model."

"Hey, she accomplished a lot in her lifetime. Not only did she create Peter Rabbit and Jemima Puddleduck, she also donated over four thousand acres of land in England's scenic Lake District to the National Trust so that future generations could enjoy its beauty."

"Nice but not good enough. Who else?"

"You never answered my question. Do they have to be dead?"

"Not necessarily."

"Fiction writers? Or nonfiction? If nonfiction, then how about Gloria Steinem? Or Erica Jong or Candace Bushnell if you want fiction?"

"I did have that one shopping spree in Italy, but normally I'm not really a shopaholic."

"That's Sophie Kinsella. Bushnell did *Sex and the City*."

"Right." They entered the Sushi Place.

The white chairs and light wood tables and floors gave the small space a bright, airy feeling. Once they were settled at their favorite table near the big windows, Faith selected the tempura shrimp maki with fried shrimp, cucumber and scallops. Megan considered the daily special before going with the miso soup, spicy seaweed salad and a selection of tamago yaki, kani and several of her favorite dynamite sushi. Faith had ordered Japanese beer before but today went with the bottled sparkling water instead, as did Megan.

"Here." Megan handed her a CD.

"What's this?"

"I burned a breakup CD for you. You liked 'I Hate Everything About You' so much that I gathered a few more songs with a similar theme."

Faith read the first few titles from the printed playlist aloud. " 'You Give Love a Bad Name' by Bon Jovi, 'Love Stinks' by the J. Geils Band, 'You Oughta Know' by Alanis Morissette, Beyoncé's 'Irreplaceable' and 'Don't Speak' by No Doubt. Thanks."

"You're welcome."

"Hey, did I tell you that I beat Caine out for a new client? On my second day on the job."

"Yes, you may have mentioned it a few

143

thousand times."

"Did I also mention that I looked into Caine's father's case?"

Megan's eyes widened. "No, that's definitely news. So what did you find out?"

"On the surface it seems like a no-brainer. Dr. Karl Hunter was a chemist working for American Research Corporation on a project to develop an affordable biofuel. He was in charge of the project. There were only three other people involved in it. Details about the biofuel were sold to a rival company. A large amount of money showed up in an offshore account in Karl Hunter's name."

"Does Caine know all this?"

"I don't know. I assume so."

"You should tell him. Maybe then he'd stop thinking his father was innocent."

"Yes, but the thing is that the case is almost too neat and tidy. My gut tells me there may be more to the story. I found a brief reference to the research assistant named Weldon Gronski vouching for Karl's innocence. He was never thoroughly interviewed, however. That raised a red flag for me. I want to track that guy down and talk to him."

"Why?"

"Leave no stone unturned."

"You don't think West Investigations botched the case, do you?"

"I don't want to think that, no. But I need to be sure. What would make a man like Karl with an exemplary record suddenly sell corporate secrets?"

"Obviously it was money."

"Why then? Why *that* particular project? He'd worked on other equally important projects."

"Did he have a gambling problem?"

"Not that I could find. Like I said, I just need some more information."

"Does your dad know you're doing this?"

"No. And don't tell him or my mom."

"I won't." Megan proficiently used her chopsticks to dip her sushi into a small bowl of soy sauce. "So when do I get to meet this Caine?"

"You don't. Why would you even want to?"

"Because he's clearly made a big impression on you."

"A bad one."

"Are you sure about that? I mean here you are, helping him investigate his father's case."

"He has no idea I'm looking into it."

"Would he approve?"

"Like I'd care."

"It seems to me you care too much. It seems Caine has made more of an impact on you than Alan did."

"And how shallow would that make me? I was engaged to Alan for almost year. And yet Caine's the one I keep thinking about."

"Maybe because Alan is out of the picture, and you keep running into Caine."

"He does that on purpose, you know."

"Have you seen him since that lunch where you conned your way into winning that client?"

"It wasn't a con. It was my knowledge of White Sox trivia."

"Right. So have you seen Caine since then?"

"No." She looked around. "But I fully expect him to show up anytime now. I wouldn't be surprised if he walked through that door."

"I would," Megan said. "How could he know about our Sushi Tuesday?"

"I may have mentioned it," Faith muttered. "Before I knew who he really was."

"Wow. Is that him?"

Faith pivoted in her seat, her heart pounding. She saw the man entering the Sushi Place. "No, that's not him."

"Too bad."

"What do you mean, too bad? You'd be

happy if he showed up here?"

Megan shrugged. "At least I'd finally get to meet him."

"He's not a nice person."

"He helped you transport your wings."

"And he never did say what he was doing standing outside the library."

"A man of mystery."

"You're my cousin. You're not supposed to take his side."

"I'm just curious about this guy who has such a strong effect on you."

"By 'strong effect,' you mean he seduced me. Do not remind me."

"Sorry."

"You know what I need? I need to get back to my worst-case scenario approach to life. Had I kept that up, then I would have had a backup plan for the wedding falling through. And I would have been suspicious of Caine in Italy."

"What if Jane Austen had thought that way?"

"She was never jilted at the altar."

"True."

"In fact, she never married."

"Yes, but she was engaged."

"For about twenty-four hours, and then she broke it off. I'm telling you — if you prepare for the worst, then you're pleasantly surprised when things do work out."

Megan shook her head. "I don't think I could live that way."

"Because you're the eternal optimist. I tried that. It didn't work for me."

"So how does your worst-case scenario fit into your new mad and bad persona?"

"I feel more in control."

"It doesn't sound like things with Caine are more in control."

"They will be when I figure out what really happened with his father."

"Going with your worst-case scenario — what do you do if you find that the agency made a mistake and that Caine's dad really wasn't guilty? How do you prepare for that?"

"I don't know," Faith admitted. "I'm still trying to figure things out." Including how she really felt about Caine.

"Is that Caine?" Megan asked.

"Cut it out. It wasn't funny the first time around."

"Hello, ladies," Caine said. "Mind if I join you?"

CHAPTER EIGHT

"Caine, I presume?" Megan said.

He nodded and smiled at her. "Megan, I presume?"

Megan smiled back. The traitor. "That's right. We were just talking about you."

Faith kicked her cousin under the table.

"What?" Megan blinked. "We were."

Caine sat in the empty chair next to Faith. Naturally that gave her a flashback to meeting him for the first time in Italy. They'd shared a table on the sunny terrace. She'd had pizza. He'd spoken fluent Italian.

Like then, he had that sexy stubble thing going on. His dark hair fell over his forehead.

"The man is stalking me," Faith reminded her cousin and herself.

"I just felt like having sushi, and someone I know raved about this place," Caine said.

"That someone was me, and you damn

149

well know it. I told you about Sushi Tuesday."

He started singing Sushi Tuesday to the
Rolling Stones song "Ruby Tuesday." He
had an awesome voice. The man could read
the phone book, and he'd sound incredible.
It was criminal.

Faith refused to be seduced. "They don't
do karaoke here," she said. "I'm sure there
are plenty of other places that do. You might
want to go eat there tonight."

He ignored her comment and instead
asked Megan, "Did your cousin tell you how
she used the White Sox to steal a client away
from me?"

Megan nodded. "Why, yes, she did."

"I did not steal a client from you! He was
not your client. He was undecided. He
made the right decision by going with West
Investigations. Does your boss know you're
here? Did he send you to spy on me again?"

"No. And no." He took the menu a server
handed him. "Thanks."

"You're not eating here," Faith said. "You
are not a sushi kind of guy."

"Really? What kind of guy is a sushi kind
of guy? Your ex-fiancé?"

"Well, yes. He was a foodie."

"And you don't think I'm a foodie?"

She remembered the delicious meals

they'd had in Italy. "I don't know you well enough to say."

"Trust me, if you can eat MREs, you can eat anything."

Trust him? No way. She'd done that once with disastrous results. "MRE?" she repeated.

"Meals ready to eat. What they hand out in the Marine Corps. I've eaten worse than MREs. Bugs. Snakes."

"Are you trying to impress me?" Faith said.

"She once ate a grasshopper on a dare," Megan said.

"I was only five at the time." Faith kicked her cousin again, warning her not to reveal any other childhood secrets and anecdotes.

Megan had a warning of her own. "Ow! If you kick me again, I'm kicking you back."

"Do you two fight often?" Caine asked.

"Never," Faith said. "You bring out the worst in people."

"Maybe I just get them to tell the truth," Caine countered before placing his order.

"Why are you here?" Faith demanded.

"I already told you. I felt like eating sushi."

"Are you totally incapable of telling the truth?"

"No."

"That's it? No?"

Caine shrugged. "You asked me a question. I answered it."

"Did you answer it truthfully?"

"Yes. I am capable of telling the truth."

"Have you ever told me the truth?"

"Yes."

"When?"

"Plenty of times."

"Be more specific."

"Why should I?"

"Because I'm asking you to."

"You already know what you think," he said. "Why should I confuse you with fact?"

"What kind of line is that?"

"It's the truth. And don't tell me that I wouldn't know the truth if it bit me."

She bit her tongue. How did he know that's what she'd been about to say? Was she that predictable? That boring?

"I'll have you know that I have a very open mind," Faith said.

Caine cracked up, almost snorting the Japanese beer he'd ordered.

"What's so funny?" Her voice was colder than the polar ice pack.

"You are."

"Wrong answer." She stood and dumped her sparkling water in his lap. He stopped laughing. She left a twenty on the table for her bill and headed for the nearest exit.

Megan scrambled after her.

Caine played it smart by staying at the Sushi Place.

"So," Megan said cheerfully once they were a block away. "That's Caine, huh? I can see the attraction."

Faith stopped in her tracks, causing the pedestrian walking behind her to veer around her to avoid knocking her down. "Attraction? You're crazy."

"What do you call that back there then? You clearly have a strong reaction to him."

"I call it aggravation and anger."

"Right. *And* attraction. I'm telling you, I saw more sparks between the two of you in the past ten minutes than I saw with you and Alan in the past year."

"Sparks cause fires. Fires cause devastation."

"I thought you were mad, bad and blonde."

"Mad and bad, sure. Not stupid."

"I'm just saying I can understand how you'd end up in Caine's bed."

Faith looked around. "We are not having this conversation in the middle of the sidewalk. We aren't having it anywhere. Change of subject."

"I can't believe you dumped your drink on him."

"He made me do it."

Megan laughed.

"What's so funny? And remember what I did to the last person who answered that question incorrectly," Faith warned her.

"That's what you said when you ate that grasshopper. You said he made you do it."

"Caine?"

"No, of course not. That kid you had a crush on in kindergarten."

"Okay. Fine. I still say Caine made me do it, and he deserved it. I don't like people laughing at me."

"I know."

"Being left at the altar that way . . ." Faith shook her head. "I don't like people laughing or feeling sorry for me."

"Well, I can tell you this much — Caine definitely doesn't feel sorry for you. I think he may be crazy about you."

"He's crazy, that's for sure."

"You're crazy," Caine muttered to himself as he returned to his table at the Sushi Place.

"I'm so sorry, sir," the server said, handing him several napkins to mop up.

"Yeah, me too."

"Faith is a frequent customer here. I've never seen her that upset."

154

"I seem to have that effect on her."

"She's a good person."

"So people keep telling me. Listen, can I have that sushi to go?"

"I'll get it ready for you." She couldn't resist adding, "Are you going to go after her and apologize?"

"No." *I'm going to go refocus my attention on what's really important: clearing my father's name.*

Caine had plenty of time to brood as he carried his takeout to a bench along the Chicago River. He needed the fresh air to clear his head.

What was he doing following Faith around like a doting dog? She wouldn't lead him to the real perpetrator of his father's downfall. At least he didn't think so. He wasn't following her because of the case. He was trailing her because he wanted to see her.

A stupid move for a man who prided himself on his street smarts.

"Is this seat taken?" a stranger asked, pointing to the empty space beside Caine on the bench before seeing Caine's fierce frown. "Uh, never mind." The man and his date hurried away.

Wise move. Caine wasn't good company at the moment. He rubbed the back of his neck where the tension was building. A stiff breeze off the lake ruffled his hair as he sat there watching the boat traffic going up and down the Chicago River — from sleek sailboats and motorized powerboats to sightseeing vessels filled with tourists admiring the view. Looking south, he could see the shiny Swissôtel on the other side of the river. Beyond that was Millennium Park and the Bean — the polished chrome sculpture that reflected the city's impressive skyline.

As far as he was concerned, Chicago held all bragging rights in the skyline department. And he didn't just think that because he was a native. Hell, the city was famous for its architecture . . . and its Portillo's hot dogs . . . and deep-dish pizza. Which reminded him, he was hungry.

He opened the container with his food and sampled one of the offerings before tossing the rest in a nearby trash container. Faith was right. He wasn't really a sushi guy. He was a burger and fries guy. A steak and potato guy. Although he did have a secret love of broccoli that he never told anyone about because that was a dorky vegetable and not a manly Marine vegetable like . . . carrots.

Yeah, carrots. They were supposed to help with night vision. Not as much as night vision goggles, of course. Vegetables couldn't compete with the tech support of the U.S. Marine Corps.

Still . . . he did have a fondness for broccoli. And that was entirely his dad's fault. Because when Caine was a kid, his dad told him that broccoli was really a bunch of small trees that a mad scientist had shrunk.

As if on cue, a little rug rat maybe three years old ran up to Caine. "Wanna see my dog-dog?"

Not knowing what a dog-dog was, Caine froze for a second before seeing the stuffed animal that the little boy was waving around.

"Victor!" His dad raced after him and scooped the kid up in his arms.

The image of father and son hit Caine hard. He remembered being swung in circles by his father on a warm summer evening. "More!" he'd yell again and again.

His dad would swing him around while laughing and telling him about centrifugal force. His dad was always a scientist at heart. Caine couldn't even count the number of times his dad would incorporate a lesson about a chemical equation into playtime. He could still hear his dad's voice saying, "Hydrogen is the first element on the periodic table . . . not to be confused with a picnic table."

Yeah, that was his dad. Karl the chemist comic Hunter.

Caine's life was forever changed by his mother's death when he was ten. His mother had been sick for several years before that — in and out of hospitals fighting cancer. She'd always wanted to go to Italy to visit her cousins there but didn't live long enough to see that dream happen. So she'd made Caine promise he'd go to visit them someday, which was why he was in Italy a few weeks ago.

He'd also promised his mom that he'd look after his dad. He'd failed with that job. Her death had devastated his dad, and the chemistry jokes had stopped for a long, long time. Instead, his father had become immersed in his work, and Caine had been left alone a lot.

Caine had joined the Marines right out of high school. His dad had supported his decision. He'd felt bad leaving his dad on his own, but Karl hadn't seemed to mind, claiming it gave him more time to devote to his work. Work that Caine had never really understood, despite his father's best efforts to educate him.

He'd wondered if his dad might not remarry, but that never happened. "Your mom was the love of my life," he'd told

Caine. "The hydrogen to my oxygen. No other molecule or woman will do."

Seeing what the loss of his mom had done to his dad made Caine determined not to display an equal vulnerability. Love killed something in you. Made you weak, not strong. These were the life lessons he learned. That, along with knowing the atomic weight of hydrogen.

Not that any of those things could help him now. He needed the skills he'd learned in the Marines: how to lock up his emotions to the horrors he saw around him. He'd heard a saying in the Corps — he wasn't sure who said it — Death smiles at everyone. The Marines smile back.

But his dad hadn't smiled back. He'd taken his own life.

Guilt shot through Caine. He should have done more, should have done *something*. Gritting his teeth, he refused to give in to the dark emotions eating at him. He couldn't afford to go there now. He had to stay focused.

Caine couldn't bring his father back to life. The best he could do was to clear his father's name.

Because he knew with every fiber of his being that his father hadn't sold corporate secrets for money. No way. He refused to believe that. And he was the only one who could prove them wrong.

That meant Caine had to keep his eyes on the mission and off Faith.

"Are you ready for your first case?" Abs asked Faith at work the next morning.

"Absolutely."

"You need to do an asset search on Douglas W. Haywood, former subprime mortgage broker. He claims he's broke and can't pay child support for his three kids. He and his wife, our client, are going through an acrimonious divorce. She's in small conference room A. Interview her and see what other information you can get on him." Abs handed over the file, which listed the bare minimum information: employment record, credit report, social security number and date of birth. "Here. You'll need these." Abs gave her a box of Kleenex. "She's a crier."

Faith entered the room to find a petite woman with short brown hair and red-rimmed eyes.

"Hello, Mrs. Haywood. My name is Faith West, and I'll be handling your case."

Candy broke into sobs.

Faith handed her the box of Kleenex. "I assure you, I'm good at what I do."

"Can . . . you. . . . break . . . his kneecaps?"

160

"I can do better than that. If he has any money, I'll find it."

"He's great at hiding things. He hid the fact that he was having an affair. I was totally clueless. I always let him handle the money. He wanted it that way. 'Don't worry, baby,' he'd tell me. 'I've got it all under control.' " Candy started sobbing again.

"I'm sorry." Faith patted her on the shoulder. "Let's see what we can do here. Do you think you can answer a few questions?"

"Maybe."

"If your husband was going to hide money, does he have any family or close friends who would help him?"

"He has a huge family, all as selfish as he is."

"I need you to write down their names, addresses and dates of birth if you know them. I also need you to confirm this is his social security number and his birth date."

"Yes, it is," Candy said before starting to write on the yellow legal pad Faith gave her.

Several minutes later, Faith asked, "What else can you tell me about your husband?"

"That he's a cheating asshole."

"Obviously, but I meant other information, like what are his hobbies or interests?"

"His only interest is to have an affair with

a twenty-year-old Hooters girl."

Faith checked the file. There was a huge mortgage due on the house they lived in, which was close to foreclosure. Three luxury cars, all in his name, all late on their payments. A time-share in Cabo San Lucas, Mexico.

"Has he taken any trips lately?" Faith asked.

"We've been separated for three months, so I don't know."

"How about before that?" Faith said. "What was the last trip you know about, and where did he go?"

"To our time-share in Cabo. For Christmas. All of us went. Our last family vacation." Candy started crying again. "I'm. . . . sor-sorry." She hiccupped. "Damn. Now I . . . I've got hiccups."

"Can I get you something? How about a glass of cold water?"

"To pour over my head?"

Faith smiled. "Hey, you've got a sense of humor. Good. That's going to help us with your case."

"How?"

"By keeping you sane through all this insanity."

"Humor helps?"

"It's a powerful aid. So are we. We're on

162

your side, and we're here to help you."

"What if the bastard really is broke? What if all the money is gone?"

Okay, here's where worst-case scenarios came into play. But Faith found it easier to apply that philosophy to her own life than to apply it to others. Especially a mom with three kids.

"Let's not cross that bridge just yet. Let me see what I can find first. Information is power."

"I could use some power about now," Candy admitted.

Faith spent the next fifteen minutes giving Candy a pep talk. When Candy left, Abs stopped by Faith's cubicle. "So you survived Candy the Crier."

"Doesn't it bother you? To see someone in pain and panic?"

"You can't get emotionally involved in every case. You can't get emotionally involved in *any* of them."

"Right. Of course not. I know that. Otherwise you'd burn out pretty fast."

Faith spent the rest of the day trying to track down any hidden assets Haywood might have stashed. All the while, she reminded herself that information was power. That applied to Faith's interactions with Caine as well. Dumping sparkling water on him didn't solve the problem. Proving the case against his father was sound was the only way to get Caine out of her life.

Saturday morning, Faith stared at the pages spread over her living room floor — a low-tech technique she'd developed for doing library projects. She was a visual thinker. She couldn't just read the information on her laptop. She needed to see what she was dealing with here. The file marked *Hunter, Karl* had plenty in it.

She'd read every page, but now she just needed to get the big picture somehow. She had a pile for each of the four people involved in the project: Karl and two other chemists along with a lab assistant. The person of most interest to her was the young lab assistant, Weldon Gronski.

Unfortunately, it seemed that Weldon didn't want to be found. He'd quit his job and moved several times in the past two years. He didn't appear to have any close friends, and none of his former coworkers had any idea where to find him. But she had an idea.

Weldon was a fan of vintage science fiction movies, and a Chicago-area theater was doing a showing of the 1951 classic *The Day*

Faith had a copy of Weldon's various photo IDs. He didn't change his appearance in any of them. He looked like what he was: a dorky science whiz with the taped glasses frames.

Later that afternoon, Faith watched the people entering the theater, searching for Weldon. Distracted as she was, she was startled when someone grabbed her by the elbow and hauled her around the corner into a quiet alley.

"Stop following me," Caine growled.

"You're the one following me."

"Get over yourself. I'm investigating my father's case."

"So am I, and I have as much right to be here as you do," Faith said.

"Beat it," he growled, showing her his war face for the first time.

Faith had to admit his expression was very intimidating, but she wasn't about to back down now.

Seeing that, Caine changed battle techniques, yanking Faith into his arms and kissing her.

CHAPTER NINE

The kiss was meant to warn Faith off. Instead, it drew Caine in, making him want her even more. She was like a land mine, hitting him when he least expected it.

Faith put her hands on his shoulders as if to shove him away. Good. She needed to end this, because Caine couldn't. Damn, she tasted fine. Why wasn't she pushing him away?

Faith gripped his shoulders harder. Now. Now she'd end it, right?

But no. Just when he thought she'd break things off, she parted her lips wider and pulled him even closer.

He was a goner.

So was she.

Their kiss became deeper, hotter. He raked his hands through her silky hair, only coming up for air long enough to change the angle of his mouth over hers before continuing the frantically intense lip-lock.

Things were rapidly spiraling out of control here. His hand was on her breast under her blouse, his thumb caressing her nipple through her sheer bra. She felt so damn good. His erection pressed tight against her.

She reached down to cup him through the placket of his jeans, her thumb grazing the bulge there.

He really should stop this. Soon. Before he exploded. But what a way to go.

His pagan elemental brain wanted to have sex. His warrior Marine brain knew this was a bad idea but wanted to have sex anyway.

Strict self-discipline was needed right now. Caine knew he should fight this. After all, he was a highly trained pro at fighting — from hand-to-hand combat to urban warfare. So why was he having such a hard time dealing with Faith?

Hanging on to his last thread of control, Caine broke off the kiss before he took her right there in the alley.

The sight of her swollen lips made his heart and other parts of his anatomy ache. Her hair was mussed from his hands, and her eyes were hazy with the remnants of passion. But she pulled herself together quickly, smoothing her hands over her hair before putting them on her hips and glaring at him.

"What were you trying to prove here?" she demanded. "That you can seduce me?"

"You seduced me as much as I seduced you."

"Me? You're the one who kissed me. Here and in Italy."

"And you were the one who kissed me back. Then and now. You slap me, you dump water in my lap, yet you still kiss me back. Why is that?"

Great question. Too bad Faith didn't have the answer. Because he could really use some answers about now. He sure as hell didn't know what he was doing with her. Kissing her hadn't scared her away at all. Instead, her sexy response shook him in a way he didn't even want to admit.

"You ruined everything," she said. "I had a plan, and you messed it up."

Caine wondered if she was referring to his father's case or to what happened in Italy.

"Does your father know you're messing with this case?" he said. "Did he send you here to interfere?"

"No and no. He knows nothing."

"You've got that right."

She glared at him. "I meant about this case."

"Again, you've got that right."

"Specifically, I really meant he knows

nothing about my interest in this case."

"Why not?"

"Because it would upset him."

Caine took a moment to digest that piece of intel. "Meaning he doesn't want you messing with this case. He wouldn't approve. He wants you to leave it alone, right? He wants you to blindly trust him when he says the case is closed. So why don't you? What's your motivation here? Are you just trying to irritate me? Sabotage my investigation?"

"I told you my motivation. It hasn't changed. I'm going to prove that my father was correct in his analysis of the case."

"What did you hope to gain by talking to Weldon? And don't even try giving me that innocent face, sunshine. I'm not buying that you're a fan of old sci-fi movies," Caine said.

"What's your interest in Weldon?"

"I asked you first."

"He's a person of interest. And now I've probably missed seeing him because of your antics."

"Right. So you should just trot on home."

She stared at him in amazement. "Trot? What am I, some kind of horse?"

"You should march on home."

"I'm not a Marine. I don't march."

"You marched out of that sushi restaurant the other night."

"I was trying to get away from you."

"Easy to do. Just stay out of my business."

"It's not just your business anymore. It's mine now too."

"Your father isn't dead."

"No," she said quietly. "And I'm sorry for your loss. I don't know if I said that before —"

He cut her off. "It doesn't matter. It's too late for an apology."

"Okay. I get that. You don't believe your father is guilty. So who do you think sold the corporate formula to a rival?"

"That's what I'm trying to find out."

"Me too."

"No, you're trying to reassure yourself that your rich daddy can do no wrong."

"That's not true."

"Isn't it?"

"No, dammit."

"Ohhhh, the librarian swears."

"And I know how to shoot," she reminded him.

"Yeah, but you haven't gone to target practice in months. I checked. There are only a handful of firing ranges in the entire area. I'll bet you've gotten rusty. Besides, you know the rules regarding concealed weapons in this state. You're not the kind to break the rules."

"I broke them with you. Big mistake."

"That's not what your kiss just said."

"Another even bigger mistake," she said. "One that won't be repeated."

"Not if you leave now."

"I'm not leaving. There's a chance I can catch Weldon when the movie lets out."

"I have no intention of allowing you to intimidate Weldon into saying whatever you want him to say."

"Me? *You're* the one into intimidation."

"You do all right."

"So what are you suggesting?" she said. "That we both work on the case?" The words were out of her mouth before she could stop them.

"Are you crazy?"

Perhaps. Perhaps she was crazy like a fox. Or so Faith tried to tell herself. She had to be logical here. "If we work together, then we can keep tabs on each other. Make sure that things are aboveboard and that you're not planting false evidence or something."

"That sounds more like something you'd do. I don't need false evidence," he said. "The truth works for me."

"So you do think we should work together."

"I never said that."

"Then what is your suggestion?"

"That you go home and keep your nose out of my business," Caine said.

"That's not going to happen. I'm here to stay," she said. "Get used to it."

"What about your job?"

"What about yours?" she countered.

"I don't trust you," he said.

"I don't trust you either, so we're even on that one. What are your other objections?"

"Too many to list them all."

"Let's try to reach a middle ground here. I'm willing to listen to your suggestions. How do you suggest we work together?"

"The same way porcupines have sex. Carefully."

"It always come back to sex with you, doesn't it," she said indignantly.

"I don't know. Does it?"

"Never mind. Let's just keep our minds focused on the facts here," she said.

"How can we, when we don't agree on the facts? You think my father is guilty. I know he's innocent."

"We both agree with the fact that Weldon was your father's lab assistant and that therefore he's a person of interest. Don't you think it's strange that he's moved so many times in such a short period? And had several employers? Why do you think that is? Do you think he has something to hide? Or is he afraid of something and wants to keep on the move?"

"If he was really afraid, he'd have skipped town. He hasn't as far as we know."

"Good point. Which leaves us with him having something to hide."

"Hold on, sunshine. Maybe the guy just doesn't like putting down roots."

"Why has he disappeared now? What has him spooked? He hasn't been back to his apartment for several days now."

"Maybe he's on vacation."

"His coworkers don't think so. They said he was on a family leave of absence but hadn't traveled out of town."

"He doesn't have any family."

"I know. So what's the plan? To wait for the movie to let out and see if he's there in the crowd?"

"The crowd?" he said. "It's not like people were lined up around the block to get in to see this flick."

"Why don't you go home, and I'll stay and watch for him."

"Yeah right, like that's going to happen," he said.

"Then you're agreed that we both stay."

"I'm not agreeing to anything."

"We've got over an hour before the movie is over. Why don't you tell me what you've come up with so far in the case?"

"Yeah right," he repeated. "Not going to happen. I'm not getting into a game of you-show-me-yours-I'll-show-you-mine with you."

"Because you're afraid that I know more than you do."

He just laughed.

She glared.

"Hey," Caine said, "if you don't want me laughing at you, then don't say such funny things."

"I wasn't trying to be funny. I was being analytical."

"Is that why you were fondling the placket of my jeans when I kissed you? Were you trying to *analyze* me? What were your findings?"

"That you're not as big as you think you are," she shot back.

"No? I think your findings are faulty." He pulled her into his arms and kissed her again.

This time she did push him away, only to haul him back and kiss him on her own terms.

Then she stepped away and gave him a cool stare.

"No," she said. "My findings were accurate."

He gave her a wry look. "You know, sunshine, sometimes you surprise me."

"Get used to it," Faith told him. She couldn't get used to the way she practically burst into flames whenever Caine touched her. She'd never felt this way before. What was wrong with her? Why couldn't she keep her cool?

At least she'd sounded like she was totally together when she'd shot that comment at him. She needed to prove that she could be focused on the case and not distracted by his seduction techniques.

"So we're agreed that we will work together, right?" she said curtly.

"Wrong," he said. "Go home and let me get back to work."

"Not going to happen. So let's go across the street to that Starbucks and get a table near the window to wait for Weldon."

She took his arm and tugged him toward the coffee shop entrance. Maybe touching him more often would make the physical contact seem more matter-of-fact and less the cause of an intense I-want-you-now volcanic need.

Faith ordered a tall soy sugar-free cinnamon dolce latte no whip no foam no sprinkles. He ordered black coffee and a brownie. They snagged the empty table in front of the window.

"So how are we going to do this?" she asked.

"Do what?"

"Work together on this case."

"We're not."

"It would be more efficient."

"Says you."

"Look, it's not my idea of fun either."

"It's not supposed to be fun," he growled.

"I'm sorry," she said quietly. "That was a bad choice of words."

"Yeah, it was."

Keeping her gaze on the theater across the street, she sipped her latte.

"How are we supposed to work together given the circumstances?" he demanded.

"I didn't say it would be easy."

"I'm a former Marine. We don't do easy."

"But you believe in teamwork, right?"

"When we're sharing the same mission, yes. Not with —"

"— the enemy?" she inserted.

"I didn't say that."

"You didn't have to."

"Don't put words in my mouth."

Her gaze moved to his mouth, his sinful mouth. He'd done some darkly sensual things to her in Italy with that mouth of his. And his recent kiss proved that what they'd shared in Positano hadn't been a fluke. The physical chemistry was still there, stronger than ever.

"Is that look for me or for my brownie?" he asked.

"Your brownie."

"You want?" He held up a small piece to her lips, daring her to take it. "How badly do you want?"

She turned up her nose, which only made his fingers brush her bottom lip and her chin. She couldn't let him see how much he got to her. She had to keep her head here and not get pulled into his magnetic field.

"How badly do *you* want?" she said.

"I've got the brownie. You don't."

"Yes, but I've got the file on your father's case, and you don't."

"And you're willing to share?"

"I didn't say that."

"I didn't think so."

"Not the entire file."

"Why not?"

"Because if my father found out . . . he wouldn't be pleased."

"If his company has nothing to hide, then he shouldn't mind."

"I am willing to share some information."

"Go ahead." He sat back in his chair.

"Only four people worked closely on this particular biofuel project. Your father was in charge of it. He had two other chemists working with him at the research facility in Joliet: Dr. Fred Belkin and Dr. Nolan Parker."

"I already knew that."

"Fred died of a brain tumor last year."

"Again, old news," he said.

"Did you know that several former employees of American Research Corporation's research facility had or have brain tumors? They're presently suing the company."

"So? What does that have to do with my father's case?"

"I don't know yet," she said.

"Are you insinuating that my father may have had a brain tumor and that's what made him embezzle money?"

"I don't know. Maybe. And what about Nolan Parker?"

"What about him?"

"What role did he play in this whole thing? Have you talked to him?"

"Not yet. I know from his earlier statements that he firmly believed my father was guilty."

"What reasons might Nolan have for saying that?"

They spent the next half hour talking about possible scenarios without reaching any conclusions. To her surprise, she enjoyed brainstorming with Caine. Once he set his hatred for her father aside, they were able to work together well.

But how realistic was it to expect him to feel any other way if he blamed her father for his dad's death? What if the situation was reversed? How would she feel if she thought his dad was responsible for her father's death? The idea gave her chills. And not the good kind.

Why had Caine kissed her earlier? Had it been to distract her? Or to make her fall for him harder?

Working with him didn't mean that she trusted him any more than he trusted her.

She looked out the window. "They're coming out of the theater."

"Weldon?"

She shook her head. "I don't see him."

They waited until the last person had departed. No Weldon.

Caine checked his watch. "Gotta go. I've got things to do." He stood and made a hasty retreat.

She wanted to follow him, but she had things to do herself. The first was to check out another lead a few blocks away. The corner tavern looked like hundreds of other Chicago neighborhood bars. This one was next to the "L" elevated train tracks and had a Singleton's Tavern vintage wooden sign that she would have expected to see outside some English countryside pub. Stepping inside, she discovered the place wasn't very busy. A blue and white neon sign behind the bar touted the fact that Pabst Blue Ribbon was on tap here.

"Are you looking for the Geek Meet group?" the bartender asked.

She nodded.

He tilted his head. "In the back on the right."

Faith walked back to the accompaniment of the "L" roaring by outside, making the floor vibrate.

A woman greeted her at the door to a large, quieter room. "Welcome." She looked down at her clipboard. "We're glad you've joined us. And your name is?"

"I didn't sign up ahead of time. Is that a problem? Weldon told me it would be okay." Faith scanned the name tags on the table beside her. Sure enough, there was Weldon's Hi My Name Is self-adhesive name tag.

"Well, we normally like people to sign up beforehand, but we do have some extra space tonight, so you're in luck. There is a cover charge."

Faith paid the amount and headed for a table where a few other people were already sitting. A red and white checked oilcloth covered the folding table, and folding chairs provided the seating. She sat and filled out her name on the supplied adhesive name tag. She was just writing the last letter in her name when a guy bumped into her elbow with his backpack, causing her to smear her *h*.

"Sorry," he mumbled, taking his backpack and setting it on the table.

His name tag said he was Marvin, but his voice said he was Caine.

CHAPTER TEN

The geeky newcomer didn't look like Caine, not with the white T-shirt and orange and green diamond weave sweater vest he wore over it. His shoulders were slightly hunched, and his hair was totally rumpled — not in a sexy way but in a hasn't-seen-a-comb-in-a-week way. He blinked myopically from behind a pair of glasses held together with tape at the right hinge.

He was good. She'd give him that. But what did it say about her that she didn't need a costume to come to the geek gathering and fit right in? Her white blouse and khaki Capri pants were pretty conservative. Maybe too much so? Was that what gave her inner geek away?

"Welcome everyone. My name is Sharon, and as you know, you're here for our monthly Geek Meet gathering. Let's get things started with a few icebreaker questions. Raise your hand if you think the Mer-

cedes symbol looks like an eclipsed confor-
mation."

A dozen hands went up amid laughter.

"Great." Sharon smiled. "How many of
you barbecue on your Bunsen burners?"

More laughter, fewer hands.

"Okay, how many of you get excited when
asked, 'What punctuation mark are you?' "

Faith's hand shot up. She knew her place
in the punctuation hall of fame. She was
definitely a question mark. Always had been.

"How many of you know the Dewey
decimal number for mathematics?"

Again her hand shot up, as did several others. "It's 510," she said.

"How about Melvil Dewey's birthdate?"

"December 10, 1851," a guy at the neigh-
boring table shouted out before Faith could.

"Right. Which leads us into the next step
— board games." Sharon pointed to a pile
of them on a small corner table. "Trivial
Pursuit or Scattergories. Take your pick.
One game per table."

Faith grabbed the last Scattergories and
brought it back to her table. Yes, she was
the Trivial Pursuit champ at the library, but
those boxes were all taken.

"Good choice," a guy in an MIT T-shirt
at her table said. "I hope you're good at this
game. We need to get a win tonight."

"You're a librarian, right?" the woman on the other side of him said. "I saw you put your hand in the air for those librarian questions. My name is Mia, and I'm a chemist," she added.

"So when she hears 'ABS' she thinks about acrylnitril-butadiene-styrol copolymer instead of antilock braking systems," MIT guy said. "My name's Ed, and I'm a chemist too."

"Do either of you know Weldon Gronski?" Faith asked.

They both shook their heads.

Faith discreetly checked the rest of the room, looking for Weldon. Half the attendees were women, so that knocked them out of the running. None of the remaining geeks looked like Weldon.

Caine aka Marvin moved his backpack off the table and dumped it onto the floor under the table with klutzy clumsiness. "Sorry," he muttered without looking anyone in the eye.

"Do you know how to play this game?" Faith asked him.

He nodded.

She kicked his ankle, not hard enough to hurt him but enough to get his attention. She regretted it a moment later when he slid his hand onto her thigh under the table.

She immediately put her knees together, which only served to trap his hand between her legs. Big mistake.

He wiggled his fingers against her.

"Is this your first time, Marvin?" Mia asked.

He nodded again, keeping his chin tucked against his chest. Meanwhile his fingers were tucked against Faith in the vee between her thighs, doing wickedly naughty things to her.

Her face and her entire body were on fire.

"Are you okay?" Mia asked her. "Is it too hot in here for you?"

Faith was incapable of making a reply. Tilting her head back, she briefly closed her eyes as her internal fireworks exploded. She tried crossing her legs. More fireworks.

Marvin/Caine took a sheet of paper and fanned her face with one hand while his other seductive hand remained under the table between her legs. The thin cotton of her Capri pants provided little protection to his erotic finger play.

"Everyone ready to play now?" Ed asked.

Faith reluctantly removed his hand from her body and returned it to his own leg before hastily pulling back her own hand and keeping both on the table in front of her. No more playing for her. What had she been thinking? Dumb question. Thinking had played no part in what had just gone on under the table. That had been purely physical. Purely, divinely physical.

Her body was still humming. No, not just humming, it was singing an operatic aria in Dolby stereo.

How was she supposed to concentrate after experiencing an orgasm in public? She didn't know where to begin. She couldn't even speak yet. At least she was no longer panting, and her tablemates had stopped giving her curious looks. None of them looked like they had a clue what she'd just gone through. She certainly hoped not.

"So," she stuttered, "uh everyone uh everyone knows . . . uh . . . how to . . . uh . . . play . . . right?"

"Oh yeah," Marvin/Caine said with a naughty grin. "I know how to play. I'm good at games. Really good."

Her laser look shot him the message, *Touch me again, and you're a dead man.*

The lazy look he bestowed upon her said, *Message received and ignored.*

"We know the rules," Ed said. "You fill out a category list with answers that begin with whatever letter comes up on the dice."

"There's only one, so actually it's a die," Mia said.

"I knew that." Ed sounded defensive. "To continue, you only score points if no other player matches your answer. The one with the most points wins. Okay then, everyone ready? I've got the timer set. Faith, will you roll the die?"

She did and then said, "The letter is *N*."

"Start!" Ed enthusiastically shouted.

Faith stared down at her category card and quickly started writing — beginning with a boy's name and moving on to U.S. cities to pro sports teams and presidents. Ned, Nevada City, Nuggets, Nixon.

But the category that provided the most heated exchanges in that first round was insects. "*Nabis capsiformis* is a pale damsel bug," Ed said.

"You made that up," Marvin/Caine said.

"Google it," Ed retorted.

"What about *Nezara viridula?*" Marvin/ Caine gave Mia an intimidating stare.

"It's a southern green stink bug," Faith replied on Mia's behalf. "I Googled it." She held up her BlackBerry. "And *gnat* is spelled with a *g*," she told Caine.

Round two proved to be just as competitive, with Marvin/Caine racking up points. Faith had heard that Marines were ultra-competitive, but she'd never been eyewitness to that trait until now. Caine's undercover geek persona was clearly proving to be more and more difficult for him to maintain. He was drawing too much attention.

Before round three, she knocked his pencil to the floor, forcing him to lean under the table to get it.

"I'll help you," she said before diving under the table to join him. "You're a geek, remember?" she whispered. "Stop being such a Marine."

"I am a Marine."

"A former Marine," she corrected him. "In danger of blowing your geek cover."

"You two okay under here?" Ed asked as he bent down to check out what was going on. "We have extra pencils on the table, you know."

"It was his good luck pencil," Faith said.

"It didn't help him spell *gnat* correctly," Ed pointed out.

Caine growled.

Faith elbowed him, reminding him that geeks don't growl unless someone challenges their equations.

"Let's resume the game." Ed sat up.

Faith shot Caine a warning look and put her finger to her lips. She then sat up so fast, she got dizzy. Caine took his time.

Ed said, "You never did tell us what you

do for a living, Marvin."

Caine shot the guy a look that said, *I eat pompous lizards like you for breakfast.*

"He can't talk about his work," Faith said.

Ed raised a bushy eyebrow. "He told you that under the table?"

Faith nodded. Caine wasn't the only one who could perfect a look of intimidation. As a librarian, Faith had that look down pat as well. And she directed it full force at Ed. "He's doing top secret research."

Ed made the mistake of laughing. "And you bought that?"

Faith grabbed Caine's arm to stop him from leaping over the table and shoving Ed through the wall.

To her surprise, Caine seemed very calm. She wasn't sure that was a good thing, however. He then casually rattled off a chemical equation so complicated-sounding that she was stunned. Ed seemed equally flummoxed. Jane Austen may have seen people flummoxed, but that facial expression was pretty hard to come by these days.

Ed shut up, and they played round three without any further problems. Unexpectedly, Faith ended up with the most points and won the game. Her prize was a Librarian Action Figure. It seemed her former profession followed her wherever she went.

Caine also followed her. She had to ask, "What did you say to Ed?"

"Something my father taught me."

"Whatever it was, it worked. I assume you're here because you spoke to the same former coworker who told me about Weldon's interest in this group," she said in an undertone.

Caine nodded and slung his backpack on with renewed confidence. The slouch was gone. But Weldon's unclaimed name tag remained on the table. He'd been a no-show yet again.

"What's next?" Faith asked Caine.

"You go home and play with your Librarian Action Figure, and I solve this case." He strode off, leaving her standing there shaking her head. The man was clearly clueless if he thought she was giving up that easily. She was a Mighty Question Mark in the world of punctuation superheroes. She had not yet begun to fight.

Okay, she was heading home now because she was clearly mixing her metaphors along with everything else. It had been a long day and an even longer evening. Time to regroup after overexplosure — er overexposure to Caine.

She'd only had a glass of Chardonnay, so she couldn't blame her messed-up thoughts

190

on her alcohol consumption. This was all Caine's fault. That orgasm had scrambled her brains. He was the reason she had to hail a cab instead of taking public transportation home.

But the car that pulled up at the curb beside her wasn't a taxi. It looked remarkably like Caine's black Mustang.

The door opened as he shoved it from inside. "Get in," he growled.

"I'd rather not."

"Do not make me come get you," he warned.

She was no fool. She got in the car. "Clearly you don't want this night to end. Why is that?"

"Because I'm not going to leave you on some strange street corner to find your own way home in the middle of the night."

"First, it's ten p.m., not the middle of the night. Secondly, this is not a strange street corner. We're on the edge of Wrigleyville. It's a good neighborhood. You know what they say about Chicago . . . that it's a big city made up of small-town neighborhoods. My Streeterville neighborhood has its own feel and history. It got its name from Captain George Streeter. He's actually got a pretty neat story." Faith was babbling, and she didn't care. "In 1886 his boat ran aground on a sandbar in Lake Michigan just offshore. He and his wife turned the boat into a houseboat and just lived there. He sold portions of the sandbar to contractors looking to dump rubble left over from the Great Chicago Fire. Eventually the landfill took shape, and since the old maps of Chicago showed the city limits ending at the old shoreline, Streeter declared the area the District of Lake Michigan and made himself governor. Then he sold small plots of the filled-in land, and a shantytown developed there. The ritzy inhabitants with mansions on the nearby Gold Coast were not happy campers, and they tried to get rid of him. But he hung on until his death in 1921. The city then used a loophole in the law to take the property from his third wife. It turns out Streeter hadn't divorced his first wife, so the marriage to his third wasn't legal. The city moved in and took over the land. But the Streeterville name remained." Realizing she sounded like a history groupie, Faith paused. She had to stop thinking like a librarian and more like an investigator.

"So you live on a landfill," Caine said.

She laughed. "That's one way of looking at it. What about your neighborhood? What's it like?"

He remained silent.

"You haven't said where you live," she pointed out.

"And I don't intend to."

"Why not?"

"I like my privacy."

"I could find out if I really wanted to, which I don't."

He responded by peeling through an orange light at the intersection and pulling into a White Castle fast-food drive-through.

"What are you doing?" Faith demanded.

"Getting food. I'm hungry."

He ordered a sack of sliders, the nickname for the four-bite, grilled-onion-soaked hamburgers that were an acquired taste. An addictive acquired taste that Faith happened to have. He opened the bag and handed her one.

He'd ordered two large Cokes without consulting her.

When he tossed a straw in her lap, she had to speak. "What is your problem to-night?"

"No problem." He reached for another slider as he exited the parking lot and turned onto the main street.

"Are you upset that I pointed out you mis-spelled *gnat?*"

His "No" was very curt.

193

"I didn't mean to embarrass you."

"Yes, you did."

Maybe she had, but only to pay him back for grinning at her the way he had after his finger foreplay had driven her over the erotic edge. That knowing I-can-strum-you-like-a-guitar grin had infuriated her. Still did. So why was she sitting in his Mustang gobbling his sliders?

What was wrong with her?

A complicated question that was growing increasingly so by the second.

She turned her attention to the case. "Why do you think Weldon got cold feet tonight? Do you think he saw us there?"

"Possibly."

"That's twice that we've gone to a viable surveillance location only to have Weldon not show up. First at the theater and then at the Geek Meet. Maybe we've spooked him. Maybe we should rethink this approach and try another way of reaching him. What do you think?"

He just grunted.

"That's real helpful." Her voice vibrated with anger. "What is your problem tonight? You're acting like part of you wants to stay with me and the other part wants to toss me out of your car."

"How did you know?"

"Because I feel the same way," she muttered while jostling the ice in her cup to cover her words.

"What did you say?"

"Because I feel the same way!" she yelled. "Are you happy now?"

"Not really."

"Me neither." She grabbed another slider out of the bag and sank her teeth into it.

"I never would have pegged you as a slider girl," he noted.

"Which just goes to show how little you know about me."

Caine knew enough. He knew she got through his defenses in a way no other woman ever had before. And that freaked him out.

So Caine remained quiet the remainder of the trip, as did Faith. Yuri was there to greet them at the door to her building.

"You sure know how to show a girl a good time." Faith shot Caine a saucy grin before hopping out of his car and marching into the building.

Yuri bent down and gave Caine a questioning look.

Caine rested his forehead against the steering wheel, looking like a man who was near the end of his rope.

"You okay?" Yuri asked.

"I need a drink," he muttered.

"I'm off duty in two minutes. Mind if I join you?"

Caine shook his head.

Twenty minutes later, they were seated in a bar, drinking beers. "So what's with the strange getup?" Yuri asked.

Caine looked down at his geeky shirt and sweater vest. He'd forgotten he was wearing them. He peeled the vest off and stuffed it in his backpack. The plain white T-shirt was more his thing. "I was doing some under-cover surveillance work tonight."

"With Faith?"

"She insinuated herself into the situation, yes."

"So you and Faith were together on some undercover mission?" Yuri said. "I find that hard to believe."

"Yeah, me too. I also can't believe I told you about it."

"Hey, I'm a fellow Marine. You can trust me."

"I can't believe you're a doorman/actor now," Caine said.

"And I can't believe you're no longer in the Corps."

"It wasn't an easy decision." Caine took a healthy swig of his Corona right from the bottle. No fancy microbrewery beers for him. The Mexican beer had been his beverage of choice since his boot camp days at Camp Pendleton outside San Diego. That seemed like a lifetime ago now. But the things he'd learned there had been ingrained into him so deeply there was no changing them now. "Not easy at all."

"I'll bet."

"I did it for my dad. Left the Marine Corps, I mean."

"You said Faith's dad was responsible for his death."

Caine nodded and swallowed another swig of Corona down a throat gone tight with emotion. "That's right."

"What happened?"

Caine wiped the condensation off his bottle with his thumb. "Jeff West accused my father of a crime he didn't commit."

"I thought Faith's dad was a private investigator not a cop."

"That's right. He was investigating a case involving corporate fraud. He thought my dad was guilty. He was wrong."

"So your dad was arrested?"

"No." Caine was finding it harder and harder to swallow. "My dad couldn't take the shame of being falsely accused. He committed suicide. An overdose."

"Shit."

"Yeah."

"What made West think your dad was guilty?"

"A shoddy investigation."

"So what's next?"

"I prove my father's innocence."

"And that's why you and Faith were on that stakeout. Did the perp show up?"

"Okay, you've been watching way too many police shows."

"So now you and Faith are working together to clear your father's name?"

"I wouldn't put it exactly like that. Has she talked to you about me?"

Yuri just smiled.

"Come on, Gunny. I've known you longer than she has."

"I don't pass on intel. What you say to me stays with me. Ditto for what she says to me."

"So she has talked about me. I knew it."

"I heard she dumped her drink in your lap last week."

"Who told you that?"

"I know one of the servers at the Sushi Place. I have a lot of contacts in the Streeterville neighborhood."

"Did you meet that asshole fiancé of hers?"

Yuri nodded.

"So what did you think of him?"

"He was an asshole."

"What did she see in him?"

"Who knows? He was smart and polished."

"I can't believe he left her at the altar that way. Do you think she really loved him?"

"Well, she was going to marry him."

"Yeah, I know but maybe . . ."

"Maybe what?"

"I don't know. Doesn't matter. It's none of my business. I need to stay focused on my father's case."

"Hard to do when Faith is working on it with you."

"She is a distraction," Caine admitted.

"I can imagine. I remember you telling me once that women got in the way if you let them get too close."

"Right."

"Do you still feel that way?"

"Affirmative."

"Well, I'm certainly in no position to be giving you romantic advice. I've been married twice and divorced twice. The Marines and marriage don't always make for a good partnership."

"But you're out of the Marines now."

Yuri nodded. "I know. But old habits are hard to break."

"Tell me about it. I still wake up in the middle of the night thinking I'm back in Iraq." Caine didn't say more, and Yuri didn't ask. There was an unspoken code between most Marines that you never referred to the bloody horror of war, but instead you sucked it up and kept going. Because sometimes the realities were just too damn difficult. Sharing emotions was not a Marine Corps thing.

Improve, adapt, overcome. Those were Marine Corps rules.

"Pain is only temporary. Pride is forever," Yuri said. "I've got the T-shirt."

"Yeah." The demons of war weren't the only things haunting Caine. His father had e-mailed him, begging him to come home. Caine had e-mailed back, saying that being a Marine wasn't a nine-to-five job. He'd made a commitment, and he had to honor that.

His dad committed suicide a few days later. December had always been a rough time for his father because it marked the anniversary of Caine's mother's death on December 7, Pearl Harbor day. "A day that shall live in infamy," President Franklin Roosevelt said. Caine's dad said the same thing every year around December 7. Caine could only imagine the demons that haunted his dad, who had never remarried nor had another woman in his life.

"She was my soul mate," he'd tell Caine, who decided at a young age that he didn't want a freaking soul mate if they could cause you such pain. Better to keep things casual. Mating for sex — okay. Mating of souls — definitely not okay. It was a code he'd followed his entire adult life.

"So you and Faith are working together. Does this mean that Faith is going to let you into the building now?"

"I have no idea," Caine said. "My focus is on the case, not on her."

Yuri just laughed and shook his head. "You keep saying that often enough, you might start believing it."

Caine sure hoped so. Because he had no intention of having his heart yanked out and stomped on. He knew better.

"Thanks for meeting with me tonight," Sara said so formally that Faith was immediately worried as she guided her mom into the condo and motioned for her to sit on the couch. "I know you're busy."

"You're my mom, of course I'd meet with you. I'm never too busy for you." Faith hugged her, but her mother didn't reciprocate. "What's wrong? Is it Aunt Lorraine? Is she still staying with you? What has the Duchess of Grimness done now?"

"No, it's not Aunt Lorraine. It's something your father has done."

"If this is about my taking the job at West Investigations —"

Sara cut her off. "It's not. Not directly."

"Are you angry with him for hiring me?"

"No, I'm angry with him for having an affair."

CHAPTER ELEVEN

Faith was speechless. Her father? Having an affair?

Faith had been raised to do all the right things: to tell the truth, to be nice to others and to respect her parents. Not to think of her father having an affair. In fact, she didn't like to think of her parents as ever having sex at all except for the one time she was conceived.

"At least I *think* he's having an affair," Sara said. "I'm not sure. I just know that something isn't right. He's done all the things that raise a red flag in cases like this — like an increase in the number of late nights when he says he's working, him not being where he says he is, a new secrecy about his actions. He's clearly hiding something."

"Well, I know he's got this war going on with Vince."

"Vince is the one who told me about the affair."

Faith heaved a sigh of relief. "Well, there you go then. If Vince told you, then you *know* it's a lie. Since when has Vince King been talking to you anyway?"

"I ran into him at a charity function I was attending on my own because your father canceled at the last minute. I was there to help the Anti-Cruelty Society."

"And Vince was there to drive you crazy by telling you that your husband is having an affair. I can't believe that you actually gave his lie any credence at all."

"I wouldn't have under normal circumstances. But things haven't been normal between your father and me for a few weeks now."

This news took Faith by surprise. "Is it because of the wedding? Because that turned into such a mess?"

"This has nothing to do with you. Our problems were not due to your wedding."

Faith wasn't ready to let herself off the hook that easily. "Still, if I hadn't been so wrapped up in the preparations, I would have noticed something . . . some stress between the two of you. But just because you're having some trouble doesn't mean Dad is having an affair. You know Vince just wants to create trouble. It's his specialty."

"I know, and if it was just Vince, I'd ignore

it. But my instincts tell me something is very wrong. I've tried in roundabout ways to get your father to talk to me, but he avoids me. I'm only asking you for your help because I don't know what else to do. That's why I want you to see what you can find out. There's no one else I can turn to. It was hard enough to come to you and admit there might be trouble in my marriage. I couldn't face telling a stranger. And I can't just come out and directly ask him. I don't know that he'd . . . that he'd tell me the truth."

Her mother never cried, not even when Aunt Lorraine would say something mean enough to test the patience of an angel, but her mother was crying now. Two big fat teardrops slowly rolled down her cheeks. "I shouldn't be dumping this on you. It's not right."

"Let me do a little digging and see what I can find out," Faith said. "I'm sure there's nothing for you to be worried about, but you'll feel better if I can prove that, right?"

Her mom nodded.

"Okay, then. Consider it taken care of." Faith hugged her.

This time her mother hugged her back. "That's what Jane Austen would do," Sara said unsteadily. "She'd reassure her mother and hug her. Not that the mothers in Austen's books were all that appealing. They tended to be self-serving and self-centered."

"Not you."

"I am being self-centered to ask you for help."

"No, you're not." Faith handed her a Kleenex from the end table. "I'm the one who was self-centered when I took off for Italy and left you here to handle the mess. Helping you now is the least I can do. Everything will be okay, you'll see."

"Thank you." Sara hugged her again, squeezing her tight, reminding Faith of the time as a child she'd gotten lost in the Marshall Field's store, and her mother had hugged her when they'd found Faith asleep in one of the empty intimate apparel fitting rooms. Faith had forgotten about that episode until this moment.

It was funny how old memories sometimes came back. Her mom had never told Faith's father that she'd wandered off, breaking a rule her parents had taught her practically from the time she took her first steps. It had been a secret between the two of them, kept all these years.

Faith couldn't say no to her mom now. She'd prove that her dad was faithful, and that would be the end of that. So here she was for a second time trying to prove her dad was not guilty of something.

"Like I said, I'm sure there's no cause for concern," Faith reassured her mom. "But I'll check things out and see what's going on with Dad."

"I knew I could count on you," her mom said, dabbing at her tears with the balled-up Kleenex.

Faith handed her a new tissue. "Of course you can count on me."

Her mom took a ragged breath before voicing her biggest fear. "What if . . . what if he *is* having an affair?"

Here's where Faith's worst-case scenario train of thought came up. What if her dad really was cheating on her mom? What if they got divorced? What if her dad took off to Bali to find himself like Alan did?

Okay, she was losing control here. And control was required to get through this tricky situation. She didn't want to go borrowing trouble. Maybe she'd have to rethink that worst-case stuff and go with something else instead. "Let's not get too far ahead of ourselves, okay? No use worrying about something that in all likelihood isn't true. Let's go with the plan that I'll find out what's wrong and clear this misunderstanding up. Think how relieved you'll be knowing that Dad isn't being unfaithful to you."

"But if he is cheating, he'd be good at hiding it. I mean the man is the top private investigator in Chicago. He'd be hard to catch."

"Yes, but I'm a former librarian, and you know one of our mottos: If we don't know the answer, we know where to find it. So don't worry. I'll find the answer." Faith just hoped it was the answer they both wanted to hear and not one that would break up her family.

"So how are you settling in?" her dad asked Faith at work the next morning. She was seated in his office to go over an insurance fraud case.

"I'm doing good. How about you?"

"Overworked and underpaid." It was a long-standing joke of his.

"Well, you're the boss. Maybe you should ask for a raise. Or take some time off. You should take a vacation. You and Mom together. Doesn't that sound like a great idea?"

"Hmmm." He'd already focused his attention on a file he was studying on his computer screen.

"When was the last time you and Mom got away?"

"Hmmm."

"Hello?" Faith rapped her knuckles on his desk. "Dad, I'm talking to you here. When was the last time you and Mom got away?"

"I don't know."

"Then it's been too long. Your anniversary is coming up soon. You should go somewhere romantic."

He gave her a look. "Like Italy?"

She squirmed. "Or someplace else. Or a cruise."

"Just shoot me now. Being stuck on a boat with a thousand other people is my idea of hell."

"Okay then, no cruise. And it's a ship not a boat. But there are plenty of other options. Isn't there someplace that you've always wanted to see?"

"Yes. The National Security Agency in Maryland, but it's a restricted area."

"And not a romantic location."

"I don't have time to take off."

"Sure you do. You're the boss. Who's going to say no to you?"

"Me."

"Let's get a second opinion," Faith said as her uncle joined them. "Uncle Dave, don't you think it would be a great idea if Dad and Mom took off on a romantic getaway for their anniversary?"

Her uncle eyed her uncertainly. "Is this a trick question?"

"No," Faith said.

"You see, he doesn't think I should leave either," her dad said.

"He didn't say that. Aunt Lorraine said you wouldn't have the gumption to go," Faith said, hoping to goad her dad into proving her wrong.

"I doubt she said gumption. She probably said I didn't have the balls to go. And I don't care."

"What's so important here that you couldn't get away?" Faith demanded.

"A number of things."

She leaned forward in her chair. "Tell me about them."

"There's no time. I've got a meeting in five minutes."

"Uncle Dave, tell him to take a vacation."

"Take a vacation," her uncle obediently said.

"There, you see? Your brother agrees with me."

"I'll think about it," her dad said absently.

"You will not. You've already wiped it from your memory banks. This is important, Dad. You really need to focus on this idea, okay?"

"I said I'd think about it, and I will." Now

he sounded irritated.

Fine. She was irritated too. The least he could do was cooperate with her here. She was trying to save his marriage. Not that she could tell him that.

Her dad had always been an uber-workaholic, but her mom was right. Now that Faith was tuned in, she was picking up weird vibes from her dad. Not necessarily "I'm cheating" vibes, not that she was sure she'd know what those were like coming from her dad. But she was getting the feeling that he was hiding something.

She could tell she wasn't going to get anything more out of him right now, so she withdrew from his office and cornered Gloria later that morning. Casually cornered her.

"My dad seems a little more stressed than usual," Faith said with daughterly concern, which wasn't faked. She truly was concerned. "Do you think my botched wedding upset him more than he let on?"

Gloria shrugged, her shoulders broader than usual in her poppy red sweater set. "As if I know what goes on in that mind of his."

"Come on, Gloria. You are such an astute woman, and you've known my father for ages . . . I mean a long time," she hurriedly edited. The frown on Gloria's face clearly indicated that she didn't like the "ages" reference. "What do you think is the cause of his raised stress level?"

"I'll tell you one thing I do know for sure. Your father has raised *my* stress level. He was always impatient, but now . . ."

"Gloria!" he bellowed from his office. "Where's that file I asked for?"

"I e-mailed it to you five minutes ago," she yelled back before returning her attention to Faith. "You see? It's little things like that. The straw that breaks the camel's back. And I'm not the only one who has noticed. Your uncle made a comment about it. A very oblique comment, because that's how Dave is. But still . . . you know it has to be pretty noticeable for Dave to see it, because he's off in his own math world most of the time."

"Thanks, Gloria." Faith grabbed her uncle's arm as he left her father's office. "Let's talk."

"I'm really busy . . ."

"I know you are, but you have to eat lunch."

"I eat lunch at my desk."

"That's not good for you."

"Has Megan been talking to you?" he asked suspiciously.

"No. Why would she? Is something

wrong?"

"My cholesterol levels were a little high. Tell her I'm eating a healthy lunch, even if it is at my desk."

Faith was alarmed by this news about her uncle's health. "Did the doctor put you on medication?"

"No, no. My numbers are slightly elevated, that's all. No need to get upset."

"Is my dad upset because he's worried about your health?"

"He's upset because he's your dad."

"So it *is* my fault."

"No, that didn't come out right. What I meant is that your dad is always upset. That's just the way he is. And, yes, he seems a tad more . . . irritable, shall we say."

"Do you think it's because of Vince King?"

"I'm sure their vendetta isn't helping."

And it probably wasn't helping that Caine was out there accusing her father of having botched the Karl Hunter investigation. That meant the sooner Faith proved Caine wrong, the better.

Friday night, and Faith had a big date. Not with a hot guy but hopefully with Weldon. She'd dressed for the occasion. Her colorful batik halter top showed off her tanned shoulders, while the black skirt she'd paired with it showed enough leg to keep things interesting.

The weather had turned hot and muggy, and storms were predicted for later in the evening. Her favorite WGN weatherman had warned viewers that some could turn severe. Her outfit was designed to keep her comfortable in what could turn into an uncomfortable situation, depending on so many things out of her control.

Faith was not surprised to find Caine casually lounging a few doors down from a northside Indian restaurant celebrating its grand reopening tonight.

The small eatery was a favorite of the elusive Weldon's. Faith could only hope that the third time of trying to find him would be lucky. She also hoped that Caine wouldn't repeat his previous distraction technique of grabbing her and kissing her or giving her an under-the-table orgasm.

She needn't have worried. Caine's scowl wasn't the least bit welcoming.

"Are you trying to irritate me?" he growled.

"I'm trying to solve this case," she said.

"No, you're trying to convince yourself that your father didn't botch it."

"My father may not have actually conducted the entire investigation himself —"

"Doesn't matter. He signed off on it."

"Because it seemed like an open-and-shut case —"

"Seemed like? Are you leaving some room for doubt here?"

"I've got plenty of doubts, and most of them center around you."

His scowl disappeared as he gave her a slow, sexy smile. "Been thinking about me again, huh?"

She looked away to prevent herself from kissing that smile off his lips. "Get over yourself." That's when she caught sight of a young man with a White Sox cap pulled low. The baseball cap got her attention, but the face beneath it cemented the deal. "Hey, that's him."

"Wait here." Caine took off.

"No way." She took off right after him. She was wearing athletic shoes meant for fast chases. She'd come prepared tonight.

"Hey Weldon, can I talk to you for a minute?" Caine said.

"There's nothing to be afraid of," Faith reassured the nervous-looking Weldon. He reminded her a little of Aunt Lorraine's Chihuahua: skinny, gangly and high-strung. His hands were tucked into the pockets of striped shorts that clashed with his plaid short-sleeved shirt, while his white socks and sandals would make a fashionista cry. On the positive side, he had really nice green eyes, and his glasses were no longer held together with tape.

"So you're a White Sox fan, huh, Weldon?" she said. "Me too."

Caine wasn't about to let her use baseball to upstage him again. "My name is Caine Hunter. You worked with my father, Dr. Karl Hunter."

"Caine is a Cubs fan," Faith told Weldon.

"I'm really not into baseball," Weldon mumbled. "Somebody left this hat on the bus."

"Still, you were smart enough to pick it up," she said. "That shows you are very smart. Brilliant, some would say."

"Would you stop with the fake compliments?" Caine glared at her.

She blinked at him with feigned innocence. "They are not fake. Are you calling Weldon stupid?"

"No, of course not."

"I've been told by people who know that Weldon here is a brilliant man."

Weldon stood a little straighter. "Who told you that?"

"People who work with you."

Weldon's expression turned suspicious. "Why are you talking to people I work with?

Do I know you?"

"Not yet, but I'm looking forward to getting to know you, Weldon." She gave him a thousand-watt smile.

"Don't trust her," Caine said. "Her father is the one who drove my dad to do what he did. She's just using you to get back at me."

"That's not true!" Faith said.

"Weldon, if you had any respect for my father, then you'll work with me," Caine said.

"I did respect your father a great deal," Weldon said.

Confidence radiated from Caine. "Then work with me."

"Look, we all want the same thing here," Faith said.

"I doubt that," Caine said.

"We want the truth."

"You only want to prove that your rich daddy was right."

"And you only want to prove that your father was innocent."

Faith glared at Caine.

Caine glared at Faith.

It took both of them a moment to realize that Weldon was gone.

Anger flew over Caine's face. "Shit. Where did he go?"

"He took off," Faith said. "Can you blame him?"

"Hell yes."

"If you'd done your research, you'd know that Weldon doesn't deal well with social confrontations."

"Tough shit."

"That's very empathetic of you. Obviously you scared him away."

"Me? You're the one who keeps getting in the way of my investigation. Why are you doing that? To prevent me from finding out what really happened?"

"I could say that you are obstructing my investigation," she said.

"Does your daddy know yet that you're sticking your nose into this case?"

The look on her face was answer enough. "Which should prove I'm not doing anything on his behalf," she said.

"No, it just means you're sneaking around behind his back."

"Pitiful," a new gravelly voice stated. "You call yourselves investigators? Amateurs. I hate dealing with amateurs."

CHAPTER TWELVE

"Who the hell are you?" Caine demanded.

"I'm a much better investigator than the two of you, that's for dang sure. The name's Buddy Doyle, and I've been working as a gumshoe long before either one of you was born. Sir Arthur Conan Doyle of Sherlock Holmes fame was my great-grandfather."

Faith was impressed. "Really?"

"Nah, but it makes a good story."

Buddy was a study in gray: gray cardigan, gray sweatpants, gray hair. He looked old and cranky, like one of those garden gnomes out to make trouble. His vivid blue eyes displayed his aggravation, while the wrinkles on his face said this was a man who'd seen it all and hadn't been impressed by any of it.

"Are you saying you're investigating my father's case? Who hired you?" Caine demanded.

"I'm not saying anything. You two have

done enough talking for an army. Amateurs." Buddy shook his head.

"What's your connection to this case?" Caine said.

"You're an investigator," Buddy replied. "You figure it out."

"I will. But it would save time if you told me now."

"Is that your way of saying that I've got one foot in death's doorway and the next foot on a banana peel?" Buddy said.

Caine blinked, clearly unfamiliar with the saying. "Huh?"

"I hired Buddy," Weldon said, reappearing as quickly as he'd disappeared.

"It's none of their beeswax, kid," Buddy told Weldon, putting a reassuring hand on the young man's shoulder while continuing his glare at Caine and Faith.

"That one says he's Karl's son," Weldon said, pointing at Caine.

"Show me some ID," Buddy told Caine before turning to Faith. "And what about you, cupcake? Who do you claim to be?"

"Her name is Faith West," Caine said on her behalf. "Her father owns West Investigations."

Buddy's bushy eyebrows rose. "The bozos who messed up the investigation and pinned the blame on Karl?"

"Did you know my father?" Caine asked.

"No, but I know Weldon, and he says Karl the Chemist was innocent. I believe him."

"Based on what facts?" Faith demanded.

"The fact that Weldon says Karl didn't do it," Buddy replied.

"Then how do you explain the fact that a sizable amount of money ended up in an offshore account in Karl's name?" Faith demanded.

"Part of the scam," Buddy said. "Did you bother to see where that money is now?"

Faith nervously nibbled on her bottom lip. "Well . . . uh . . . no . . . uh, not yet."

"It was transferred out within hours of my father's death," Caine said.

"By you?"

"No, not by me."

"I don't understand," Faith said. "Who else had access to that account? I didn't see anyone else's name on it."

"It was transferred to a holding company, which transferred it to another holding company," Caine said. "Pretty complicated paper trail."

"Karl barely had the patience to balance his own checkbook," Weldon said. "He was not a banking expert. No way."

"Wasn't your ex-fiancé a banker?" Caine asked Faith.

"Yes, but he couldn't have had anything to do with this case. I hadn't even met him yet when the situation with your father occurred. It doesn't make any sense that he'd be involved. You're not being logical."

"She's probably right, but I'll check it out anyway," Buddy said. "What's this bozo's name?"

"Alan Anderson," Caine said.

She smacked Caine's arm. Hard. "Stop doing that."

He didn't even blink let alone flinch. "Doing what?"

"Answering for me," she said. "I can speak for myself."

"Maybe we should go inside," Weldon said nervously. "And talk about things."

"And eat," Buddy said. "I'm starving."

"Some of the food here may be a little too spicy for you," Weldon said.

"You mean for an old geezer like me? Don't you worry. I've got a cast-iron stomach." Buddy patted his abdomen proudly.

They entered the crowded establishment and were shown to a table for four in the back. Studying the menu, Faith asked Weldon, "I see they describe themselves as specializing in Indian and Nepali cuisine. What are some of your favorites?"

"Vegetable korma, any kind of curry, aloo

ghobi. And of course the naan and the raita and all the condiments."

They ordered an assortment of appetizers for starters — from vegetable samosa to chicken momo, dumplings filled with grilled chicken marinated in garlic, ginger and Nepali spices. They also added a selection of tandoori appetizers at Weldon's insistence.

"Tandoori is marinated meat cooked in a very hot tandoor, which is a clay oven with a really hot fire inside," Weldon said.

"The kid knows all kinds of trivia like that," Buddy said proudly.

"So does Faith," Caine said.

For their main courses, Faith and Caine both ordered the tandoori roasted chicken. The more adventurous Buddy ordered the spicy shrimp vindaloo, while Weldon went with his favorite, the spicy kerala fish curry.

The appetizers were a big hit, but it was the main course that really made an impression . . . on Buddy.

"Son of a . . . buck!" Buddy reached for his bottle of Bud even as his eyes watered and his face turned red. "That's hot!"

"I tried to warn you," Weldon said.

"I know. That was close. I almost broke my vow. I gave up cursing, you know," Buddy said.

"For Lent? We're past that now," Weldon said.

"Not for Lent. For good," Buddy said.

"An interesting choice," Caine said. "Why'd you make it?"

"It's personal," Buddy growled in that gravelly voice of his. "Let's stick to the case. I'm assuming we all know that Fred Belkin died of a brain tumor last year."

"Was there anything suspicious about his death?" Caine asked.

"Not that I could find. Why?" Buddy asked. "What are you thinking? That someone is knocking off everyone involved with the biofuel project?"

"That would include me," Weldon said with a gulp.

"Don't panic yet, boyo," Buddy told him.

"I know you think Karl wasn't guilty, but do you think he would commit suicide?" Faith had to ask.

"I don't know," Weldon said.

"Why have you been hiding out, Weldon?" Faith said. "Avoiding your apartment and work?"

"Because someone has been following me."

"You were already out of your apartment and off work when I started trailing you," Faith said.

"Same here," Caine said. "Did you see the person trailing you?"

"No, but I did," Buddy said. "Unfortunately I didn't get a good look at him. Medium height, medium build, his shoulders were a little hunched like he spent time bent over books or something. He didn't have the military bearing that Caine here has."

"Unless Caine is going undercover," Faith said. "In which case he can hunch his shoulders with the best of them."

"You were in the Marines, right, Caine?" Buddy said.

"Yes, sir."

"I was in the army myself," Buddy said. "You Devil Dogs are a crazy bunch."

"We like to think so, sir."

"So where are you staying now, Weldon?" Faith asked.

"Somewhere safe," Buddy said.

"What about the other guy? Nolan? Could he be following you?" Caine asked.

"I doubt it," Weldon said. "Yeah, he was angry that the project was canceled after Karl's death. The company that stole the information went bankrupt and never followed up on the biofuel ideas."

"Nolan is still in the area," Faith said. "And he's still working as a chemist in the biofuel field. Have you talked to him, Weldon?"

"No. We never really got along very well."

"He's a prick," Buddy said. "I tried talking to him and didn't get anywhere."

"Maybe he'd talk to me," Faith said.

"Why?" Buddy asked. "Because you're a woman?"

"And a former librarian," Caine said.

Buddy raised both bushy eyebrows. "No kidding. I'm impressed. But I doubt Nolan would be."

"It can't hurt to try," Faith said.

"Unless he's the one who framed Karl," Buddy said. "In which case he could hurt you quite badly."

"We'll go talk to him together," Caine said.

"Maybe we should just speak to him over the phone," Faith said.

"Good luck with that," Buddy said. "He ignored all my calls. I had to go see him. He was not a happy camper."

"Let me take care of Nolan," Caine said.

Faith gave him a look. "We're in this together, remember?"

"You seem like strange partners to me," Buddy said.

"We're not partners," Caine said.

"What are you then? Rivals?"

"No," Faith said. "It's . . . well, it's sort of complicated."

"I can see that."

"I'd like to make a toast." Weldon raised his glass. "To Karl, the comic chemist."

They all raised their glasses. "To Karl."

"Did he tell you those chemistry jokes at work?" Caine asked Weldon.

He nodded. "What do chemists call a benzene ring with iron atoms replacing the carbon atoms?"

"A ferrous wheel," Caine said with a grin. "Why do chemists like nitrates so much?"

"Because they're cheaper than day rates," Weldon said with a matching grin.

Buddy groaned.

"What is the dullest element?" Weldon said.

"Bohrium," Caine said triumphantly before giving Weldon a fist bump.

"Those are good memories," Weldon said wistfully.

"Yeah," Caine said.

"Bad jokes, though," Buddy grumbled.

As they all laughed, Faith was left wondering whose dad — hers or Caine's — would ultimately be found guilty. The possibility that her dad might have botched the investigation wiped the smile right off her face. Because that gut feeling she'd had in the beginning that something was off with the way this case was handled just kept increasing bit by bit. In addition to that, she still didn't know if her dad was cheating on her mom. She needed to find the truth on both issues.

On Monday, Faith met up with Caine a block from their respective office buildings.

"Didn't want to risk being seen by your father, huh?"

"He was already suspicious that I took off an hour early."

"I told you I could handle Nolan myself."

"And I said we need to do this together."

"Because we don't trust one another. I see you've donned your undercover geek attire," she said.

"Sometimes you talk like a show on PBS."

"Sorry."

"Don't be. It's kind of cute."

She didn't want to be cute. She wanted to be strong. "You know the cover story, right?"

"Right."

Nolan didn't live far from the downtown campus of the University of Chicago. It was a bit of a trek, but it was a nice day, so they walked it. Caine was unusually quiet. So was she. Her thoughts were focused on the role she'd be playing in this scenario.

They reached Nolan's home and waited outside until he arrived. She knew from her research that he always came home at the same time every evening, which made her plan easier. Sure enough, he showed up right on time. She approached him with her hand out.

"Dr. Nolan Parker?"

He nodded and ignored her hand.

"Hello, sir," Faith said. "My name is Andrea Morehead, and I'm writing an article about research chemists in the Chicago area who are working on biofuel projects. I'd love to interview you for the article. I tried calling you, but your voice mail was full."

"Right. I've been meaning to fix that. I've been too busy." With his receding hairline, rimless glasses and big ears, Nolan reminded her a bit of one of the Teletubbies. The yellow one.

"I'm on a very tight deadline for this article, so if you want to be included, I'd have to interview you right now," she said.

"Who's he?" Nolan pointed at Caine.

"He's my photographer."

"This is very unusual."

"I understand. I just thought I'd give you a chance to be included in this article featuring the best and the brightest. But if you don't have the time . . ."

"I didn't say I didn't have the time. No article about the best and the brightest would be complete without me."

The guy clearly didn't lack self-confidence.

"I can spare you a few minutes." He made the simple words sound condescending. "We can talk out here."

They stood on the brick steps leading to his building. He didn't invite them in. Why not? What was he hiding?

"My wife has the flu. I don't want to disturb her," Nolan said.

"Okay." Faith started with the easy stuff, his background, where he went to university. She'd done her research on him, so she knew a lot already. "I understand you worked at the American Research Corporation for a time."

"That's correct."

"Were you in charge of the biofuel project there?"

"No, but I should have been. They put an inferior person in charge, and he ended up ruining everything."

Faith saw the tic in Caine's jaw. Not a good sign.

"The guy was unstable," Nolan continued. "ARC never should have trusted him. I knew from the beginning that he was no good."

"How could you tell?" Faith said.

"He was unstable, like I said. He ended up committing suicide, you know. Set the project back by two years. But now I'm working for a new company, and we're really making a lot of strides in this field. Of course, I can't give you details, because the material is classified by my employer, and you probably wouldn't understand it anyway, unless you held an advanced degree in chemistry and had years of experience."

"I got a C in high school chemistry," Faith admitted. "I'm not a science person. I'm more into words."

"Humph." Nolan gave her a disapproving look. "We need more young people to go into the fields of math and science. We need chemists and engineers."

"What character trait makes you a good chemist?"

"Curiosity and a willingness to experiment and the intelligence to figure out what works. You can't be a weakling in this field. That was Karl Hunter's problem. He was weak."

Okay, now Caine had two tics in his clenched jaw.

"Thank you, Dr. Parker. You've been very

helpful."

Caine stepped forward, and Faith wasn't sure if he was going to take Nolan's picture or hit him with the camera. As it was, he took a flash photo that had Nolan blinking myopically.

"We're done. Thank you again," she called out over her shoulder as she grabbed Caine and started down the steps.

"Wait!" Nolan said. "When does your article come out, and where will it be published?"

"I'll leave a message on your voice mail with the details."

As they walked away, Faith noticed the sheer curtains on the main floor of his duplex move.

"Did you think that was strange?" she said.

Unlike Buddy, Caine apparently hadn't given up cursing, because he swore a blue streak.

"Okay, I may have gotten a C in chemistry, but I did get an A in biology, and I don't think what you're threatening him with is actually physically possible," she said.

Caine took a deep breath, and then his expression went hard and cold. Faith shivered despite the sticky eighty-degree weather. If her father had messed up, he was in deep shit.

■ ■ ■ ■

Faith's caseload picked up at work, and the next day was more hectic than usual. Her newest client was Lisa Farmer, a young woman worried about her boyfriend, a Chicago Streets and Sanitation worker named Robbie Hillsboro. "He's started acting strange. He ups and leaves in the middle of dinner or whatever we're doing. He just says he has to leave, and he won't tell me why. I get a large inheritance when I turn twenty-six in a few months. My grandfather made a fortune on nuts. You know, peanuts, cashews, that kind of thing. I don't have anything to do with the business, but he left me a sizable amount of money. Robbie doesn't know anything about it. At least I don't think he does."

"So what do you want us to do?"

"Find out where he's going when he takes off. If there's another woman, I need to know."

"We can do that."

Lisa's story wasn't that unusual. These days, there was a con around every corner. As the economic times got rough, there were always those who did whatever it took to get cash.

The problem was that after only a few weeks on the job, Faith saw these cases all the time. It would be easy to get burned out or cynical from all the bad things she saw going on: husbands cheating on wives, wives lying to husbands, employees stealing from their bosses, bosses using company funds for their own use.

The trick was to stay uninvolved, as Abs had told her. So Faith tried to simply focus on finding the truth, to discover what really happened.

That brought her back to Caine's father's case. After their dinner the other night, Faith had asked a forensic accountant friend of hers to try to track down the missing money in that offshore account.

She had to keep her investigative work on this matter from her father. She also couldn't let her dad know that she was trying to figure out what was going on with him. So that meant two big cases had to be top secret, while she still completed the workload on the rest of her cases so no one would get suspicious. It also meant she often got home after seven, as was the case tonight.

She was hoping the pouring rain would hold off until she reached her condo, but it didn't. Although the heaviest commuter traffic had lessened, the sidewalks were still crowded, and umbrella wars were won and lost. Her White Sox umbrella stood up well to the battles along the way and didn't bow to the city's famous wind that blew sheets of rain almost horizontally into her face and mangled other, weaker umbrellas. Hailing a cab was impossible in this weather, so she trudged on along with her fellow Chicagoans. The locals were accustomed to freaky weather that could easily go from serene to severe and back again.

Yuri stood ready to open the door for her the second she reached her building, soaking wet and exhausted. "You need an ark to go out in this weather," he said with his customary big smile.

She closed her umbrella and wiped the rain from her face before emptying her mailbox and dumping the contents into her Golden Book tote bag. Not only did she still need a new tough author mentor, she needed to get a new professional tote bag. But who had time?

"This didn't fit in your box." Yuri handed her a large, thick envelope.

"It's from the library." She ripped it open to find a pile of handmade cards from the regulars of her story time group. "WE MISS YOU," they wrote over and over again. Maria Sanchez had put a Love Your Library Post-it note on one of them: "You're not replaceable, please come back."

Faith sighed. "You walk away, and they pull you back in."

"Sounds like the Chicago mob," Yuri said.

"Al Capone had nothing on Maria Sanchez. She's very determined. Like your friend Caine."

"Did you two have another fight?"

"No. Did he tell you we had?"

"No."

"What did he tell you?"

"Nothing."

"Then why did you think we were fighting?"

"Because you're always fighting."

"Not always."

"No?"

"No. We actually worked together the other night and were cordial."

"Cordial?" Yuri sounded skeptical.

"I was cordial. Caine was Caine."

"He's good at doing that, being Caine."

"He certainly is. The man has definite trust issues."

"Is he the only one?"

"No. I have the same issues. I question his motivation. He questions mine. It's just all so crazy. I never used to be into crazy."

"And now?"

"I'm eating the man's sliders and sharing tandoori appetizers with him. What does that say about me?"

Yuri grinned. "That you have good taste."

"Maybe, but I'd rather have good judgment." And anyone with good judgment would know she was playing with fire by working with Caine.

The next day, just before five, Faith decided it was time to confront her dad directly. Not that she planned on asking him if he was having an affair. But she needed to start a conversation that would give her some clues. So she cornered him in his office, trying to look and sound casual while doing so.

"Did you see that story online about work spouses?" she asked.

"No."

"It was interesting. Who do you talk to about work?"

"My brother Dave."

"Who else?"

"Gloria."

Faith tried to imagine Gloria as a work spouse but couldn't. She saw her more as a mix of Jewish mom and drill sergeant.

"Anyone else? Do you talk to Mom about work?"

"Not really."

"Why not?"

"Because she's not interested. What's this about?"

"I told you. I saw this article online about work spouses."

"You mean couples who work together?"

"No, I mean the person at work you confide in and how it can lead to more intimate relationships if you're not careful."

"I don't think you have to worry about that with Dave and me," her dad noted dryly. "In fact, I can guarantee it."

"So those are the only two people you confide in about work stuff? Dave and Gloria? No one else?"

"I don't know. From time to time I may talk about a particularly difficult case with one of the investigators."

Aha! "Has that happened lately?"

"No."

"What about Renee from Human Resources?"

"What about her?"

"Weren't the two of you working together on a new employee handbook?"

"Yes."

"She's a very attractive woman."

"Yes, she is. Her partner, Marta, thinks so too." Her father eyed her suspiciously. "Has your mother been talking to you?"

"About what?"

"About me working too much?"

"Has she said anything to you?" Faith countered.

"She doesn't appreciate the responsibilities involved in running a business this size."

"She might if you talked about it with her."

"Right. I'll add that to my to-do list. Right after I visit Disneyland."

"I'm trying to have a serious conversation with you here."

"I don't have time for serious conversations right now."

"You never have time."

"Now you do sound like your mother. Look, I've got to go. I've got a dinner appointment."

"With a client?"

"I'll be late if I don't leave right now."

It was only after he'd left that she realized he'd never answered her question. So she did what any PI daughter would do. She followed him.

Fifteen minutes later she was seated in the corner of a prestigious restaurant. A screen of greenery separated the room where she was seated from the adjoining one where her dad was studying some paperwork and sipping his wine.

She was so focused on him that she didn't notice Caine until he sat at her table. "Why are you trailing your father?"

She didn't even bother asking Caine why he was trailing her. She'd gotten accustomed to his knowing her every move. "None of your business."

Caine said, "If it has something to do with my father's case —"

"It has nothing to do with that. It's personal. So go away."

Before he could, Gram joined them. "What are you two whispering about over here in the corner?"

CHAPTER THIRTEEN

Faith tried not to panic. Her grandmother did not have the quietest voice in the world. What if she was the dinner date Faith's dad was expecting? What if she wasn't? "Shh, Gram."

"Don't shush me. You're not a librarian anymore. Why are you over here skulking in the corner with this sexy man? Why don't you join your father? I'll tell him you're here."

"No." Faith grabbed her grandmother's arm. "Don't do that. Please."

"Why not?"

"Because. I don't want him to know I'm here."

Gram eyed Caine. "Do I know you?"

"No. I'm Caine Hunter."

"Ah. The ex-Marine who works for our rival."

"Former Marine," Caine corrected her.

"My husband fought in World War II. He

was in the U.S. Army. I was twenty years younger than him, but there's just something about a man in uniform. Have you seen him in his uniform?" she asked Faith.

"Grandfather? Yes, I've seen photos of him —"

"No, I mean this former Marine here. Caine. Have you seen him in his uniform?"

"No."

"Good. Don't you go trying to break my granddaughter's heart," Gram said. "She's had enough trouble in her life lately. She doesn't need a former Marine messing things up. Even if you are good-looking. Don't you go trying to seduce her in some dark corner."

"He's not," Faith said.

"You mean you dragged him into the corner?" Gram raised an eyebrow. "Well, I heard you were becoming more forceful since returning from Italy."

"There was no dragging done by either one of us."

"So what are you two doing here? If you plan on getting intimate, you should really go get a room."

"That is not going to happen."

"I'm no prude, but I don't think you two should be making out in the corner."

"We weren't. We're not going to."

242

"Then what are you doing?"

"Working."

"Working?"

"Are you meeting Dad for dinner, Gram?"

"No."

"Then what are you doing here?"

"This is my favorite restaurant. I was going to meet Zoe. You know her. I play bridge with her. Anyway, she just called and canceled."

Faith was so focused on her grandmother that she didn't see Buddy until he joined them at the now-crowded table. "What are you two amateurs up to now?" Buddy demanded.

"Who are you?" Gram demanded.

"Buddy Doyle at your service, ma'am." To Faith and Caine he said, "I've got a table a few feet from here. You can still see your mark, but you won't be drawing attention to yourselves."

"Do you work for West Investigations?" Gram asked.

"No, I run my own operation. And I do a better job of it than these two youngsters."

Gram took offense at Buddy's words. "My granddaughter is very good at what she does."

"Nonsense." Before Gram could get more upset, Buddy added, "You're much too young to have a granddaughter."

Faith's grandmother smiled. Her spiky haircut was softly styled, and the Chanel suit she wore gave her an elegant look. Instead of a string of pearls, she wore a button on her lapel that said Save the Polar Bears.

"Shall we move now before we generate more attention?" He pointed to his table. He was right. It did have a better vantage point. The greenery shielded their move.

Once at his table, Buddy gallantly held out a chair for Faith's grandmother. "You know my name now, but I still don't know yours."

"Ingrid West."

"Ingrid. That's a lovely name."

"It's Swedish."

"I know."

Caine nudged Faith, who stood there in disbelief, watching Buddy flirting with her grandmother. "Sit," he said.

He belatedly held out a chair for her.

She sat.

Caine took the seat next to her.

Buddy opened the menu, gave it a quick once-over and slapped it back onto the table. "Who can afford to eat at a place like this?"

"I'd be glad to treat you," Ingrid offered.

"That's kind of you, ma'am, but I could never take money from a woman. It wouldn't be right."

"I'll buy you dinner," Caine said.

Buddy hurriedly grabbed the menu. "In that case, I'll have the filet mignon."

Faith could practically see Caine gulp. The filet was one of the most expensive things listed, with a price of over forty dollars.

"And I'll have the Caesar salad to begin," Buddy continued.

There went another eight dollars.

Caine put on his war face, and Buddy decided not to push him any further.

Until it came time to order drinks. "I'll have whiskey, neat," Caine said.

"Make that two," Buddy said.

Caine yanked the menu from him and handed it to the server.

Faith tried not to grin as she ordered the grilled salmon for her grandmother and herself. "We'd like a separate bill for the two of us."

"Wipe that smile off your face, sunshine," Caine whispered in her ear. "Your dad's got company."

Her gaze darted to her father's table. He was standing to welcome a beautiful woman with an intimate smile. The woman had the smile, but now her dad did too.

That was no way to smile at a client. Maybe she was an old family friend that Faith didn't know about? Just back in town after years away?

"Who's that woman with your father?" Gram demanded.

"A client," Faith immediately said.

"Really?" Gram didn't sound convinced. Didn't look convinced either. "Are you sure?"

"Absolutely."

"Is that why you didn't want to join him? Because he was having a business dinner?" Gram said. "Then why were you two spying on him?"

"We weren't spying. Dad wouldn't approve of me eating dinner with Caine," Faith said.

"That's true," Gram said. "But I like you," she added, patting Caine's hand.

"Thank you."

"But that could change in a split second if you mess up," Gram warned him.

"Understood."

"She knows the Swedish mob," Faith told Caine.

"They are better than the Finnish mob," Buddy said, for which Gram gave him a look of deep gratitude.

"Thank you," Gram said. "I've been trying to tell my family that, but they don't believe me."

"Young people these days." Buddy shook his head. "They think they know everything when they really know nothing."

"Even worse, they think *we* know nothing," Gram said.

Buddy nodded. "Pitiful, isn't it? And wrong on so many levels."

"You're a very smart man, Mr. Doyle."

"Oh, call me Buddy, please."

"Is there a Mrs. Doyle?" Gram asked.

"My wife, bless her soul, passed away ten years ago."

"I'm sorry for your loss. My husband died several years ago as well."

"You have my deepest sympathy."

"Thank you." Gram smiled at him. "That's kind of you."

"So what are you doing here, Buddy?" Faith said.

"Trailing you two," he readily admitted.

"Why?"

"Curiosity." He returned his attention to Faith's grandmother. "As you could tell from my earlier comment, I don't usually frequent places like this. I'm more a corned beef and cabbage kind of guy. Have you ever had it at O'Sullivan's?"

Gram shook her head.

"Oh, you are really missing something special. Would you care to accompany me there some evening for dinner?"

Faith couldn't believe how fast the guy moved. She'd had him pinned as a grumpy old guy in his gray cardigan. Yet here he was in a black suit, white shirt and green tie with little dark shamrocks on it. She was impressed.

So was her grandmother. "That sounds lovely, Buddy." She beamed at him.

Buddy beamed back.

"Are you going to let him get away with this?" Caine whispered in her ear.

She shivered. His lips brushed her skin through the silky cover of her hair.

"Did you check him out?" Caine added softly.

"Look at those two lovebirds," Buddy said. "Whispering sweet nothings in each other's ears."

Faith shook her head to both Caine's question and Buddy's teasing comment.

When Caine moved his hand to Faith's thigh under the table, she nearly jumped out of her seat.

"You okay, hon?" Gram asked.

"Fine." She shoved Caine's hand away and gave him a stern look filled with furious warning. No way was she having an orgasm in front of her grandmother. Faith would be in therapy for years. Decades. She'd never recover.

Faith couldn't relax for the rest of the meal. Part of her was keeping an eye on her father and his dinner date. No inappropriate touching there that she could see.

No inappropriate touching from Caine either. Both he and Buddy behaved with gentlemanly manners.

But Faith still couldn't let her guard down. What if her grandmother told her dad about this dinner with Caine? What if Gram told him that Faith and Caine seemed to be spying on him? What if Buddy took Gram out on a date? Faith would have to do a background check on him as soon as she got home. Unless she checked her Black-Berry now and did a search. The disapproving look Gram shot her when Faith reached for her phone had her putting it back in her new leather tote. No more Golden Book tote bags for her.

You are a confident, competent professional investigator, she silently told herself over and over again. *You know what you're doing and are good at it.*

Too bad Faith didn't believe a word she was silently saying, no matter how many times she said it.

■ ■ ■ ■

Faith considered the fact that Abs had invited her to the newest trendy hot spot for drinks after work on Thursday to be a positive sign. Ever since Abs had given Faith the Haywood case, Abs had seemed increasingly suspicious of Faith's motives for working at West Investigations. Maybe Faith was just being paranoid. She really did want to be more like Abs, who had the ability to remove any emotional attachment to a case. Abs had the kind of natural cynicism that came in very handy in this line of work.

Abs held the door open and motioned Faith inside, where the bold lime green, hot orange and azure blue light panels against the walls provided a colorful backdrop to the curved bars. Given the cutting-edge decor, Faith was surprised to hear classy crooner Frank Sinatra singing about doing things his way.

Abs was clearly no stranger to the place. "It's cocktail night," she said before leading Faith to a small table along one wall beneath a lime green light panel. "You've got to try their Mounds martini."

"What's that?"

"A chocolate martini with coconut rum."

"Sounds good."

"I've had their Kobe beef sliders, if you're hungry," Abs said.

Her comment reminded Faith of Caine telling her he wouldn't have pegged her as a slider girl. She hadn't heard or seen Caine for two days now, not since her grandmother had caught them in the corner and Buddy had joined them.

"I'm not hungry." Liar, liar. She was hungry for Caine — for his kiss, for his touch. She crossed her legs and uncrossed them again at the erotic memory of his under-the-table moves.

"You okay?" Abs asked.

Faith nodded before turning the spotlight onto Abs. "So, where do you see yourself five years from now?"

"Why?" Abs asked suspiciously.

"No reason. Just making conversation."

"Then where do you see yourself five years from now? Married with kids?"

"Surely you've heard that I didn't have very good luck in the marriage department. I'm focusing on my career now." The firm statement was meant as much for herself as for Abs.

"Me too."

"You're very good at what you do," Faith said. "I'm really envious of the way you're able to stay so focused. You don't seem to hesitate or question yourself."

"Hesitation is for wimps, and I'm no wimp."

"Right. I'm not a wimp either," Faith said.

Abs didn't appear convinced about that.

"I'm not." Faith took a large sip of her Mounds martini. "Mmmm good."

"Nice girls don't get the corner office . . . unless they are the boss's daughter."

"I didn't take the corner office. I turned it down."

"Which proves my point," Abs said. "Nice girls don't get the corner office."

"I'm not always nice."

Abs's expression was skeptical.

"I'm not."

"Name one time when you were mean."

"This afternoon I didn't hold the elevator for a guy."

"You're kidding, right?"

"I know it was mean."

"Not even in the ballpark of mean."

"You're not a Cubs fan are you?"

Abs shook her head. "Baseball is too slow for me. I'm a hockey fan."

"I'll have another one of these Mounds martinis," Faith told the server as she walked past. "I can be tough," she told Abs.

"Yeah right."

"You could teach me to do better."

"I'm not sure you have the natural ability required."

"Sure I do," Faith said. "I might not have in the past, but I'm mad, bad and blonde now."

"Toughness isn't a matter of hair color." Abs took a sip of her own drink. "Did you cry watching *Marley & Me*?"

"Of course. Who wouldn't?"

"I wouldn't. That's why I'm tough and you're not."

"That can't be the only requirement. I ran the Chicago Marathon one year."

"That's not tough. That's a waste of time."

"No, it wasn't. Getting engaged to Alan was a waste of time."

"Love stinks."

"I know. I have the song on my breakup CD. My cousin Megan burned it for me."

"That was nice of her," Abs said.

"Yeah, she's very nice."

"Just like you."

Their argument continued as Faith polished off two more martinis.

Caine was sitting in a tavern with Buddy and Weldon going over details of his father's case when his cell phone rang. Checking the caller ID, he saw it was Faith. She never called him.

"I'm calling about Faith," a strange woman said. "Your number is listed as her ICE."

Caine had entered his number in her ICE — in case of emergency — contact file on her BlackBerry himself back in Italy.

"What's wrong?" he demanded.

"She's had a few too many Mounds martinis. I called the first number listed for her ICE contact but got her mom's voice mail, so I called you. I'd just put her in a cab myself, but I don't know her address, and she's not real clear on that info at this point. I could get her address from her driver's license, but I'd feel better if someone she knew well took care of her. Can you come get her? I don't even know your name."

He had no intention of telling her his name. "Where are you?"

She told him.

"I'll be there in fifteen minutes," Caine said.

"A problem?" Buddy asked.

"Nothing I can't handle. Sorry to cut this short."

"No problem. Go do whatever you have to do."

Caine had no trouble finding Faith in the trendy martini bar. She was dancing by herself to Dean Martin's "Ain't That a Kick in the Head." He used the term *dancing* loosely, as it actually looked like she was just bouncing around not quite in time to the music.

He could tell by her loopy smile that she was totally out of it. "Caine!" She threw her arms around him, nearly knocking him over. "Tell Abs that I can be a real bad girl. Tell her I'm touch. Er tough."

"She's tough," Caine said, keeping an arm around Faith as he grabbed her purse and led her toward the door.

"Bye, Abs." Faith wiggled her fingers over her shoulder.

"Wait," Abs called out. "Aren't you Caine Hunter? I don't think it's a good idea for you to take her —"

"It's fine," Caine told Abs in his that's-a-direct-order voice. "She's safe with me."

The place was crowded, but at his dangerous scowl, the upscale clientele parted to give Caine a path to the nearest exit.

"They have fancy sliders here," Faith said. "That's nice."

"No, it's not. And I'm not nice either."

"No, you're drunk. Get in." He held the Mustang's passenger door open for her and guided her inside, lifting her legs and swinging them into the car. His fingers lingered beneath her silky thighs as the skirt she wore hitched up.

Reminding himself that he was not the kind of guy to take advantage of a drunken woman, he tugged her skirt back down to a respectable level and closed the door.

She opened it again. "Don't you love that Dean Martin song?"

"Not really." He shut the door.

She opened it again. "How come?"

"I'm more a Guns 'N' Roses guy." He closed the door, and this time he locked it remotely. He'd already activated the kid's protection option that allowed the driver to control the locks and windows.

She was leaning halfway across his seat when he got in. "If you don't like Dean Martin, why did you come here?"

"To get you." He drove off before the valet parking attendant could demand a bigger bribe to allow him to temporarily park in front of the trendy place.

Faith seemed incapable of sitting upright or staying on her own side of the car. He couldn't get to her condo fast enough. Yuri would be there . . . but he wasn't.

"Where's Yuri?" Caine demanded.

"He's off tonight," the beefcake young guy in the doorman uniform said. "And you can't park there. The underground parking

256

garage entrance is around the corner."

Caine might have trusted Yuri to get Faith upstairs to her condo, but no way was he trusting this cocky dude.

The garage entrance required a security code. "What's your password?" he asked Faith.

"Austen. Jane Austen," she said in her best 007 voice.

Once he parked his Mustang, Caine had a hard time getting Faith out of the car. Finally he had to practically lift her out and scoop her into his arms. She rested her head on his shoulder, her silky hair brushing his chin. "Nice," she murmured.

It was way beyond nice and entering downright dangerous territory. Caine kept his eyes fixed on the elevator ahead of them and not on her cleavage, which was generously displayed the way her wraparound dress had parted.

He hit the elevator button with his elbow. Thankfully, the doors opened immediately, and he stepped inside. A short ride took them to the lobby, where he had to transfer to another elevator.

He knew her address from the research he'd done on her back in Italy. She lived on the twelfth floor, unit 1209.

He slid her to her feet in front of her door.

"Where are your keys?"

"In here." She jiggled her purse . . . and giggled. He realized then that he hadn't heard her giggle since before they'd slept together in Italy. He also realized he really missed her giggle. She may have laughed at him after she'd swiped that client by using her Sox fan status, but it didn't have the charm of her giggle. What had he been talking about before? Oh right, her keys.

"Get them out," he said.

"Okeydokey." Her bumbled search proved unsuccessful.

Sighing, Caine took the purse from her, or attempted to, but she refused to relinquish possession.

"Just wait," she told him. "Hold your hand out."

He reluctantly did so while holding her upright with his other hand on her shoulder.

"Here." She leaned against him and started piling things in his hand. Her lipstick, her wallet, pepper spray, her iPod, a paperback romance novel. "I found them!" She dangled them in front of his nose.

"Great." He dumped her stuff back in her purse and took the keys to open her door.

"Why are the walls moving?" she said.

"Because you drank too many Mounds martinis. What the hell is a Mounds martini anyway?"

"Chocolate and coconut just like the Mounds candy bars. Yummy."

Why was she looking at him when she said "Yummy"? Was she talking about the drink or him? "Where's your bedroom?"

She tsked and shook her finger at him. "In your dreams, Mr. Marine."

Actually her bedroom *had* been in his dreams . . . or her bed, to be more exact. With her in it . . . naked on black satin sheets.

Caine had no trouble finding her bedroom, which was straight down the hall from the living room. He had significantly more trouble getting Faith to go to bed. That's when he made his first mistake.

CHAPTER FOURTEEN

The last time Faith had had too much to drink, she'd had too many mojitos with Megan and ended up on a plane to Italy . . . where she'd slept with Caine.

Now here she was again. Sleeping with Caine.

She sat up in bed, groaning and clutching her head. They hadn't had sex, had they? No. She was sure they hadn't. Pretty sure. Sort of sure.

Okay, don't panic. Breathe.

She wasn't nude. That was a good thing, right? She was wearing underwear and a baggy White Sox nightshirt that she didn't remember putting on herself.

She closed her eyes and tried to imagine herself in some happy place like the Comfort Café eating blueberry pancakes. Yummy.

Except she was still a little queasy. Yucky.

Wait . . . had Caine helped her when she'd

thrown up last night? Had he held her hair back from her face when she'd barfed? Had he gently wiped her face with a cool washcloth?

Yes. She was sort of sure he had. Pretty sure. Damn sure.

The memories came rushing back. He'd been nice to her. Kind. Caring.

Why? What was his master plan? And how had he ended up here at her condo anyway?

She didn't realize she'd spoken that last question aloud until he answered.

"Your friend Abs called me." His voice was husky with sleep, making it sexier than ever.

"Why?"

He sat up next to her. The sheet slid down to his waist, revealing his bare chest. "Because she thought you needed help."

"But why call *you?*"

"I may have been listed as one of your ICE contacts."

"No way. I'd never list you."

"I entered my name on your list when we were in Italy. In case something happened."

She was offended. "You touched my BlackBerry?"

"Yes."

"But we didn't have sex last night, right?"

"What? No."

"Good. That's good." She took a deep breath. "Tell me I took my own clothes off and put this nightshirt on."

"You took off your own clothes and put your nightshirt on."

"By myself?"

"By yourself."

"Are you lying?"

"Yes."

"Do I want to know what happened?"

"Probably not."

She groaned.

He rubbed her back. "Want some aspirin?"

"I want a hot shower." She climbed out of bed.

So did he. He was wearing jeans that hung low on his hips. "Need some help?"

She shook her head then wished she hadn't. "I had no idea chocolate martinis packed such a punch."

"How many did you have?"

"I'm not sure. I wasn't paying attention. Three, maybe four, I guess. Too many."

Faith felt much better after she had a shower and washed her hair. Her purple silk robe slid against her bare skin with soft insistence. Her senses felt as if they were on high alert, and it was all due to the half-naked man on the other side of the bathroom door.

She supposed she should count her blessings that he hadn't gone to bed commando. She still vividly remembered his towel falling from his hips at the hotel in Positano, leaving him standing nude before her.

She still didn't know why he was sleeping in her bed. That would be her next question. First she needed to brush her teeth for about five minutes. There. Now she was ready to face him. Not that her robe provided much protection.

To her relief, Caine was no longer in her bedroom. She smelled coffee being brewed. Closing and locking her bedroom door, she quickly got dressed. Today was a workday, and she was running late.

A pair of black knit pants and a bright turquoise top restored her sense of control, strengthened by the skillful application of makeup. Her hair obediently fell into place, although one section did stubbornly refuse to behave. Exasperated, she tossed down the brush and headed for the kitchen. She needed caffeine.

Caine handed her a mug with cream and lots of sugar just the way she liked it. His remembering how she liked her coffee shouldn't have been a big deal, but it was. It would be rude to ask him why he'd stayed the night right now. In the end, she didn't have to, because he told her.

"You didn't want me to leave last night, in case you were wondering. You'd only stay in bed if I would stay there with you. Then you got sick, and I couldn't leave you alone that way," he said.

"You were nice to me."

"You don't have to sound so surprised." He propped one hip against her granite counter while he sipped his own mug of coffee. He'd given her the What Would Jane Austen Do mug and kept the Hello Kitty mug for himself. "I can be nice when the situation warrants it."

"Yes, but you were nice to *me*."

"I've been nice to you before. I helped you with your wings. And helped you take flight at the Geek Meet."

"Don't remind me," she mumbled into her coffee. "I can't believe you did that. I can't believe I let you."

He just smiled at her. That's all he did, yet it was as if he touched her intimately all over again.

She tore her gaze away from the magnetic visual hold he had on her. "I've got to go, or I'll be late for work."

"Same here," he said before rinsing his mug in the sink and setting it in the dishwasher. Alan never did that. He always left his dirty dishes on the counter for her to clean up.

Faith had reached the point where she believed Alan had done her a favor by leaving her at the altar. Well, maybe not a favor per se. But she was definitely better off without him. She knew that now.

She didn't know how to describe her feelings for Caine. She watched the muscles across his back ripple as he tugged on his T-shirt. She'd barely recovered from that when he placed his hand on the small of her back to guide her into the elevator a few minutes later. The bottom line here was that Caine's effect on Faith was ten times stronger than any Mounds martini could ever be, and she had no idea how to deal with that fact.

Faith was still trying to recover her equilibrium when she sat down in her cubicle. She had yet to decorate it. The space certainly had none of the tchotchkes of her previous one. There were no posters here. No Jane Austen mugs. No tiaras or magic wands or wings.

Instead, she had a *Wild Words from Wild Women* daily calendar, and that was about it as far as personal touches went. Faith dutifully turned the page to today's quote by Dr. Laura Schlessinger, syndicated radio shrink. "If you stick your head in the sand, your butt is in the air."

Faith was pondering the ways that applied to her life when Abs joined her in the cubicle. Being Abs, she got right to the point. "If you promise not to tell your father that I got you drunk, then I won't tell him about Caine."

"You didn't get me drunk. I got myself drunk. Those martinis tasted so good, but I had no idea they were so potent."

"Well, sure, if you drink four or five of them on an empty stomach."

"I didn't have five."

"That's irrelevant. The big question here is why was Caine listed as one of your ICE contacts?"

"It's a long story."

"Fair enough. But we're agreed that you won't tell your father, and I won't tell your father, right?"

"Sounds good to me," Faith said.

"That doesn't mean you can't talk to me. Are you and Caine working together on his dad's closed case?"

"I don't want to talk about it."

"I can understand why. Your father would have a hissy fit if he knew."

"You can't tell him."

"So now that's two things I'm not supposed to tell him," Abs said. "That you're seeing Caine *and* working on his father's closed case. You'd owe me big time for keeping those things silent."

Faith didn't like the sound of that.

"Why are you interested in the case anyway?" Abs said. "I mean, I can understand why Caine would find it hard to accept that his dad was guilty, but what's up with you? *You* don't think his dad was innocent, do you?"

"I don't know."

Abs shook her head. "I warned you about getting emotionally involved in a case."

Faith didn't waste her time denying her emotional state of mind. "Haven't you heard of trusting your gut?"

"Yeah, I've heard of it. I just don't believe in it."

"Come on. Surely you've had a case where you sensed something was wrong?"

"You mean like feminine intuition?" Abs scoffed.

"Intuition period."

"Intuition is fine if you're reading palms but not for investigative work. We have to discover the facts. Emotions weaken your objectivity and adversely affect your judgment. So much for you being tough."

"Sometimes taking the easy way out is just that. Easy. It's much tougher to question decisions."

"Which just leaves you indecisive. The case is closed. There's no bringing Caine's father back from the dead. You should leave it alone."

"Why are you so vehement about this? Do you know something?"

"Yes. I know you're making a mistake in digging up the past."

"Why?"

"Because I don't think you're tough enough to face what you might find out."

"What do you think I'll find?"

"My intuition tells me it won't be something good," Abs said in a mocking voice before walking away.

Which left Faith wondering what Abs was hiding and how it affected this case.

Caine called Faith three days later on Monday as she was walking home from work. The "Don't Stop Believin' " ringtone had a new meaning for her now. It didn't just apply to baseball but also to her convoluted feelings for Caine.

"Just a heads-up that I'm going to be doing a surveillance on Nolan Parker tonight," he said. "So don't mess it up."

So much for Caine being nice to her. "I won't mess it up. Thanks for inviting me to join you."

"I'm not inviting you. I'm telling you not to interfere."

"The best way to ensure that is to include me in the surveillance process. Two sets of eyes are better than one. Remember, I'm the one who got Nolan to speak to us in the first place."

Silence.

"Are you still there?" she said.

"Be ready in fifteen minutes."

She had to sprint the last block, but she was wearing her commuter shoes, so she made it in time to race inside and change her work outfit into something much more casual and nondescript.

She had her hair stuffed into a baseball cap, and it wasn't even a White Sox one. Just a plain navy blue cap to go with her plain navy blue T-shirt and plain jeans.

"Is it safe to assume that I have permission to let Caine in the building?" Yuri asked her as she paused at the building's front door.

"It's not safe to assume anything where Caine is concerned," Faith said.

"Oh no. What did he do now?"

"Nothing."

"I thought you two were . . . uh . . . getting along better."

Faith sighed. "You heard he spent the night, right?"

Yuri didn't reply.

"It isn't the way it looks."

"I don't judge," Yuri said.

"He was just being nice."

Yuri nodded. "Right."

"I know it's hard to believe."

"Nearly impossible," Yuri agreed.

"Really, he was just being nice. I'd had too much to drink and got sick, and he stayed to make sure I was okay. That's all it was."

"If you say so."

"I do. And don't say anything to anyone else about this."

"I wouldn't dream of it." Yuri held the door open for her as she hurried outside to hop into Caine's Mustang.

"Is this surveillance on foot or are we tailing him by car?" she asked, swinging her backpack onto the floor in front of her.

"The car," Caine said.

"Then you really should have a more inconspicuous vehicle, preferably something blue."

"Why? Is that your favorite color?"

"No, it's the most common car color. I've

been doing my research. Brushing up on my PI skills."

"This isn't meant to be a training mission."

"I don't mind training you," she said.

"That's not what I meant."

"Oh, you thought you'd train me." She laughed. "I can assure you that's not necessary. You still haven't told me why you're doing this surveillance tonight. Did something happen?"

"Nolan called Fred Jr. today and asked for a meeting tonight."

"How do you know that?"

"I talked to Fred Jr. today. Met him."

"You didn't tell me you were going to do that."

"I'm telling you now."

"Where's Buddy tonight? Will he be tailing us?"

"No. He's taking your grandmother out to dinner at O'Sullivan's tonight."

"She didn't tell me that."

"I guess you don't know everything then, do you?"

"I didn't say I know everything." She almost added that she knew where to find information she didn't know, before remembering that was a librarian's line. And she was no longer a librarian.

271

She had checked out Buddy, however. He was a Chicago cop for twenty years, as was his son and even his grandson Logan. After retiring, Buddy opened his investigation business over two decades ago. He was seventy-eight, owned his own home and had no major debt.

Which she supposed made him okay to take out her grandmother.

"What was your impression of Fred Jr.?" Faith asked.

"A brainiac chemist following in his father's footsteps. Not as bad a pain the ass as Nolan Parker. Fred Jr. made no derogatory comments regarding my dad."

"Was he as . . . uh . . . confident as Nolan?"

"That wasn't confidence Nolan displayed. That was self-aggrandizement."

"Agreed."

"A famous football coach once said empty barrels make the most noise."

"So you're a football fan as well as a Cubs fan?"

Caine eyed her suspiciously. "Why do you want to know?"

"No reason. I was just making conversation."

"We don't make conversation on surveillance."

"By 'we,' are you referring to Marines or PIs? Because I've actually had my PI license longer than you've had yours. Not that I'm bragging or anything."

"Right. You're just being self-aggrandizing."

"I am not." She socked his arm. "Take that back."

"And you hit like a girl."

"Only when I want to. You know I'm capable of doing much worse." She shot him a look, reminding him of what she'd done to him back in Positano.

He rubbed his chest and nodded his acknowledgment before parking down the street from Nolan Parker's home.

"You see how much better it is when we work together instead of against each other?" Faith was feeling surprisingly optimistic tonight. She wasn't sure why. Maybe because today she'd successfully completed the case about the Chicago Streets and Sanitation worker who took off to take ballroom dancing lessons whenever his second cousin, a dance instructor, was available. It turned out that Lisa was a huge fan of *Dancing with the Stars,* and this was Robbie's way of hoping to impress her with his skills. Faith hadn't discovered anything to indicate that Robbie knew about Lisa's inheritance or that he was in any kind of financial difficulty. A happy ending for a change.

So far that wasn't true for the Haywood case. Faith hadn't finished her investigation yet, but it appeared that Douglas Haywood really had lost millions. Both parties were presently seeking counseling to see if there wasn't a way to stay together until the economy improved to prevent further financial losses. The counseling seemed to help defuse their situation somewhat. Not that Faith had given up on her asset search yet.

She wasn't one to give up easily.

"Why the look?" Caine asked.

"What look?"

"Are you bored?"

"No."

"I am."

"Gee, thanks. Answer me this. Why is it that no one wants to talk to us like normal people? Why do we have to keep following them around to get answers? Don't they realize it makes them look suspicious?"

"They don't care."

"Well, they should."

"Consider it a chance to improve your PI skills."

"As I've stated previously, my PI skills are fine, thank you very much. I fooled you in

Italy, didn't I?"

"Hey, what happened to those sandals of yours? The ones you had made there for you?"

"I left them in Positano."

"That's a shame. They looked good on you."

His compliment made her realize how small the interior of the car really was. She reached for her backpack. "I, uh, I brought some food for us."

"Oh yeah? What do you have?"

"Trail mix and baby carrots."

"Rabbit food. I got the good stuff." He reached into the storage console and removed some beef jerky and a small bag of Doritos.

She shuddered. "How can you eat that?"

"Easily. Watch me."

Before he could take a bite, Nolan strolled out of his house and headed toward his car, a Prius.

Faith nudged Caine and whispered, "It's blue. I told you it's the most common color for a car."

"We have to make out," Caine replied, dropping the junk food and tugging her into his arms.

"What?"

"He's looking this way. Pretend we're

making out, but keep an eye on him."

Caine's mouth was millimeters from hers, and she was supposed to stay calm enough to watch Nolan? Talk about self-discipline. She nervously licked her lips, which made Caine growl softly.

"He's pulling out." Her words sounded unintentionally erotic. But maybe that was just her. Her mind seemed overwhelmed by sex at the moment, which is why she didn't protest when Caine kissed her hard for a quick second before following Nolan, keeping a car or two space between them.

Nolan's vanity plates — IMGenius — made tailing him a breeze. He pulled into a convenience store about three miles away.

"He's meeting Fred Jr. in a convenience store?"

"Maybe he's picking up some beef jerky and Doritos," Caine said as he parked in the opposite end of the strip mall.

"He doesn't strike me as the beef jerky type."

"You're right."

"Shouldn't we go in there after him?"

"Fred Jr.'s car isn't here yet."

"Maybe he parked it somewhere else."

"Nope. He just pulled in." Caine peeled his T-shirt off, revealing the navy blue wife beater tank top he wore beneath it. He yanked on a pair of aviator sunglasses and a Cubs baseball cap. "Showtime."

"What about me?"

"You wait here." He was gone before she could protest.

He wasn't the only one who could change their appearance in a heartbeat. She peeled off her own T-shirt to reveal a slutty halter top with bedazzled nipples on it, a gag gift from her bridal shower. She donned a pair of cat's-eye sunglasses rimmed with rhinestones and popped some gum in her mouth as she stepped out of Caine's Mustang.

She found Caine standing in front of the condom section. She slipped her arm around his waist. "Shopping, baby?" Her voice was low and husky as she went for a porn-star sound.

His initial double take made her feel good, but the anger she felt emanating from him made her heart skip. Or maybe it was the way he grabbed her and pulled her close. "You disobeyed orders," he growled against her cheek.

"You're not in the Marines anymore," she growled right back before freezing at the sound of Nolan's voice.

"I think our phones are bugged."

"Why?" A man with a nasal male voice asked the question. This must be Fred Jr.

Both men were in the opposite aisle.

"Maybe something to do with the ARC case," Nolan said.

"But you're not involved in the lawsuit."

"I know. But it feels like someone has been following me. How about you? Have you felt the same thing?"

"Yeah, I have."

"Who do you think it is?"

"I don't know. Maybe Karl's son the Marine."

Caine didn't say a word, but she felt him stiffen, and not in a sexy way but in a warrior-ready-for-battle way.

"Why the hell would Karl's son be following me?" Nolan said.

"I don't know," Fred Jr. said. "Maybe it's not him. Maybe it's the lawyers. Maybe they've got investigators checking out anyone who worked at ARC's research facility during that time."

"Yeah, maybe."

"Since I am suing them, that's probably who's following me," Fred Jr. said.

"You should have warned me," Nolan said. "I wouldn't have arranged to meet with you if I'd known you were being tailed. Don't call me again."

"Hey, you're the one who called me," Fred Jr. said.

But Nolan was already on his way out the door, which Faith could see. She and Caine hurried out after him and got in the Mustang in time to trail Nolan back to his home. They had to park a block and a half away because there was nowhere else open.

Faith discreetly discarded her gum before speaking. "So what did we learn from that encounter?"

"Several things. That Nolan thinks his phone is bugged and that he's being followed. Fred thinks he's being followed too."

"Do you think the lawyers defending the chemical company hired investigators to check Fred and Nolan out?"

"It's possible, I suppose. Buddy claims he hasn't bugged anyone's phone and that if he was tailing Nolan and Fred, they'd never know it."

"Our company and Vince's are the two major investigative firms in the city. If the lawyers were going to hire someone, you'd think they'd contact one of our companies."

"Your company already has a track record with my father's case, so odds are that they'd want someone fresh."

"Like Vince?"

Caine nodded. "I'll see what I can dig up."

"Okay. What else did we learn from their meeting?"

"That you can't follow orders." Caine turned to give her a steamy stare. "And that you look sinfully hot in that halter top."

Thoughts of the case flew out of her mind. "Take your Cubs cap off," Faith said.

"Why?"

"Because I can't kiss a man wearing a Cubs cap."

Caine whisked the cap off.

She grinned at him. "I didn't say I was going to kiss you now, just stating a fact."

"You're bad. Has anyone ever told you that?"

"No." She was rather pleased with herself.

"Maybe you should take off your sexy halter top."

"Because you can't kiss a woman wearing a sexy halter top?"

"I'd rather kiss one without a top."

"Forget about it."

"Is that your best *Sopranos* impersonation?"

"I'm afraid it is."

"That's okay. You're good at other things." With each word, he came closer, until his lips rested on hers, and he was kissing her.

She kissed him back before coming to her senses. "Wait, what about Nolan?"

"I don't want to have sex with Nolan. I want to have it with you."

"We are not having sex in the front seat of your car."

"How about the backseat?"

"No, not there either."

"So you think we should just park and make out? Sounds good to me."

"What about the surveillance?"

"Finished for tonight." His hand stole beneath her halter top. "Now I'm on stealth mode."

"Mmm, you're on seduction mode."

Speech was replaced with hot, wet kisses. Damn, Caine was a fine kisser. The best. That tongue of his should be labeled dangerous to a woman's peace of mind and definitely dangerous to her common sense. Faith hadn't made out like this as a teenager, and now she realized what she'd been missing. There was something to be said for slowing things down and enjoying every second. While his mouth consumed hers, his hand leisurely rubbed and caressed her breast under the minimal cover of her sexy halter top.

The sound of yelling dragged Faith from her passion-induced haze. An elderly woman driving a boat-sized old Cadillac had pulled alongside them before apparently getting out and banging on their windshield. "Do that hanky-panky stuff somewhere else. I need this parking space!"

CHAPTER FIFTEEN

Twenty minutes later, Faith dumped her backpack on the floor just inside her front door and headed straight for the kitchen. She'd tugged her navy T-shirt over her slutty halter top before entering her building. She really didn't need any of her neighbors seeing her in that wild outfit.

Her stomach growled as she opened her fridge. She hadn't had any dinner, and she was hungry.

Yeah, you're hungry, her inner voice mocked. *Hungry for more of Caine's kisses.*

Her life was rapidly turning into the Tale of Two Faiths. One part of her knew she was playing with fire by responding to him. Yet the more time she spent with Caine, the harder it was to resist him. He'd apologized for not being able to take her to dinner tonight because he had to work on another case for King Investigations.

That brought her to the second part of

her conflicted self. This was the logical part filled with questions. How was she supposed to believe that Caine wanted her for her and not just as a way of exacting revenge on her father by breaking her heart? Her gut told her that wasn't the case, but how could she trust her own judgment when the choices she'd made, like getting engaged to Alan, were clearly mistakes? Could she really afford to risk getting badly hurt by making another mistake? Could she just have blind faith that things would work out with Caine?

Despite her name, blind faith had never come easily for Faith. It all went back to that worst-case scenario thinking. The one time she'd abandoned it, she'd been left at the altar. So much for blind faith.

The worst-case scenario here was too bad to even contemplate right now. So she instead focused her attention on scrounging up some food. She clearly needed to place another order with Peapod to have more groceries delivered. As it was, the contents of her fridge consisted of the usual condiments, English muffins, blueberry jelly, organic yogurt, skim milk, leftover asparagus quiche from the Comfort Café, a bag of light Caesar salad and something wrapped in foil that she was afraid to open.

The choice was clear: quiche and a salad.

She curled up on her couch with her plate and watched two episodes of her guilty pleasure, the cartoon *Jane and the Dragon*. Now that she was a PI, she probably should have been watching *CSI* or *NCIS* or something involving investigative work.

So sue her. At the moment, she needed to watch the show based on the books by Martin Baynton.

Besides, it wasn't as if Jane was a wimp. She was a girl who wanted to be a knight, not a lady-in-waiting. Come to think of it, Jane was actually a kick-ass kind of girl. Sure, she got help sometimes from the court jester and a dragon, but they were sidekicks.

Faith had trouble sleeping that night, and when she did doze off, she had nightmares about dragons with swords and Caine laughing at her fears before kissing her, leaving her aching for more.

Faith went to work the next morning with dark circles under her eyes. She'd tried to cover them up with makeup, but cosmetics could only do so much.

"A rough night?" Abs asked with a knowing smile.

"I was working," Faith said.

Gloria walked by before back-stepping to pause, shake her head and click her tongue at Faith. "You should have worn red today."

Gloria smoothed a hand down her poppy red shirtdress. "It makes you look good even on bad days."

It did occur to Faith that as the boss's daughter, she really should get a little more respect around here. She needed to work on that . . . on a day when she wasn't so exhausted. On a day when she'd slept well instead of tossing and turning most of the night, reliving every kiss, every caress that Caine had ever given her.

Sure, she'd refused to have sex in his car, but what did that really prove? That she still had some remnants of common sense and self-discipline left? So what? The bottom line here was that her feelings for Caine refused to go away and just seemed to grow stronger every time she saw him, every time she kissed him, every time she let him caress her.

"You're not still pining after Alan, are you?" Gloria asked.

"No," Faith said. "Definitely not."

Gloria nodded. "Good. I'm glad to hear that."

"Maybe she's pining after someone else," Abs said.

"Don't be silly. It's too soon for her to pine after someone else. Isn't it?" Gloria asked Faith.

"Right." Faith prayed her face didn't turn as red as Gloria's dress.

"Faith isn't slutty like that," Gloria said.

Which reminded Faith of the halter top she'd worn last night into the convenience store. What would Jane Austen think . . . ?

No, no, Faith wasn't going there. Dressed like that, Faith should have wondered what Madonna would think. No doubt the Material Girl would approve.

Not that Faith could see Madonna as her mentor, despite loving her song "Jump." Going from Jane Austen to Madonna would be too big a jump for Faith. Or would it?

Hmmm, she'd have to consider that later.

She spent the morning working on the asset search for the Haywood case. Candy Haywood had mentioned that they'd owned a time-share in the Mexican resort of Cabo San Lucas, so Faith was searching for possible bank accounts or additional real estate in that area. Her search wasn't just under Douglas Haywood's name but under his father's name, his brother's name and even his brother-in-law's name. None of them had the kind of funds that Haywood had once possessed . . . and might still possess. When she turned up nothing, she started on the females in his family, beginning with his mother.

"Bingo." A big bank account, as in seven figures, in a Mexican bank under his mother's name.

Faith was so happy she stood and did a happy Snoopy dance.

"Yeah, that makes you look real tough," Abs said.

Faith didn't care what Abs thought. She immediately called Candy Haywood's attorney and gave him the info, e-mailing him all the details. So much for Douglas Haywood being broke.

Now, if Faith could only be as successful regarding the investigation into her dad's behavior. He'd given her the password to check into the company credit card account when he'd given her a card. She'd already checked and didn't find any suspicious activity by her father. No charges for florists or Victoria's Secret or jewelry stores. No hotel room charges. Nothing to raise any red flags.

She told her mom as much later that evening when she phoned her.

"So you haven't found one single thing that's suspicious?"

Faith paused a second too long.

"I knew it!" her mom said. "Tell me right now."

"It's probably nothing."

"Then there's no problem telling me about it."

"I'm just afraid you'll make more of it than you should. It's no big deal."

"Let me be the judge of how big a deal it is."

"You have to promise me first that you won't go off the deep end."

"Jane Austen would not have her mother make a promise like that."

"She might. But I'm not Jane Austen. I'm thinking I might be more like Madonna."

"You're thinking of adopting a child?"

"No. Not like Madonna that way. Never mind. The only thing I observed was dad having dinner with a client."

"What client? A female?"

"Yes, a female."

"A good-looking one?"

"I suppose . . ."

"What's her name?"

"I don't know."

"Then how do you know that she's a client?"

"Dad said he was having dinner with a client."

Thump thump thump.

That didn't sound good. "Mom, what are you doing? Where are you?"

"In the kitchen."

"What was that noise?"

"Me whacking the phone against the counter. Maybe I should hire someone else for the job. Maybe it's too much for you."

"It's not too much for me."

"Maybe you've got so many other cases that you don't have the time to devote to this one."

"Of course I have the time."

"Really? Because I'm not sure you're giving this the priority it deserves."

Faith felt more than a twinge of guilt. It was true that she'd spent more time on Karl Hunter's case than she had investigating her father.

"I knew it. I'm right, aren't I?" her mom said.

"I'll do better. I promise."

"Please don't let me down."

Faith's heart ached at the sadness in her mom's voice. "I won't."

She worked until the middle of the night, trying to find something about her dad that would give her a clue as to what might be going on, but she found nothing. Surely that was a good sign?

"It sounds like Nolan Parker is a hot dog searching for mustard," Buddy said as he and Caine sat in one of Chicago's many

South Side Irish pubs late Wednesday night.

At Caine's blank look, Buddy explained. "It means he's in search of attention."

"If he framed my dad, why would he be looking for attention? Which reminds me, you're telling me the truth when you say you aren't bugging his phone, right?"

"That would be illegal."

"That doesn't answer my question."

"You're absolutely right."

"I need to know if it's you or if there's someone else in this mix."

"And I need to keep some things private. You're not my client. Weldon is."

"Does that mean that if Weldon is responsible for framing my dad, you won't tell me?"

"You met the kid. Do you think he framed your dad?"

Caine rubbed his forehead. "I don't know what I think. I checked and haven't found any record of any other investigators tailing Fred and/or Nolan. So that leaves you. You tailed Fred and Nolan to find out if they were the one tailing Weldon. Am I right?"

Buddy just smiled. "Have another Guinness." He signaled their server. "By the way, I did check out Faith's ex-fiancé, and he had no connection to your dad's case. But you knew that already. You just said it to push Faith's buttons, right?"

Caine shrugged. He would have preferred his Corona over a Guinness, but Buddy had insisted on the Irish beer. He'd also insisted on dodging a direct answer to Caine's question, but Caine could read between the lines . . . at least as far as Buddy was concerned. The rest of Caine's life still felt pretty messed up, and reading between his own lines was a blurry business. Caine silently admitted he was guilty as charged about wanting to push Faith's buttons. But that wasn't the only thing he wanted to do to her. "Another Guinness isn't going to clear my brain."

"Maybe not, but it makes a soul feel good, and I have a feeling your soul could use some cheering up."

Buddy might be an old guy, but he was right on the money with his observation. Caine was having a hard time dealing with the situation. The case had gotten more complicated. In the beginning, Caine's only goal was to prove his dad's innocence. Now Faith was in the mix. Caine already had enough guilt to last a lifetime without failing his father again.

Caine was a Marine. And failure wasn't an option for a Marine. Not even for a former Marine.

Caine had spent over a third of his life in the Corps. He'd been trained to do what had to be done. He was part of a brotherhood that left no one behind. Yet he'd left his fellow Marines behind when he'd gotten out. A shitty decision to make. He'd been between a rock and a hard place. Not unusual for him. During his deployment he'd dealt with far worse.

He'd had to wait two long years after his father's suicide before his obligation to the U.S. Marine Corps was completed. He couldn't wait any longer. He had to prove his dad was innocent of the charges against him. He owed his father that much. He owed him so much more.

So why was he finding it so hard to adjust? His honorable discharge was three months old. Ninety-seven days, to be exact, since he'd gotten out. He'd been lucky that Vince King had hired him. So many vets coming back were finding it hard to get work.

Vince was practically drooling at the thought of having West Investigations' reputation stomped on, which would happen if Caine could prove his dad was innocent after all. That's why Vince didn't mind that Caine was spending so much time on his dad's case. Yes, Caine was putting in extra hours to work on additional cases, but his main focus was his dad's case.

Your dad's case and *Faith,* his conscience taunted him. *You've focused on both.*

Yeah, that was a problem Caine didn't know how to solve. Faith seemed genuine in her quest to discover the truth, but he wondered how long that would last once they proved her dad was wrong. What would she do then?

Would she still kiss him with wild abandon then? Trap his hand between her legs after he gave her an orgasm? Give him that sexy smile of hers?

Caine doubted it.

He was a warrior. He knew all about the need to fortify perimeters so they were well-protected. Yet he'd been unable to strengthen his defenses so that Faith couldn't get past them. Why? Was she deliberately trying to distract him so he couldn't stay focused on the case?

His gut told him no. But then his gut was close to another part of his anatomy that ached to have sex with her. Was he guilty of thinking with his dick?

In Positano he'd worried about that. Worried that she'd gotten to him. Weakened him. Since then, his attraction for her had only grown more powerful.

"You're staring at that Guinness as if it

holds the secrets of the Holy Grail," Buddy said. "You thinking of that gal of yours?"

"She's not my gal," Caine said curtly before adding, "sir."

"Stop calling me sir. Makes me feel old. And don't you be telling me I *am* old."

"I wouldn't dream of it."

"But you were dreaming of Faith."

"Not dreaming, no."

"What then?"

"Analyzing."

Buddy shook his head. "Boyo, men have been trying to analyze women since Adam and Eve. Don't waste your time. It can't be done."

"Whenever someone tells me something can't be done, that makes me more determined to prove them wrong."

"That's a Marine thing," Buddy said.

Caine didn't deny it.

"What did your dad think of you joining the Marines?" Buddy asked.

"He was okay with it."

"Just okay? Not bursting with pride?"

"He was a chemist not a warrior."

"Did he want you to follow in his footsteps and become a chemist too?"

"No, he let me do my own thing."

"From what I've heard, he was pretty torn up after your mom passed."

"He never recovered from her death."

"Do you think he committed suicide to be with her?"

That possibility ate at Caine. "I don't know."

"His suicide was only a few days after the anniversary of your mother's death." At Caine's look, Buddy added, "I do my research."

Caine's throat tightened. "I can't say what he was thinking."

"Did he write you anything that could give a clue?"

"He sent e-mails."

"What did he say?"

"Not much. He'd tell a joke or two. Say work was keeping him busy, that sort of thing. No details."

"Did you keep the e-mails?"

Caine shook his head. He wished he had. Hindsight was twenty-twenty.

He'd only kept one e-mail, the final one his dad sent. It had simply said "I'm sorry. I can't go on."

By the time Caine returned from a recon mission and got to read the e-mail, his father was already gone.

Caine had been trained to serve his country first and foremost. He'd done everything the United States Marine Corps had asked of him. Now it was time to put his father first — even if it was too little, too late.

"You know what I missed when I was in the army?" Buddy said. "Sliders. How about you?"

"What did I miss? Being able to walk outside without body armor and a helmet. Being cool. In Iraq it got as hot as a hundred and forty-five degrees Fahrenheit, and then add the body armor." Caine shook his head as if trying to dislodge bad memories. "I missed driving a car without looking around at people and everything suspiciously. Those are just some things."

"Sounds rough."

"It was no picnic, sir."

"I told you not to call me . . . Oh, I get it. You don't want to talk about it the same way I don't want to be called sir."

Caine nodded. "That's right."

"Message received loud and clear." Buddy took a sip of his Guinness. "I couldn't help but notice that you always choose a seat facing the exit and also against a wall if you can manage it."

"Old habits are hard to break."

"Yeah, I sat in that seat myself for a long time, but I figured you need it now more than I do."

"It's not a matter of need." At Buddy's

look, he said, "Okay, maybe it is. Let's change the subject."

"So I understand you're living in an apartment in Oak Park now."

"I don't *live* there. I'm staying there temporarily." A Marine buddy had lent him the place while he was deployed. It was furnished, barely. A black leather recliner, large flat-screen HD TV, a bed and a table. It served Caine's purposes perfectly. "How did you know where I'm staying?"

"I told you, I'm a darn good PI. I also know that former Force Recon Marines with your skills and knowledge are in high demand by private security contractors willing to pay big bucks. I'm assuming you took the job with King Investigations because of your father, but do you plan on staying with them once this case is solved?"

"I don't know."

"Haven't thought that far ahead, huh?"

"Affirmative." Caine had a hard enough time dealing with the present without dealing with the future. Time enough to worry about that after he cleared his dad's name.

Wednesday night Faith sat on the floor of her condo, her feet tucked beneath her yoga style as she ate beef and broccoli from her favorite Chinese takeout while reviewing the progress made on Karl Hunter's case. She was burned out from investigating her father's situation and needed a break. Besides, if Karl's case was the cause of her father's changed behavior, then the sooner she completed Karl's case, the better.

In between bites of food, she wrote on the yellow pad perched on her bent knee. She could have put her notes on her BlackBerry, but when she was really focused, she reverted to pen and paper.

1. Weldon thinks/believes Karl is innocent.
2. Weldon thinks/believes someone is following him besides me and besides Caine.
3. Caine sleeps with me then doesn't call me for three days.

Faith crossed that one out. "Focus," she told herself. "He slept in the same bed. We didn't have sex. And, yes, he still hasn't contacted me since we made out in his Mustang on Monday night. That has nothing to do with Karl Hunter's case. Okay, it does a little, because Caine is Karl's son. But, really, sex has no place in this equation. Stick to the facts."

4. Weldon hired PI buddy to prove Karl's innocence.
5. Buddy and Weldon don't like Nolan Parker.
6. Nolan jealous of Karl. Why didn't he invite us in when I interviewed him? That was weird. And who was tweaking the curtains inside his home, watching us?
7. Nolan calls Fred Jr. and asks for a meeting. Is Nolan paranoid, or is someone really tapping his phone? Is it Buddy?
8. Fred Jr. thinks his phone is being tapped because he's suing the research company for giving his dad a brain tumor that killed him.
9. What is Abs's connection, if any?
10. Why does Caine kiss me in his car and not call me?

Faith vehemently crossed those words out, almost ripping the paper in the process.

She was supposed to be reviewing Karl Hunter's case, not reviewing every time she'd made out with Caine. She needed to stay focused here. What kind of investigator was she to allow herself to be distracted?

She knew what an old pro like Buddy would say. "Buckle up, buttercup," he'd

growl in that grumpy voice of his. "Brood-
ing is for amateurs."

"You know the Cure Cancer Charity Ball is
this Saturday night, right?" her dad said at
work Thursday afternoon.

Faith had actually forgotten all about it.

She must have displayed her panicked
face, because her dad said, "Don't even
think about trying to back out. I've reserved
a table for eight. Your mother and I, Dave
and Megan, my mother and her date and
you and your date."

"Gram's got a date?"

"Yes. She wouldn't tell me anything about
him. My mother can be stubborn at times."

"What about the Duchess of Grimness,
Aunt Lorraine?"

"She's swimming with the fishes."

Faith was momentarily speechless. Sure,
he was no fan of Aunt Lorraine. No one
was. But was her father capable of doing
something like that? Her thoughts took off
like a rocket. Had the woman her dad had
dinner with been a hired assassin? Was that
why he'd been preoccupied?

"You killed her?" she whispered.

Her dad laughed. "No, but don't think I
haven't been tempted after the stunt she
pulled at last year's charity ball. She's

definitely persona non grata there. I meant she's on vacation down in the Caribbean, swimming with dolphins. I hope she doesn't punch one of them."

"Yeah, I hope so too. Getting back to the charity ball. Megan doesn't have a date?"

"She's got her dad. I thought you and Alan would round out the numbers."

"That's not going to happen."

"Obviously. I reserved these tickets nearly a year ago. I couldn't anticipate what would happen with Alan the Ass. So just bring someone else instead."

She was quiet. She could imagine what her father would say if she suggested Caine as her escort.

Her father frowned. "Unless that's a problem? You're over Alan, right?"

She nodded.

"Then what's the problem?"

"No problem." She'd find someone. And she had to get a dress. No worries. She had forty-eight hours.

The once-passive Faith who let her family clean up her wedding mess had been replaced with the new, active Faith who took care of herself . . . with a little help from her doorman.

"Yuri, I need a big favor." Faith had cornered him as soon as she entered her condo building after work. "I need a date for this Saturday night for a charity ball."

"You don't want to ask Caine?"

"I'm attending with my father. He books a table every year. So, no, I can't ask Caine."

"Understood."

"I thought maybe one of your actor friends might be willing to attend with me. Everything is paid for. They'd have to have a tuxedo because it's black tie, but I'd pay for the rental."

"I think I know just the man for the job." Yuri pulled out his iPhone and got online to Facebook before turning the screen to her. "His name is Dylan Donovan."

"Does he really look like that?"

"Yep."

"I'm sorry, that was shallow of me."

"Of course he wouldn't be oiled and shirtless. And he wouldn't have his jeans undone the way he does in this photo. Do you want me to give him a call? He owes me a favor."

"Sure," she croaked before clearing her throat. "I'd appreciate that." She certainly appreciated the picture of Dylan Donovan. Her mouth was dry and her palms damp. This charity ball might turn out to be better than she'd expected, providing Dylan was available.

"He's agreed to the gig," Yuri said. "What

time do you want him to pick you up?"

"Um, seven thirty. Does he need a tux?"

"No, he has one."

"Tell him thanks."

"No problem. Dylan could use the exposure."

Exposure got her thinking naughty thoughts. Maybe she was getting over Caine if she could drool over another guy. That was a good thing, right? Who knew at this point? She couldn't figure out her complicated relationship with Caine right now.

"Do you need anything else?" Yuri asked. "Do you have your dress?"

"No."

"Several young actress friends of mine rave about this new Oak Street boutique." He showed her the store's website with examples of their clothing.

"Thank you so much, Yuri!" She hugged him. "I'll head right over there now."

The boutique had the perfect dress for her: a classy black strapless full-length sheath with a sweetheart neckline. She felt so proud of herself for getting both a dress and a date in a matter of two hours that she splurged and got a beautiful jewelry set with a layered amethyst necklace and matching large teardrop dangle earrings.

Friday flew by with new cases and work

piling up. She wanted to treat herself to blueberry pancakes at the nearby Comfort Café Saturday morning but worried she wouldn't fit into her dress that night if she did. So she nibbled on a granola bar instead. Later that afternoon, her manicurist suggested black cherry chutney nail polish for her mani/pedi. Faith agreed and also splurged on a facial.

But nothing she did erased the fact that she hadn't talked to Caine since they'd made out in his car Monday night. Which was fine with her. She didn't care.

Okay that was lie, and she was trying not to lie to herself anymore. So she did care, but she'd get over it. Naturally she'd be concerned that Caine might be off on some rogue mission with his father's case without consulting her. Of course, if he had consulted her, it wouldn't be a rogue mission.

She was still trying to recover from her father telling her that Aunt Lorraine was swimming with the fishes. She hoped Caine hadn't done anything drastic or illegal. Maybe she should call him to find out.

Right. Like he'd tell her if he'd done something wrong. She removed her hand from her BlackBerry.

Forget Caine and concentrate on getting through this event tonight.

Faith had considered getting her hair trimmed but was afraid of messing up the haircut she loved so much and looking like a wreck, so she left it as it was. She spent a lot of time preparing for the charity ball. Her hair was styled, her underarms and legs were shaved, her body moisturized with Stella McCartney's sexy and stylish lotion. Studying her reflection in the mirror, she decided that she'd never looked better in her life.

She was ready to go when Yuri called to inform her that Dylan was downstairs waiting for her.

"Showtime," she whispered as she entered the elevator, momentarily flashing back to when Caine had said the same word before heading into the convenience store during their surveillance. No, tonight wasn't about Caine. Tonight was about the first major public appearance of the "new" her. Many of the people there tonight were guests at her wedding over a month ago. But they'd never seen the mad, bad and blonde version of Faith. Which left her with only one thing to say, courtesy of Buddy: "Hold on to your hats, honeypies."

CHAPTER SIXTEEN

Faith stepped out of the elevator in the foyer downstairs and found Dylan Donovan waiting for her. He looked stunning in a tux and was driving a black Porsche.

"Thank you so much for stepping in and agreeing to help," she told him.

"No problem." He caught her glancing at the car. "It's used. I borrowed it from a friend of mine for the night. My Jeep doesn't go with my tux."

"Right." Then she worried that she sounded snobbish. "Not that there's anything wrong with a Jeep."

"Wouldn't go with your dress either. You look beautiful."

"Thank you. So do you. I mean you look nice." *Shut up, Faith. Next you'll be telling him some story about Bertha Palmer and one of her numerous charity balls.* Thank heavens the ball wasn't at the Palmer House this time but was instead taking place at McCormick Place. Otherwise who knew what trivia Faith might have come up with about the hotel's original owners.

Dylan's manners were impeccable. He held her hand as she got into the Porsche and closed the door for her. Once they arrived at their location, he again helped her out of the low-slung sports car.

The organizers outdid themselves with the large ballroom's decorations, transforming it into a magical place decked out in shades of silver, black, teal and white. Teal linens and rose-filled mirrored boxes decorated the tables.

Faith's parents were already seated at the table. Only then did she realize that this was the first time she'd seen them together since her canceled wedding. Her mother looked lovely in a conservative navy blue full-length gown. Her father looked at ease in his tuxedo. But he wasn't paying attention to his wife. Instead, he was talking to someone else. Thankfully it wasn't the beautiful mystery client but an older man with silver hair.

Faith's mom smiled with relief when she saw Faith. "Megan and her dad are at the silent auction table making some bids."

Faith introduced Dylan as a friend of hers. He charmed her mother and impressed her dad. Faith's grandmother arrived shortly thereafter with her date, Buddy.

But Faith was most surprised and dismayed by the fact that Vince King sat two tables over, looking very much like a king holding court. And his right-hand man Caine was right there beside him.

"Can you believe it?" Faith's dad said. "I'm sure Vince arranged things so he'd be near my table to taunt me. Do you know what his latest dirty trick is? He's spreading rumors that I'm having an affair. Can you believe that?"

"Yes." Faith prevented herself from nervously glancing at her mother.

"The man has no shame," her dad continued. "No sense of honor or dignity. He'll pull whatever dirty trick he can to get what he wants."

"What does he want?"

"Me gone."

"Would he hurt you?"

"He's too cowardly. He'd much rather ruin me."

Faith couldn't read her father's expression.

"Maybe you two should dial back your rivalry," she said.

"Don't worry about it." He patted her bare shoulder before frowning at her cleavage. "That dress is a little low-cut, don't you think?"

She rolled her eyes. "The days of you telling me what to wear are long past."

"At least Faith doesn't have tattoos," Gram said. "And that dress is gorgeous. Angelina Jolie wore something like it to the Oscars one time. Angelina has tattoos. Faith has excellent cleavage, don't you think so, Dylan?"

"Yes, ma'am."

Dylan was speaking, but Faith felt Caine's eyes on her. Sure enough, he was looking at her, but she couldn't tell what he was thinking. He was too damn good at keeping secrets. And he looked too damn good in a tux.

He had a beautiful woman on his right. Who was she? His date? It didn't matter. Despite making out with him in the front seat of his Mustang, Faith was supposed to be trying to get over him. Yet her reaction to Caine in a tux was ten times that of the incredibly handsome guy sitting next to her.

Dylan was the perfect companion. He made pleasant conversation, even if a lot of it was about him. He didn't deliberately say things designed to drive her nuts. He didn't offer her sliders, didn't slide his hand beneath the table to make her fly, didn't brush his thumb over her lips.

But he was a great dancer. After their delicious three-course dinner, she accepted his invitation to hit the dance floor. An orchestra with a male singer provided the music.

Faith was doing just fine until the song changed to the Righteous Brothers classic "Unchained Melody," and Caine cut in. They were on the opposite side of the dance floor, away from both the West and the King tables.

Dylan took one look at Caine and correctly decided he was a man who wouldn't take no for an answer. Still, Dylan checked with her to make sure it was okay, and she admired him for that.

"Who's the pretty boy eye candy?" Caine asked.

"He's my date just like your girl eye candy is your date."

"Wrong. She works for Vince. She's not my date."

"She looked like she'd like to be your date."

"What about you? What would you like?" He lifted his hand higher up her back until his fingers rested on her bare skin. The brush of his caress sent shivers of delight up and down her spine. He gently pulled her closer, resting his chin on the top of her head, sliding his fingers between hers rather than simply clasping her hand.

What would she like? She liked the way Caine smelled, a clean citrus scent that took her back to Positano and the night she'd first met him. For once she didn't focus on his betrayal but on the incredibly powerful chemistry between them. She hadn't imagined it.

She knew Caine felt it too.

They swayed to the music. She was totally wrapped up in his embrace, in his presence, in his magical hold on her. The music was slow, but her heart was racing, and all her senses were on high alert.

Their forbidden dance was brought to a premature end by Faith's father, who pulled her out of Caine's arms. "Are you crazy? What are you doing?"

"I'm dancing. You're making a scene."

"Let them be," Gram ordered as she and Buddy two-stepped beside them. "Do not make a scene, Son." She glared at Faith's father. "Go back to the table and behave. And leave Faith alone."

"You don't know who he is," Faith's dad said, only to be interrupted by Gram.

"I know all I need to know. Now let's dance."

Faith's father angrily returned to their

table. Faith returned to Caine's arms. Gram returned Caine's smile of gratitude.

"You okay?" Caine asked Faith, his breath stirring strands of her hair.

She nodded, but her hands were trembling. "I'm feeling a little like Juliet. I just don't want to end up like her."

"She wasn't a tough blonde like you."

"Abs says I'm not tough."

"Because she's hard and tough."

"And I'm not?"

"No. But I am."

She smiled up at him. "So I've noticed."

"How soon can we leave?" he said.

"I can't just dump Dylan. But he has to leave early because of a previous engagement. I planned on taking a cab home."

"Plan on sharing that cab with me."

"You didn't drive?"

Caine shook his head. "Not tonight." He brushed his lips across her cheek before whispering in her ear, "Wait for me."

Faith's magical haze was blown out of town by the cold blast of her father's anger once she returned to their table. "I can't believe you were dancing with him after what he's done."

"Was that Caine?" Faith's mom asked.

Faith nodded.

Her mom gave her a look of commiseration.

Gram returned to the table to give her son a look of reprimand.

Faith was amazed to see that her dad actually squirmed in his seat.

"You should have been dancing with your wife instead of trying to make trouble," Gram said.

"I wasn't trying to make trouble," he protested. "You don't know the whole story. He works for King Investigations."

"Your archrival yada yada yada." Gram shook her head. "I know. I also know that life is too short to have such hatred. Don't let it erase the love in your life."

The next hour was awkward as Dylan made his escape, stopping near the exit to pick up a bodacious babe who'd been eyeing him all night.

"Looks like your date just dumped you," Aunt Lorraine appeared out of nowhere to tell Faith. "Seems to be a repeating pattern with you and men."

"I thought you were swimming with the fishes — I mean the dolphins," Faith said.

Aunt Lorraine sat in the seat Dylan had just vacated. She looked like Cruella De Vil, the villainess from the Disney classic *One Hundred and One Dalmatians.* "I was, but I flew back this afternoon. My flight was late, or I would have gotten here sooner. You don't think I'd miss this event, do you?"

"I thought they forbade you from attending," Megan said.

Sure easy for her to make a comment like that. Aunt Lorraine wasn't her aunt.

"That was a misunderstanding." Lorraine gave Megan a vulture glare. "Why are you here with your father? You couldn't find a man either, Megan?"

"You know what?" Faith stood. "I've had enough."

The older woman sniffed her disapproval. "I should hope you would have had enough of picking losers."

"I've had enough of you, Aunt Lorraine," Faith said. "I've had enough of this. I'm leaving now."

Megan said, "I'd join you, but I have my eye on a couple of silent auction items that haven't come up yet."

Faith glanced over her shoulder to see Caine seated at the table with his gorgeous coworker hanging on his arm and almost drooling over him.

She'd once told Caine that she wasn't a Marine, and therefore she didn't march, but she did march right out of that ballroom, head held high, shoulders back, posture

315

perfect. She didn't look left or right. She just kept going.

She'd reached the cab line when Caine suddenly appeared by her side. "I told you to wait for me."

"I don't take orders from you. I don't take orders from anyone. You got that?" She bounced her index finger off his sternum.

He lifted her hand and kissed it.

His romantic gesture caught her off guard. Usually he moved in like a commanding warrior, seducing and conquering.

"Having a bad night?"

She nodded.

"Let's see if I can't make it better." He guided her into the cab and slid in beside her. He gave the driver her address and then turned to look at her in the darkness. A second later he was kissing her.

He began slowly for a change. He seductively nibbled at the corner of her mouth, the fullness of her lower lip. He was wooing her and doing a damn fine job of it too. No Austen hero could have done it better.

Cupping her face with his hands, he made her feel treasured. Made her feel special. Made her feel wanted. Made her want him even more.

She parted her lips, inviting him in, and he increased the intimacy of their kiss. He slowly explored with a talented gentleness that sensitized every touch point from the tip of her tongue to the roof of her mouth.

Meanwhile he slid one hand through her hair while his other hand stealthily found the slit in her dress and moved up her thigh to rub her feminine mound through the silk of her sheer underwear. The need grew inside her, doubling time and time again, until it exploded out of control. She clutched his crisp shirt in her fists as she was swept away by everything. Suddenly she was horizontal on the backseat of the cab, his tautly aroused body pressed against hers.

His mouth consumed hers — hot and wild. Gone was his earlier slow approach. Now the kiss was all about escalating passion.

Caine traced her cleavage with his fingertip before freeing her right breast from the captivity of her strapless dress. He brushed his thumb over her nipple, then lowered his head. His darkly erotic tongue-lashing made her womb weep with pleasure.

Gasping his name, she tilted her head back and banged it on the cab's door handle. The pain brought her to her senses. Wiggling out from beneath him, she hurriedly stuffed her naked breast back into her dress.

"We are not having sex in the back of a cab," she said.

"Right." He moved away slowly, reluctantly, to the far corner of the seat.

As the cab came to a halt in front of her building, she turned to face Caine. "Would you like to come up with me?"

Caine leapt out of the cab and quickly tugged her out before shoving a handful of bills through the open window at the cabbie.

They sprinted to the elevator, which unfortunately was already occupied, so they couldn't make out. Not in front of Mrs. McGee, who lived one floor below Faith and sat on the board of the Operatic Society.

But Caine was very creative. He stood closely behind Faith in the far corner from the silver-haired grande dame, trailing his fingers down Faith's back left bare by the low-cut gown. The second Mrs. McGee got out and the elevator doors closed, Caine and Faith were at each other. His lips didn't leave hers as they rushed to her door a few feet away. She fumbled to unlock her door.

Once inside, he turned her against the closed door and held her hands above her head as he kissed her lips, her jaw, her shoulders and the curve of her breast. He shifted against her, letting her feel his arousal through his dress pants and her silky gown. A gown that was getting in his way. He released her hands to find the hidden zipper in the back, undoing it in one go so that the gown was released and fell to the floor. She stood there in nothing but her jewelry, her stilettos and her black silk tap pants. He kissed his way down, starting at her breasts, which he treated to lavish attention. He kissed her navel, her hipbone, the top of her thigh. He caressed the back of her knee with his fingertips before trailing down to her ankles and her stilettos. Kneeling before her, he removed them from her feet.

His next mission was to retrace his path back up her leg directly to the lacy hem of her tap pants. He brushed his thumb against her most sensitive mound, letting the silk magnify the pleasure.

Her hands shook as she tugged him to his feet and undid the zipper on his pants. He growled his pleasure as she fondled him.

"Condom," she gasped. "Do you have one?"

He quickly retrieved one from his wallet. She shoved his pants and black briefs out of the way and helped him roll it on. He shoved her black silky tap pants down to the floor before lifting her in his arms. She wrapped her legs around his waist as he surged into her. He had her pinned to the door as he consumed her moan of pleasure with a kiss so hot she almost came right there and then.

He pumped in and out, in and out, with ever-increasing speed. The friction was erotic and deeply satisfying. She couldn't breathe, couldn't think. She could only feel. Pressure increasing, building, building. So close, so close . . . there! *Yes!* Her orgasm consumed her, the spasms like a powerful internal earthquake.

With one final thrust he came, tilting his head back before leaning his forehead against hers.

It took Faith a while to come back to earth, and when she did, she had her feet back on the ground but only for a second as he swept her into his arms and carried her to her bedroom.

"Do you have more condoms in your wallet?" she asked.

He nodded.

"Did you think you'd get lucky tonight? With me or with that gorgeous woman hanging all over you?"

"No. The Marines trained us to always be prepared, which means carrying a condom whether you think you'll need it or not." He left to retrieve his wallet and returned to her side to nuzzle her ear with his lips.

"I'm no longer your one-night stand," Caine said.

"What are you?"

"The man in your bed."

"And what am I to you?"

"Trouble. The best damn trouble I've ever had in my entire life."

"This isn't smart."

"Maybe not," he said. "But it sure feels good."

"What are we going to do?"

"I thought I just showed you. Give me a few minutes, and I'll show you again."

"I'm not talking about sex."

He pulled back to stare down at her. "Is that all this is for you? Sex?"

"What is it to you?"

"I asked you first."

"So what?"

"So you don't really want to talk any more than I do. I think you'd much rather I did this . . ." He brushed his thumb over her clitoris, sending her flying back into the orgasmic outer limits.

The next afternoon, Faith stood beside her cousin Megan in the enclosed dark area of the Smith Museum of Stained Glass Windows at Navy Pier. "What's wrong?" Megan said. "You only suggest coming here if you're upset."

"I didn't come here after I was jilted."

"No, you went to Italy instead. So I guess this is now your second choice stress haven. Unless you plan on returning to Italy in the near future?"

"No."

Faith slowly made her way to the collection of Tiffany windows, pausing in front of her favorite landscape. The artificial light behind the large panels made them glow like jewels, the way Caine was able to make her glow with an inner throbbing light that was hot and vibrant. She took a deep breath and tried to keep her mind off sex. It wasn't easy. Caine had left early that morning, kissing her on the cheek and telling her he'd be in touch. "Did you know this is the only stained glass museum in the country?"

"Yes, I know. I'm the one who told you that. What's wrong with you today?"

That was a complicated question, because not only was Faith still totally distracted by the memory of making love with Caine several times last night, but she also had the disturbing feeling that she was being stalked. "Did you feel like someone was following us?" Faith glanced over her shoulder. The museum was tucked away in the far end of Navy Pier. Most people didn't even know of its existence.

"Hundreds of people followed us here," Megan said. "I mean, come on. It's Navy Pier, one of Chicago's top tourist destinations, on a beautiful sunny Sunday afternoon. Of course the place is packed."

"I meant on the walk here from my condo."

"No, I didn't notice anything. Why?"

Faith shrugged. "It was just a feeling."

"Do you still have it now?"

"Not as much."

"If someone really is following you, then maybe wandering around in an out-of-the-way place that's on the dark side isn't the best move."

Faith shook her head. "No, it's fine. Just my overactive imagination. Besides, I've got pepper spray in my bag."

"What's got you so jumpy? Did you find something in the case about Caine's father?"

"I'm discovering things, and none of them make me feel good. Well, one thing did, but it wasn't about his father's case. It was about Caine."

"I saw the way he was eyeing you at the ball last night."

"I didn't mean to ignore you last night.

We didn't get to talk much."

"That's okay. You were on the other side of the table with your date, divinely yummy Dylan."

"He's an actor."

"You didn't go to an escort service, did you?"

"No. Dylan is a friend of Yuri, my doorman."

"That dress of yours was also hot."

"Yuri again. He hooked me up with this new boutique on Oak Street. I know you prefer vintage clothes, or I would have told you about it."

"Maybe I should move to your building."

"You only live two blocks away."

"We were both lucky that our inheritance from Granddad helped us get our condos."

"I still miss him," Faith said.

"Yeah, me too. I couldn't believe Gram brought a date to the ball. He seemed like a nice guy."

"He's quite a character."

"I'll say. He was trying to set me up on a blind date with his grandson, Logan, who's a cop."

"What did you say?"

"I said no, of course. You know I don't do blind dates anymore. Especially not with a cop. Not with my history."

Faith nodded her understanding. Megan might be the optimist in the family, but even optimists had their line in the sand that they wouldn't cross.

"What do you say to lunch at the Comfort Café?"

"Yes! You know I love the food there."

The café, specializing in comfort food with a twist, was located halfway between Faith's and Megan's condos. Its convenient location wasn't the only reason they ate there a lot. The food was delicious. Their light and fluffy blueberry pancakes were to die for. Their famous French toast stuffed with cream cheese and marmalade sprinkled with powdered sugar was another big hit.

They managed to snag a table in the far corner. Despite the fact that it was past the main lunch crowd, the café was always popular. They were too late for the breakfast specialties, but the lunch selection was just as mouthwatering. Faith went with one of her faves, the homemade mac and cheese with shallots, Gruyère and mascarpone cheese while Megan had her favorite Hilltop Salad composed of organic spring greens, candied walnuts, gorgonzola cheese and other goodies with a yummy raspberry chipotle vinaigrette.

"Okay, now talk." Megan speared a dried

cranberry. "I saw Caine follow you out of the ballroom last night. Did you two hook up?"

Faith blushed.

"You did. OMG. Your dad is going to have a cow."

"OMG we sound like the Gossip Girls. Did my dad see Caine follow me?"

"I don't think so. He was finally dancing with your mom. What's going on with those two? I definitely sensed some tension there. Between your parents, I mean. We both already know about the tension between Caine and your dad."

"My parents are going through a bit of a rough patch at the moment, but they'll come through. I'm sure Aunt Lorraine's sudden appearance didn't help."

"She was almost shown the door because she sneaked in without a ticket. Your dad had to buy another ticket for her to avoid another scene."

"Great. She does have this unerring ability to show up at the worst possible times and say something awful."

"Her words clearly didn't upset you enough to avoid Caine."

"You've got that right."

"So how did things go?"

"They went well."

"Only well?"

Faith smiled. "Awesome, incredible, mind-blowing."

"Does this mean you two are a couple?"

"I don't know." Faith moved her mac and cheese around the dish with her fork. "There are still a lot of things we have to work out yet."

"That's an understatement."

"Let's talk about something else. Hey, did I tell you that I recently discovered the neatest sculpture? A lot of people like the Calder or the Picasso. Others love the Bean by Anish Kapoor in Millennium Park. But I think my new favorite statue is the tree-hugging torso in front of the John Hancock Building. Most people don't even notice it, set into the ground at the base of a tree the way it is. But I like it."

"You're avoiding talking about Caine," Megan said.

"Guilty as charged," Faith said. She refused to feel guilty about what she'd shared with Caine last night. Guilt played a large part in their relationship. She suspected Caine felt guilty about his father's suicide, and she sure felt guilty about her father's possible role in that. She was also guilty of falling for Caine despite her best efforts not to. Not a smart move.

■ ■ ■ ■

Monday morning, Faith's BlackBerry
started vibrating the instant she sat down in
her cubicle. She didn't have it set to ring-
tones when she was at work. She hoped it
was Caine, who'd stopped by her condo last
night and made love to her again and stayed
long enough this morning to make breakfast
for her, but a quick glance at the screen let
her know that the call was from her friend
Sherry Weiss, the forensic accountant.

"You're not going to believe this," Sherry
said. "Another forensic accountant is checking into the same account you asked me to
investigate. I've got her name, but I don't
know who hired her."

Faith Googled the woman's name and
found a photo of her. It was the woman her
dad had dinner with when Faith had spied
on him.

Tired of beating around the bush, Faith
went directly to her dad.

"Why did you hire a forensic accountant
to look into Karl Hunter's case?"

"Who says I have?" he countered.

"Don't bother denying it. I saw you having dinner with her. Unless you're having
an affair with her?"

"What? No!"

"Then you'd better tell Mom that."

Her dad blinked in confusion. "Tell her I'm not having an affair with a forensic accountant? Why would she think that?"

"Because you've been acting strangely, showing all the signs of a husband cheating on his wife. Come on. As the wife of an investigator, you don't think she knows all the signs? The late nights, the preoccupation, the secrets, the guilt. But it wasn't caused by another woman, was it? It was caused by Karl's case, right? You were having second thoughts about it. Admit it."

"Okay, I admit I had a few concerns. But I can't talk about it now. I've got an important meeting across town. We'll discuss this later."

"Later *today*. I mean it, Dad."

He nodded. "I promise."

As soon as he left, Faith stayed in her father's office and made the call to her mother. "He's not having an affair. I saw him having dinner with a female client, and I discovered today she's a forensic accountant Dad asked to look into Karl Hunter's records."

"I thought that case was closed two years ago."

"It was, but it's been reopened now. That's

why Dad's been so strange. Because there could be more to this case than we originally thought."

"But that poor man committed suicide."

"I know."

"Is that why Caine was dancing with you at the charity ball? Was he asking you about his father's case?"

"Naturally he's interested in the investigation."

"He looked interested in you. Very interested. First you meet him in Italy, and then you hook up with him here."

Faith hoped her mom didn't know what the current definition of *hooked up* meant.

"Yeah, well, um, I just wanted to tell you that Dad is not having an affair," Faith said. "Vince King was just trying to make trouble. He's very good at that."

"You didn't tell your father that I thought he was cheating, did you?"

"Of course not. Well, not exactly. I'm not sure how I worded things or precisely what I said, but I told him to call you, which I'm sure he'll do."

"I'll look forward to that," her mom said.

Faith was looking forward to talking to her dad about Karl's case, but instead of calling her, he sent her a text message. "Urgent. Don't tell Caine. Need you to come to . . ."

She recognized the address. It was Nolan Parker's house. Why would her father want her to join him there? She called his cell, but it went right to voice mail. That left her with only one way to find out what was going on — by doing what her father asked.

She took a cab to Nolan's house and climbed the front steps. The door was ajar, and her knock opened it wider. She stepped inside. "Hello?"

She was grabbed from behind and a gun stuck in her side. "Welcome to the party," a man growled.

CHAPTER SEVENTEEN

"What's going on?" Faith couldn't breathe. She told herself not to panic and not to pass out. She'd skipped lunch. She was light-headed. She was scared spitless. "Where's my father?" The voice hadn't sounded like Nolan's, but she'd only heard him two times in her life. "Nolan?"

The man holding her laughed as he grabbed her bag and tossed it in the far corner. "Guess again."

The high-pitched voice rang a bell, but she couldn't place it at the moment. Having a gun held on her didn't make for the clearest thinking. "Who are you?"

"Fred Belkin Jr. at your service."

Sure, now she could place him. She'd overheard him briefly talking to Nolan at the convenience store. "Where's my father?"

"He's tied up at the moment."

Faith didn't like the sound of that. "Does

Nolan know about this? Is he here with you?"

"No, this is a one-man operation." Fred Jr. kicked the front door all the way shut while keeping the gun pressed against her.

"Then why are we meeting here?"

"Because it's quiet. Nolan is in Portland at a chemical conference, and his wife is visiting her mother in Buffalo. I offered to house-sit and take care of his parakeets while he's away. He'd just fired his last pet sitter. Good parakeet caregivers are hard to find, you know."

"I don't understand."

"I don't either. Parakeets are not that demanding compared to other companion animals."

"I mean I don't understand why you're aiming a gun at me. Do you think I'm going to upset the birds?"

"You're certainly trying to upset the applecart. That's a strange phrase, isn't it? And not really applicable any longer in the twenty-first century. I mean, no one has applecarts anymore."

"Is my father here?"

"Of course he's here. I already told you that he's tied up."

"Where?"

"I'll show you. Walk straight ahead and go

into the first room on the right. And don't try anything, or this gun may go off prematurely."

He shoved her ahead of him. She walked into an almost-empty room to find her father sitting in an upright chair, bound by duct tape around his ankles, his wrists and his mouth. He was unconscious, and he had a bloody bruise near his temple.

"Dad!" She took a step forward.

Fred Jr. pulled her back before shoving her into the opposite corner of the room. Waving the gun at her, he said, "Don't make me hurt you."

"I don't understand." Her voice was unsteady.

"I took his phone and texted you on it. Simple, really. Don't worry. He's still alive. For now."

"Why are you doing this?"

"Because you made me do it. Sticking your nose into my business."

"Is this about your lawsuit against ARC?"

"There is an indirect connection."

"I don't work for ARC. Neither does my father. We don't represent them or their attorneys."

"I know that." Fred Jr. glared at her. "Do you think I'm stupid?"

"No."

"Good. Because I don't think you're stupid. You used to be a children's librarian. A noble profession. You should have stayed in the stacks."

Faith was having similar thoughts herself at the moment — along with the panic that threatened to consume her. She focused on the rise and fall of her dad's chest. He was still alive.

"You really should have let sleeping dogs lie. Another strange saying. But it's true. You should have left Dr. Hunter's suicide alone."

She was frantically trying to put things together here and make sense out of it all. Why would he say that she should have left Dr. Hunter's suicide alone unless . . . "Was it a suicide?" One look at Fred Jr.'s face, and she had her answer. "It *wasn't* a suicide." She followed her gut here. There was no pride in Fred Jr.'s eyes to indicate he was responsible. Abs may have scoffed at trusting instincts, but Faith didn't have much else to go on. "Your father was the one who framed Dr. Hunter."

"I didn't know about that until after the fact. My dad had a brain tumor caused by working for ARC, yet they refused to acknowledge their culpability. He knew he was dying, and he wanted ARC to pay."

"But why frame Dr. Hunter? Why make him pay?"

"He was collateral damage. My dad thought the accusations alone would be enough to tip Dr. Hunter over the edge because he was already depressed. But my dad couldn't be sure. So he took matters into his own hands."

"Karl Hunter didn't take his own life, did he? Your father killed him."

"Gave him an overdose and made it look like a suicide. It was the perfect cover."

"It was murder!"

"Hey, it's not my fault. I wasn't part of my father's plans. He only confessed all this on his deathbed. Even then I wasn't sure if it was real or the tumor talking. Then I checked the bank account he told me about. He warned me to keep transferring money into various holding companies so no one could find it. But then you sent your damn accountants looking for it. I had to stop you."

She wanted to know how he'd known the accountants had been hired by them but decided she had more pressing issues at the moment. "Listen, you said it yourself. This isn't your fault. We can work this out."

"No, we can't."

"You don't want to do this." She wasn't

sure what "this" was, but given the fact he had a gun, none of the options appeared favorable. "You can stop this."

"I'm in too deep. I can't stop now."

"Yes, you can. I'll help you. You weren't involved in the murder. And you still have the money. You can return it —"

"Are you crazy?" He waved the gun at her with increasing agitation. "When am I ever going to get a chance for that kind of money again?"

"It's blood money."

"My father deserved that money, and he left it to me. He wanted me to have it."

"What do you plan on doing?"

"Well, clearly I have to get rid of you and your father. And then there's Karl's Marine son. Caine. Yes, Caine. He'll have to be taken out too."

"You can't spend your father's money if you're in prison."

"I have a plan. I shoot you and your father. Then Caine when he comes. Then I wipe my prints from the gun and put it in Caine's hand. He'll be blamed for going off the deep end and shooting the two of you for causing his father's suicide and then shooting himself."

"But his father didn't really commit suicide."

"He won't know that. Besides, he'll be dead. You too. So you've got nothing to worry about."

Yeah right. Because she'd be dead. The one day she wore underwear with a hole in it. Hadn't her mother always warned her not to do that? Because that was the one day you'd end up in the ER. Or the morgue.

In the mysteries she'd read, the heroine had always known what to do, how to cope. They never had to pee like Faith did right now.

Abs had once warned Faith never to travel with a full bladder because it could rupture in a car accident. Apparently Abs's cousin was an EMT and told her gruesome stories.

Faith crossed her legs and ordered herself to stay calm and concentrate. No good wondering what Jane Austen would do in this situation. She'd never have gotten into this situation to begin with. Smart woman, that Jane.

Faith had pepper spray in her bag, but Fred Jr. had taken it from her and dumped it by the front door. She wished she had that stun pen she'd seen on the Internet. But she didn't.

"Now we get you tied up like your father," Fred Jr. said, "and then I text Caine using your phone, just like I used your father's."

Her phone was dead. She'd forgotten to charge it. She had a feeling Fred Jr. would not be pleased with this news, so she was in no hurry to share it with him.

She could tell by his moves that Fred Jr. was not used to handling a gun, which made him more dangerous in some scenarios and less so in others.

Faith hadn't used a weapon since she'd left Las Vegas two years ago. She told herself it was like riding a bike. Her father had trained her well.

She looked over at her dad, checking to make sure he was still breathing. He was. She had to get the gun away from Fred Jr. But how? He'd hardly be willing to just hand it over. She'd already tried logic. That hadn't worked.

"Lie on the floor." He waved the gun at her. "It's time to tape you up. Too bad there's only one chair in here. Nolan really needs to decorate the place, don't you think?"

"Please, Fred —"

"Fred *Jr.* On the floor right now! Or I shoot your father."

Faith dropped to the floor and realized she had one chance here. When Fred Jr. stood above her, smiling down at her, she took it.

■ ■ ■ ■

Caine hopped out of his Mustang, furious with Faith for not telling him she planned on visiting Nolan. Thank God he'd placed a small tracking device in her purse after they'd had sex last night.

He really didn't need her pulling this kind of crap right now. He was messed up enough as it was, torn between love and loyalty. Wait a second. Love? He loved Faith? How the hell did that happen? He'd been so damn careful *not* to fall in love with her. Just because he'd had sex with her didn't mean he was in love with her. Just because her giggle made him smile didn't mean he was in love with her. And just because the thought of her not in his life made his gut clench didn't mean he was in love with her.

It meant he was an idiot.

Who was he kidding here? He frigging *was* in love with her. And he was going to kiss her senseless for taking a risk, going rogue this way on her own.

The sound of a gunshot from inside Nolan's house froze Caine's heart and instantly threw him into Marine mode. He pulled a knife from its sheath in his boot and headed up the stairs to the front door.

It was unlocked.

He heard Faith talking. Thank God. She was alive. For now.

"I don't like to brag, Fred, but I'm a crack shot, so I wouldn't recommend pissing me off right now. Do not move!"

"You're lying. You wouldn't shoot me."

"She probably would," Caine said as he entered the room. "And even if she wouldn't, I sure as hell would."

"She and her father were trying to kill me," Fred Jr. said. "They didn't want me telling anyone about the money. They wanted it for themselves."

"That's a lie," Faith said.

"Why don't you give me the gun, sunshine, and you take my phone to call the police," Caine said.

Faith readily made the switch. She was afraid she might be tempted to shoot Fred Jr. after what he'd just put her through. Her plan had worked as she'd hoped. Fred Jr. stood at her feet with the gun in one hand, the duct tape in the other. She'd kicked up, landing a direct hit on Fred Jr.'s family jewels with her pointy-toed polka-dot shoes. He'd squeezed off a wild shot that hit the ceiling before dropping the gun and bending over in pain. She'd scrambled to get the weapon before he did. She'd succeeded. Barely.

"Your dad didn't commit suicide," Faith told Caine in a rush. "It was his father, Fred Belkin. He killed your father and staged it to look like a suicide. Fred was the one who sold the information to the rival company. He was angry with ARC for giving him a brain tumor."

Caine was having a hard time processing this news as Faith spoke to the 911 dispatcher while using a Swiss Army knife from her bag to free her dad. But one thing came through loud and clear. His father had been murdered.

Seeing the dangerous look on Caine's face, Fred Jr. dissolved in hysterical tears. "It wasn't me! I didn't kill him. My father did. Don't shoot me!"

Buddy arrived with the police minutes later. "Picked it up on the scanner," he told Faith. "Been busy, buttercup?"

Unable to speak, Faith dashed for the bathroom, vowing to never leave her home or office again without first emptying her bladder. A better daughter would have stayed by her father's side, but the EMTs said he was fine as she raced past them. At this point she was just so relieved that no one had been killed that she could hardly see straight.

An hour later, seated beside her father in the ER, her relief doubled with the news that her father had suffered a mild concussion from being hit on the head with a blunt object but otherwise was okay. Faith had yet to reach the okay level, especially when Caine walked in.

He'd driven her to the hospital in his Mustang, bombarding her with questions she wasn't always sure how to answer. "Why were you there?"

That one had been easy. "My father texted me to come."

"Does he usually text you?"

"Not often, no."

"That should have been your first clue something was wrong," he'd said. "Next time someone texts you like that, phone them to verify it."

The last time someone had texted her, it had been Alan, and she could hardly have phoned him to verify that he'd sent the message. Besides, he'd texted her several times after that about his belongings until she'd blocked him.

"What exactly did Fred Jr. tell you?"

She'd repeated the words as she remembered them. "That his father confessed on his deathbed that he'd been the one to give your father an overdose, making it look like a suicide. He wasn't sure if his father was hallucinating because of the brain tumor, but when he checked out the bank account his father told him about, he found the money. That Fred did all that because he was angry with ARC for giving him a brain tumor. Not wanting to get caught, he used your dad as a cover for his own crime."

Caine had yet to say anything about his feelings regarding the revelation that his father hadn't committed suicide after all but had been murdered by Fred Belkin. But then Caine rarely shared his feelings. He buried them. When he put that war face on, there was no telling what his thoughts were.

Caine stood near the entrance to the ER bay where Faith's dad was situated, as if he'd rather not enter.

"Are you okay?" she asked him.

"Hey, I'm the one with the concussion," her dad said with a weak smile.

"You're the one who botched the investigation," Caine said.

Uh-oh. Faith hoped the two men she loved wouldn't stage a *High Noon* showdown here in the middle of the emergency room. Her knees started shaking. Not because she was afraid of a showdown, but because this was the first time she'd really acknowledged that she loved Caine.

She'd heard stories about near-death experiences changing you, making you reassess your life, stripping away your defenses and forcing you to face the truth.

She loved Caine. He hated her father. Not a good mix.

"Guilty as charged. We messed up," Faith's father said. "I'm sorry, Caine. You have every right to be angry. I should have verified the investigation myself instead of delegating it to someone else. That was a mistake."

"One of many." Caine's voice was curt.

"So what do you intend to do?"

"I don't know yet." Caine turned on his heel and walked out.

A hard rain started to fall as Caine stood above his father's grave. The flowers he'd brought bowed beneath the force of the sheets of water. Rain ran down his face, soaking his clothes. He didn't mind the discomfort. He welcomed it.

Pain is just weakness leaving your body.

The Marine Corps had taught him that. Taught him how to deal with death too.

Yet here he was, at a complete loss, not knowing how to express the explosion of feelings ripping him up inside. Still, he felt he needed to say something to his father.

"I don't know if it's better that you were murdered and didn't commit suicide. How sick is that?"

Caine scrubbed his hand across his face. Those weren't tears, dammit. It was the rain. Just the rain.

"I totally bought the story that you'd taken that overdose. I knew you didn't do what they accused you of as far as the money and all that shit. But I thought you really had committed suicide, and I felt guilty as hell that I didn't save you from that. I promised Mom on her deathbed I'd take care of you. Did you know that?" His voice cracked, and his throat clamped shut as he tried to regain control. "I failed you."

He scrubbed his face again. "I'm sorry, Dad." Bending his head, he slowly dropped to his knees. Lightning flashed above him, and thunder shook his world.

Caine traced his father's name carved into the granite headstone. The man responsible for his death was already dead, so Caine could find no revenge there.

Caine had set out to clear his father's name, never guessing what that mission would entail. Everything had seemed so black and white in the beginning. Faith's father had driven Caine's dad to kill himself.

346

No apology could make up for that. No amount of regret.

But now he knew that wasn't really what happened after all. Yes, Faith's father still bore some responsibility for botching the investigation. But Faith was the one who'd uncovered the truth. She'd continued asking questions, even when Caine had tried to get rid of her, to scare her away.

Instead, he was the one who'd been scared shitless when he'd heard that gunshot outside Nolan Parker's house. Gunfire was nothing new to him, although he was more accustomed to the rapid fire of automatic weapons. What was new was his total terror that Faith had been killed.

She hadn't melted under pressure. No way. She'd stood with that weapon in her hand, as mad as hell, an Amazon warrior in polka-dot shoes who'd rushed to the bathroom the instant things were over, muttering something about not wanting to wet her pants.

Faith was such a strange combination of vulnerability and strength, of power and empathy, of primness and passion. And he loved her, God help him.

Caine had spent so much of his life refusing to open himself up to that kind of intense emotion. No soul mate for him.

He slowly moved his hand over the dates on his father's gravestone. A higher power would decide Fred Belkin Sr.'s final resting place, and the justice system would take care of Fred Jr.

Caine knew one thing for sure regarding his dad. "You're finally with Mom again."

Setting the flowers on his father's grave, he released the pain and the guilt, silently acknowledging how much he loved and missed his dad and finally admitting that the salty wetness on his face wasn't really caused by the rain after all.

Faith had no idea where Caine was. She'd checked the waiting room, and he wasn't there. She couldn't blame him for taking off. He needed some time alone to process the fact that his father had been murdered.

She still didn't know how Caine knew she was at Nolan's house. She'd have to ask him next time she saw him. *If* she saw him again.

The investigation was over. Did that mean that his relationship with her was over? Did he consider it to even be a relationship? They'd never really clarified that issue. She knew she loved him. She didn't know how he felt about her.

She knew he wanted her. She knew she still pictured him as her Dark Knight. She knew he had the ability to touch her in ways no one else ever had or could. And not just physical ways, although those were awesome. But in other ways — like the way he grinned at her over the top of her Hello Kitty mug. It took a tough man to carry that off.

Her thoughts were interrupted by her mother's arrival to the ER. She hugged Faith before going to her husband's bedside. Tears ran down her face as she cupped his face with her hand.

"You heard I'm not having an affair, right?" he said. "As if I'd ever cheat on you." He shook his head then groaned. "Bad move."

"I'm sorry," Faith's mom said.

"No, I'm sorry for not telling you what I was doing reopening the investigation into Karl Hunter's case. I screwed up badly," he said. "The facts, or what we thought were facts, were too neat and tidy. I should have caught that. Faith caught it. She's good at her job."

That might be, but Faith was no longer sure that working for West Investigations was the right job for her after all.

She left her parents together and caught a cab home. It had been one hell of a day that got worse when she arrived at her building to find her runaway groom, Alan, standing there waiting for her.

He eyed her new blonde, bad self uncertainly. "Faith, is that you?"

She nodded.

"Good news. I'm baa . . . ack." As if expecting a hero's welcome, he opened his arms to her.

CHAPTER EIGHTEEN

When Faith didn't run into his tanned arms, Alan appeared taken aback. He stood there, perfectly groomed as always, his light brown hair expertly gelled, his eyes greener as a result of his tinted contact lenses. "What's happened to you?"

"What happened to me? I got over you, that's what happened. As well as being held at gunpoint this afternoon, but that's another story. What are you doing here? If you've come to pick up your Wagner opera CD collection, you're about a month too late."

"I didn't come for my CDs, although I can't believe you got rid of them." Seeing the dangerous look on her face, he hurriedly said, "Never mind. I copied them onto my iPod, so that's okay. It's just that for sentimental reasons I really liked that set . . . Never mind. I can see talking about that upsets you. I came back for you."

"Then you've wasted a trip."

"Are you still angry about the wedding thing?"

"The wedding thing? You mean dumping me at the altar? Yeah, I'm definitely still pissed about that."

"Okay, so I may have made a mistake."

"*May* have?"

"Definitely did." He gave her a toothpaste ad smile. "But I'm back now."

"So what?"

"So we can pick up where we left off."

"No, Alan, we can't."

"Well, not *exactly* where we left off. Not with that big wedding."

"Not with any wedding. You said I was boring."

"Nonsense. I didn't use those words exactly." He pulled out his iPhone. "I kept a copy of the text message. Look, here it is." He turned the phone to show her the screen.

She shoved it back at him. "I don't need to see that. And I sure as hell don't need to see you. Go away."

"You don't mean that."

"Yes, I do."

"But we were about to get married."

"*Were* being the operative word here. That's all in the past."

"How can you throw away the two years

we had together?"

"You threw it away. But you know what? You did me a favor, although I would have preferred that you told me you were having doubts instead of taking the coward's way out."

"I am not a coward."

"You wanted excitement and adventure. You didn't want me, and you didn't have the nerve to tell me that to my face."

"I was trying to spare your feelings. Telling you to your face seemed rude."

She stared at him in disbelief.

"And I was trying to find myself," he said. "I was confused."

"I don't care."

"Okay, you're upset with me. I get that now. I'm more self-aware than I was before. I'm a better me."

"Bully for you."

"I'm a better me, so I can help you become a better you."

"You can help me by leaving me alone," she said.

"You don't mean that. You don't want to be alone."

"She's not alone." Caine appeared out of nowhere to stand by her side. "The lady is with me now."

Alan was not a happy camper. "Who the

hell are you?"

"The man who's going to make your life hell if you don't beat it right now."

Alan retreated a few steps and gave Caine a wary look. "I'm her fiancé. I deserve an explanation."

"You're her ex-fiancé, and you deserve to have your ass kicked."

"He's not worth the trouble." Faith grabbed hold of Caine's arm.

"It's no trouble," Caine growled. "It would be my pleasure."

"He's a former Marine," Faith told Alan. "I don't know how much longer I can hold him back, so you'd better get out of here while you can."

"If I leave now, I'm not coming back," Alan warned. "This is your last chance."

"No, it's your last chance, Alan," she said. "Leave while you still can."

He angrily walked away.

Faith turned to Caine. "You came back."

Caine nodded.

"I wasn't sure you would."

Yuri stepped outside to join them. "Is it safe to let Caine in the building now?" he asked.

Faith didn't know how safe it was, but she was no longer looking for safe. She was looking for love . . . and answers.

So was Caine. At least he was looking for answers. She had yet to discover his thoughts about love.

"Did you know Alan the Asshole was coming to see you?" Caine asked once they were inside her condo.

"No." She sank onto her couch. "I had no idea. I thought he was still in Bali."

"Are you still in love with him?"

"Did it look like I was still in love with him?"

He shrugged. "You were pissed, but that doesn't mean you don't still love him."

"Well, I don't."

"You're sure?"

"I'm positive. Look, can we change the subject, please? I have a question for you. How did you know that I was at Nolan's house?"

"I put a tracking device in your purse last night."

"Why?"

"To keep track of you."

"Because you don't trust me."

"It's not a matter of trust. It's a matter of security."

"By the time you got there, I had the situation under control," she said.

"Yeah, you did."

"I am glad that you showed up, though,"

she admitted. "An extra pair of hands in a case like that is a good thing."

"Sure."

"You were my backup."

"Looks like I was."

"And still are, showing up the way you just did to get rid of Alan. Not that I couldn't have taken care of him myself."

"Right."

"Sometimes it's nice to have backup."

"Yes, it is." He started pacing. "I should have provided backup for my dad. I should have known that I was investigating a murder and not a suicide. But my dad's last e-mail to me said he was sorry and he couldn't go on. If that doesn't sound like a suicide note, I sure as hell don't know what does."

"Is that all he wrote?"

Caine nodded. "Two sentences. That's it."

"Fred Belkin could have sent that e-mail from your father's laptop. It didn't say anything specific."

"You're right. My dad would have said something about joining my mom. He loved her so much. Too much."

"How can you love someone too much?"

"Trust me, it's possible."

She wondered if Caine hadn't inadvertently just given her a key to his inner self.

If he thought his father loved his mother too much, it made sense that he wouldn't want to make the same mistake. And he definitely made it sound like a mistake, like love was something to be avoided.

She should ask him about that now. She really should. But she wasn't ready to hear his answer yet. So instead she referred back to the case. "I thought someone was following me when Megan and I were at the stained glass museum the other day. Do you think it was Fred Jr.?"

Caine nodded. "He did babble something about that while you were in the bathroom before the police took him away. You should have told me about it earlier."

"I thought I was just being paranoid or something."

"He was also the one tailing Weldon."

She paused for a moment before quietly saying, "I looked for you at the hospital today, but you'd left."

"I went to the cemetery. Did you know my dad liked model trains? He collected several of them. They're packed up in a storage unit. He hated celery and liked watching *NCIS* on TV. I'd forgotten that kind of stuff. The little things. He taught me to love broccoli. I never told anyone else that. And he made these weird fried egg and ketchup sandwiches."

Faith knew Caine's staccato sentences were a sign of his stress. Blinking back the tears, she softly said, "I wish I'd gotten the chance to know him."

"He was a good guy. A special guy."

"I'm sure he was. After all, he had a son who's a pretty special guy."

"I thought my dad wasn't tough enough to fight off the depression that sucked him in every year on the anniversary of my mom's death. I thought he was weak to give in instead of fighting." Caine's voice grew hoarse with emotion. "But he wasn't weak. He was murdered."

"I'm so sorry."

"Yeah." He stopped pacing and sat on the couch next to her. "Me too." He gently wiped away the tears rolling down her cheek. "Don't. Don't cry."

"I'm sorry. I'm usually tougher than this."

"I know you are." He kissed her. Words were abandoned in favor of caresses that started out tender and became increasingly passionate until he carried her to her bedroom and made love to her with a deep desperation that had her gasping his name as she came again and again.

"I'm so glad you're okay!" Megan grabbed

Faith the instant she opened her front door the next morning. "I'm sorry I didn't call first. I had to come see for myself." She looked over Faith's shoulder. "Am I interrupting something?"

Faith turned and caught sight of her blouse still draped across her couch where Caine had left it last night when he'd undressed her. "No. Caine left before I woke up this morning."

"Our parents are kind of nervous about what Caine's going to do next."

"Me too." He'd made love to her with a newfound sense of intensity that both thrilled her a lot and unnerved her a bit. Was that his way of saying good-bye? He'd left without waking her. He'd never done that before.

Back in Italy he'd threatened to make her father pay big time for falsely accusing his dad. She didn't know if he still planned on doing that, and she hadn't felt right about asking him after he'd shared his memories of his father with her following his visit to the cemetery.

"Did he say anything?" Megan said. "Give you any clues about his plans?"

"Not really." Faith smoothed the red wraparound jacket she'd worn her first day at West Investigations. Today she teamed it with a black pencil skirt and comfy shoes. Lifting her hand, she touched the cameo she'd bought for herself in Positano. This was the first time she'd actually worn it. "I've got to get going, or I'll be late for work."

"You could take a day off. Don't you need some time to recover?"

Faith really needed time to figure out what to do next. And not just regarding her relationship with Caine but the rest of her life as well. Last night she'd dreamed she was back at the library, and she felt happy. She woke this morning wondering if she'd tossed the baby out with the bathwater by leaving the library.

"I may have made a mistake," Faith said. "I mean, I've made plenty of them, but . . ." She shook her head. She didn't have the words yet, because she hadn't made a decision. Once again she was the Queen of the Question Mark in the Punctuation Hall of Fame but lacking any answers. "Never mind. Come on. Walk down with me."

They stepped into the elevator together. "Did you hear that Alan showed up yesterday?" Faith said.

"No. He had the nerve to come here?"

"I didn't let him in the building." Faith pushed the button for the lobby. "I've got to say it felt really good to kick him to the curb."

"Good for you." Megan shared a fist bump with her. "You go, girl!"

Faith arrived at work to find Gloria waiting for her. "I'm so glad you're okay!" Gloria hugged her tightly before standing back to look at her outfit approvingly "Red. Good for you. Show the world who's boss."

"Her father is the boss," Abs said as she joined them. "I heard you had a busy day yesterday. Wilder than story time at the library, I'll bet. I can understand how a hostage situation can spook you."

"I'm not spooked," Faith said. She wasn't having second thoughts because she was afraid. She was having second thoughts because she thought she was going to die at Fred Jr.'s hands, and that made her reassess her life. All this time, Faith had wanted to be more like Abs. But looking at her now, Faith suddenly realized that was no longer the case. She didn't want to be permanently emotionally detached like Abs . . . And that's how Faith would eventually become if she stayed here on a full-time basis.

Talk about an aha moment. She'd just had one, big time. She did still have a few questions for Abs, however.

"Why did you warn me off investigating

Karl Hunter's case?" she said. "What was your stake in this?"

Abs eyed her with newfound respect. "You're suspicious. Good. That's a good thing."

"That doesn't answer my question."

"You kept going on about intuition and trusting your gut. I don't work that way. If the case was flawed, that meant your intuition stuff was right, and I'm not happy with that. I prefer the world based on facts. It may not always be right, no system is. But it works for me."

"It doesn't work for me," Faith said.

Abs nodded. "Yeah, I figured."

"A gut feeling?" Faith teased her.

Abs smiled. "Something like that."

Faith wasn't looking forward to telling her father about her decision. And it was now a decision. She was a children's librarian at heart. That didn't make her weak. It made her strong. She loved watching kids' eyes light up at story time or finding a new book for a beginning reader. Hooking books with kids gave her a sense of satisfaction that she'd found lacking in her new job.

Sure, finding that missing money for Candy Haywood's divorce case had felt good, but those moments were too few and too far between all the other nasty stuff.

And, yes, she enjoyed research, but she'd rather research what a sixth-grader who loves horses should read next.

It turned out she was more like Jane Austen after all. A new kick-ass version of Jane Austen.

Her dad showed up in the office later, right after lunch.

"I thought the doctor said you were supposed to take it easy," Faith said as she trailed after him.

"I am taking it easy. I took the entire morning off, during which time your mom and I booked a trip to England for our anniversary."

"That's great."

"So how are you holding up today?" he asked.

"We need to talk."

"I was afraid of that." He sat in his ergonomically designed chair behind his desk. "You've decided to go back to the library, right?"

"How did you know?"

"You'd be safer."

"I'd be stronger," she corrected him. "Because I'd be following my heart. That's not to say that I'm not willing to help out around here from time to time. But this isn't where my passion lies."

"I got the feeling from the way you were looking at him that your passion might be with Caine. Is that right?"

"I'm not ready to talk about Caine yet."

"Notice I'm not asking you to talk to him on the company's behalf."

"Good. And before you ask, no, Caine didn't have anything to do with my returning to the library."

"I can't say I'm not disappointed that you're not staying, but I can understand. Maybe Caine would like to work with us. He's a good investigator. Not as good as you, of course. He could make sure we don't screw up again like we did with his father's case."

"You'd have to talk to Caine about that." Faith went around the desk to hug her dad. "I'm glad you're okay. When I saw you unconscious in that chair with blood on your face . . ." She shivered.

He stood and gave her a giant bear hug like he used to do when she was a kid. "And I'm glad you're okay." He patted her back. "I know I don't say this often enough, but I do love you, you know. And if being back at the library is where you want to be, then I'm for it a hundred and ten percent."

Faith sniffed back the threat of sentimental

tears. "Thanks, Dad. I love you too." She had yet to figure out how her love for Caine and her love for her father could coexist peacefully. But she was determined to figure it out somehow.

"You're back!" the kids shouted as she walked in on afternoon story time at the library later that day. The three- and four-year-olds gathered around her like sheep returning to the flock.

"Thank God!" a frazzled Maria said. "I'd just about given up hope."

Faith was surprised to see that Maria was handling story time. Usually the branch manager had plenty of other duties to fill her time. But Maria did have five kids. She should be able to manage story time with one hand tied behind her back. Come to think of it, her kids were all older. There was an art to dealing with little ones this age.

"I should have called first," Faith said. "But I wanted to talk to you face-to-face."

"Just tell me you're back."

Faith nodded. "If you'll have me."

"Great. Here, finish this." Maria handed her the book she'd been reading.

"*Charlotte's Web*?" Faith shook her head. "I've got something else in mind." She reached into her Golden Books tote bag and pulled out her *Scaredy Squirrel* book.

"We thought you were never coming back," one little kid said.

"Never say never," Faith said.

"Why?" a little girl named Latisha asked. "Is it a bad word?"

"No, but you never know what could happen next."

"You just said never."

"Yes, I did. Never mind."

The kids giggled. "You said it again."

"You're right." Faith grinned. Damn, it felt good to be back. "So let's find out what Scaredy Squirrel is up to now."

"I told you West had messed up the investigation on your father's case," Vince crowed. "Time to break out the good booze and celebrate."

"No, thanks." Caine didn't feel like celebrating.

Vince shrugged and poured himself a generous splash of high-priced Scotch from the Irish crystal decanter on his mahogany sideboard. "Well, I'm going to celebrate. Why aren't you smiling?"

"Because my father was murdered."

Vince frowned. "So? You knew he was dead. Dead is dead. The bottom line here is about West Investigations screwing up royally. I've scheduled a press conference for later this afternoon. I want you to get all emotional and tortured about how West ruined your dad's life. Then you can announce you're suing them."

"I'm not going to sue them."

"Why the hell not?"

"Because I'm done letting you use my father as a pawn in this war you've got going on with Jeff West."

"I would have thought a man like you, a former Marine, would know how to wage a war."

"I know this particular war isn't worth it."

"It is to me. And it used to be for you too. What changed? Wait, let me guess. It's the girl, right? You got whipped by a fancy piece of tail —"

Caine grabbed Vince by his Armani suit lapel and growled, "Watch what you say about her. Not another word."

Vince just shook his head in disappointment. "Never allow your emotions to affect your business decisions."

Caine let him go. "Call off the press conference."

"Why should I?"

"Because you played a part in this mess. You sabotaged the investigation by bribing

367

the West employee originally in charge of the case not to dig any further. Oh, yeah, I know about that. The guy doesn't work there anymore. He isn't even in this state anymore. But I tracked him down and convinced him to talk. I have a copy of his sworn deposition. I really don't think you want me flashing that at your press conference."

"West still had the chance to review the case for himself, and he didn't."

"There's plenty of guilt to spread around," Caine agreed.

"I thought I could count on you. I thought your hatred of West equaled mine. But no, they got to you. Weakened you. I hate weakness. Weak people ruin everything. They always let you down. You've let me down, Caine."

"Same here, Vince. Same here. By the way, I quit."

"Going to work for the enemy now?"

"I don't know."

"If you tell him about the deposition you have, I'll sue you until you don't have a penny left to your name. You signed a confidentiality agreement when you came to work for me," Vince shouted after him as Caine left. "Don't forget that."

Caine had no intention of forgetting

anything. He was still working on forgiving. With that thought in mind, he crossed the street to visit West Investigations. He called ahead first. "We need to talk," Caine told Jeff West as he entered the high-rise building. "I'm on my way up."

"I'll be waiting," Jeff said.

Jeff was standing by his open office door when Caine arrived. "Faith isn't here right now," he told Caine. "Just in case you were wondering."

Caine didn't say anything. He took the chair facing Jeff's desk and waited until the other man was seated before speaking. "I'm not going to sue you, if that's what you're worried about."

"I'm glad to hear that. Again, I can't express how sorry I am that this case wasn't handled better. I've been reviewing the work done by one of our employees, and I have the feeling that Vince King played a part in there. The person involved no longer works for my company. Even so, I should have caught the problem when I reviewed the case. I didn't. I'm not trying to pin this on King or heat up the vendetta he has against me. I will, however, be much more vigilant regarding cases and employees in the future. But the bottom line is that even if King had a hand in messing up the case, I should have caught that. The buck stops here with me."

Caine bluntly said, "I no longer work for Vince King."

"Faith no longer works for me," Jeff said just as bluntly.

Caine couldn't hide his surprise at this news.

"She didn't tell you?"

He shook his head.

"She's gone back to the library. She says that's where her heart lies. She's a damn good investigator, as are you. If you want a job here, it's yours. I'd be honored to have you."

"Thanks for the offer, but no. I've got other plans."

"Involving my daughter?"

"Some of them. I've had enough of the investigative business. I want to work with returning Marines, help them merge back into civilian life — get jobs, health care, affordable housing, social support, family therapy. I've talked to a couple former Marine buddies of mine who are setting up a nonprofit organization."

"I'd be honored to make a generous donation to such a worthy cause," Jeff said.

"You can't make up for what happened to my dad by writing a big check," Caine said.

"I know that." Jeff looked older than his

years. "Believe me, I know that. And I'll regret to my dying day that I didn't detect something was wrong."

Caine knew what his father would want him to do. He'd want him to forgive. "Even if you had, there's no guarantee that you would have caught Fred Belkin in time to stop him from murdering my father."

"That's generous of you to say."

Caine cleared his throat. "There's another matter I wanted to discuss with you as well. It's about Faith. I've got this plan." Caine told Jeff about it. When he was done, he said, "What do you think?"

Faith's dad smiled and nodded. "I approve."

Two weeks later:

"I've never been to a Crosstown Classic game," Caine told Faith as they stood in line outside Comiskey Park aka U.S. Cellular Field. He was wearing jeans, a Cubs T-shirt and baseball cap and garnering jeers from the White Sox fans nearby. "The Cubs versus the White Sox. A classic rivalry. Well, we know which side you're rooting for."

Faith was wearing a White Sox jersey along with black shorts, her black Keds and plenty of sunscreen. It was a hot summer day.

Caine shook his head at the White Sox mascot.

"That's Southpaw," Faith said.

Caine tried to think of something nice to say about the tall fuzzy green thing. "It must be hard being green."

Faith socked Caine's arm. "Be nice."

"That was me being nice."

"I can't believe you got tickets for the Scout Seating section two rows behind home plate."

Caine shrugged. "I've got connections."

"You must have. You do realize that this is the place to watch baseball, because White Sox fans actually do watch the game. Cubs fans are at Wrigley to see and be seen and to download apps onto their iPhones."

Caine narrowed his eyes at her. "Those sound like fighting words to me."

"Just wait and see."

"You can count on it."

She could also count on Caine and have faith that it would be okay. She'd learned more about Caine in the two months since she'd first met him in Italy than she'd known about Alan after two years. She certainly knew Caine moved fast. He'd already made a lot of headway with his nonprofit organization to help returning

Marines. He was determined to make a difference.

He'd definitely made a difference in her life. He'd opened up to her in ways she'd never expected. Not that he'd ever be the kind of guy to bare his soul, but he let her see him as he was.

They'd spent all their spare time together, but Caine had yet to say how he felt about her. He'd shown her, though, in so many ways. She told herself to be patient, to enjoy the romantic road they were traveling together and not jump ahead to some happy ending. She needed to live in the moment.

"When you're in the Scouts Seating section, servers bring your drink and food to your seats, you know," she said.

"So now it's all about the food? I thought it was all about the game."

"It is."

"You're not going to order sushi, are you?"

"No, although they do offer it here."

"That's just wrong. Ballpark dogs and beer. That's baseball food."

"Speaking of baseball, there have been some memorable Crosstown games over the years. In 2008 Mark Buehrle threw for seven innings and struck out five. Then there was that infamous game in 2006 when Cubs player Michael Barrett punched A. J.

Pierzynski, and the White Sox won in a shutout seven to nothing."

Their seats were great. Faith was nearly hoarse by the time the seventh inning stretch came around with the obligatory "Take Me Out to the Ball Game." As soon as that was over, "Don't Stop Believin' " started playing in the background.

Caine turned to Faith and peeled off his Cubs T-shirt to reveal a White Sox one beneath. "I'm a new man because of you," he said.

She blinked. "You don't have to change because of me."

He dropped to one knee and removed a pair of sandals from his backpack. They were identical to the pair she'd left behind in Positano.

"You know the story of Cinderella, right? Well, think of this as a kind of reverse Cinderella, because you're not down on your luck, and I'm no prince, but I've got sandals from Positano meant just for you, made for you."

She stared at him in disbelief. The sandals looked exactly like the ones she'd left behind, only this pair was new. Afraid she'd been hit with a foul ball and was dreaming, she looked up and saw, on the other side of the field . . . wait . . . was that them on the

JumboTron? No way she'd dream that.

Faith heard the ballpark announcers say over the loudspeaker system, "What is that guy doing? He's got a pair of shoes in his hand."

"Looks like he may strike out with that offering," the other announcer said.

"I love you, Faith," Caine said. Reaching into his backpack again, he removed a ring box this time. "Will you marry me?" He looked at her expectantly. "What do you say?"

Her Dark Knight was proposing? He loved her? What would Jane Austen do? She'd say, "Yes, sir, I shall marry you," instead of shrieking, tugging Caine to his feet, and kissing him so hard he nearly dropped the ring.

And it was an incredible ring; she saw that now as he slid it onto her trembling finger. He'd chosen an antique Edwardian setting with intricate lacy filigree work and a beautiful diamond. Jane Austen would definitely approve. So did Faith.

"I don't need a prince," she said fiercely. "I need backup. You're my backup."

"And you're mine."

She kissed him amid cheers and applause from the stadium crowd.

"Wait, it looks like this guy may have hit a

home run after all," the announcer said. "And now, let's get back to the game."

Faith was in a fog until the game ended with the White Sox winning by a narrow margin — five to four.

When she and Caine reached the special exit for their section, they were greeted by Buddy and Weldon.

"I'm trying to convert Weldon to the joys of baseball," Buddy said before thumping Caine on the back in congratulations. "Holy cow! That was some game, huh? And did you see some crazy guy proposing? Looked a lot like you."

"It was me, but you knew that." Caine grinned.

So did Faith, who hugged both Buddy and Weldon before being engulfed in a huge hug by Megan. "That was so romantic! Jane Austen would be so proud."

Faith nodded. "Yeah. I didn't know you were at the game today."

"I'm not the only one." Megan stepped aside to reveal Faith's parents standing behind her.

Faith's mom was crying and laughing at the same time.

"I told you this was a good idea," Faith's dad told Caine.

"You said it was a *brilliant* idea," Caine

corrected him.

"Yeah, well, I guess this means I should start planning another big wedding," Faith's dad said.

"Actually, Caine and I were thinking of eloping," Faith said.

"That's right. How does Las Vegas sound?" Caine said.

"Today?" Megan yelped.

"Not today," Faith said. "But soon. And you're all invited."

When Caine pulled her into his arms, Faith knew this was meant to be. No doubts, no reservations, no strikes, no outs. She'd won big time. She'd won it all.

We hope you have enjoyed this Large Print book. Other Thorndike, Wheeler, Kennebec, and Chivers Press Large Print books are available at your library or directly from the publishers.

For information about current and upcoming titles, please call or write, without obligation, to:

Publisher
Thorndike Press
295 Kennedy Memorial Drive
Waterville, ME 04901
Tel. (800) 223-1244

or visit our Web site at:

http://gale.cengage.com/thorndike

OR

Chivers Large Print
published by BBC Audiobooks Ltd
St James House, The Square
Lower Bristol Road
Bath BA2 3SB
England
Tel. +44(0) 800 136919
email: bbcaudiobooks@bbc.co.uk
www.bbcaudiobooks.co.uk

All our Large Print titles are designed for easy reading, and all our books are made to last.